I0579919

The Styx Trilogy
Book Two

Outcast Shadows

by
Rose Corcoran

To
all of my aunties
who read and loved
my books, and encouraged
their creation

Preface

♠◆♣♥♣◆♠

The Story So Far

When a goblin curses Princess Emmaline and turns her into a rabbit, she and her court magician, Bostwick, must travel through the goblin homeland of Ataxia to find a cure.

After a year of searching, they finally hear about the Domino of Nonpareil, a mask that allows the wearer to become anything he wishes. When they arrive at the Domino's home, Styx Castle, they meet a human maid named Millicent and the goblin queen, Delilah, who haughtily refuses to part with the Domino. Bostwick tries to steal the mask, but is caught red-handed. Delilah offers him a deal: work in the castle as a butler for 100 years, or be cursed. Having no other options, Bostwick agrees to take the job.

As he and Emmaline experience life in Styx—much of which is spent cleaning the derelict castle— they come across the map of Styx, which would cause actual devastation to the country if destroyed by a member of the royal family. Bostwick also encounters a cat named Sebastian who claims to be a goblin that was cursed by the Styx family and is in need of the powers of the Domino to regain his true form.

During an incident involving some rabbit-eating wyrms, Bostwick sees Millicent using magic. The maid reluctantly tells him that she wanted to go to Melieh's Academy of Magic, but was barred after failing an entrance exam; the test results claimed she was a "criminal psychopath". After some inner turmoil, Bostwick agrees to teach Millicent himself. Sebastian offers to lend a hand.

Through magical training, Millicent, Bostwick, and Sebastian form a close bond, but Emmaline is suspicious of the cat's intentions. She tries to question him about why he was cursed, but doesn't learn much, except that he is much older than any normal cat or goblin.

Delilah, meanwhile, sets her sights on matchmaking and begs Millicent to wear a gaudy pink dress in an effort to woo Bostwick. This plan, of course, goes horribly wrong. Bostwick insults the dress, Emmaline blurts out that Millicent has a crush on him, and Millicent runs off in tears. Realizing that her plan was a disaster, Delilah magically steals Millicent's entire memory of the event.

This is the last straw for Bostwick, who steals the Domino and enlists Sebastian's help in an escape plan. When Sebastian transforms to look exactly like a former ruler of Styx, Emmaline puts it together: he is Styx royalty, so he can destroy the map and annihilate the country to get his revenge.

In a final confrontation, however, Sebastian attacks Millicent, threatening to kill her unless Delilah tears up the map. The queen does so, and Sebastian turns into a shadow, wraps around Millicent and the map pieces, and disappears with them through Bostwick's top hat. The castle starts shaking and is transported to a country called Catawampus, apparently because that is where Sebastian dropped one of the map pieces. Instead of punishing Bostwick for betraying her, Delilah decides that they must focus on retrieving the scattered map pieces, rescuing Millicent, and making Sebastian pay for his crimes.

The Cast

Bostwick von Dogsbody: Seventeen-year-old human magician, serving a one-hundred-year sentence as Delilah's butler. Sarcastic, grumpy, and currently guilt-ridden over getting Millicent kidnapped. Secretly loves poetry.

Emmaline Camellia: Fourteen-year-old human princess who stepped on a goblin's tail (by accident) and was turned into a white rabbit. Sensible, but still a kid. Has been taught history and politics by her tea inspector, Mr. Charles.

Delilah Glossolalia of Styx: Goblin queen. Capricious and chaotic, but definitely cares about her friends and her country.

Millicent Minikin: Sixteen-year-old human maid, also a magician. Originally learned magic from old, handwritten books. Meek and kindhearted. Most notable physical feature is her green hair, the result of a spell gone awry.

Sebastian: A goblin-turned-cat-turned-goblin again. Doesn't like to talk about his past and prefers brooding or reading by himself. Has sophisticated and polite mannerisms, but also occasionally resorts to kidnapping.

Balder Spleenbeck: A Gremlin criminal who attempted to blow up Styx. Small stature, huge ego.

Table of Contents

Prologue

260 Years Ago

The full moon rose in the eastern sky, visible above the outer walls of Melieh's Academy of Magic. Professor Leech had finally given up his nightly watch to go stop a fight between two students just indoors, which was a setup, of course. Now sure that they would not be interrupted, Alistair called the rest of the students to the center of the courtyard.

Since the end of the day's classes, they had been surreptitiously gathering out there, some pretending to study while others conversed about seemingly carefree subjects whenever a teacher passed. Two had even brought a picnic blanket and food to have the excuse of staying out late to enjoy the romantic evening. Now they formed a small ring of eleven around the pale, dark-haired boy who stood next to the statue of a Styx goblin, not saying a word. One by one, the oil lamps in the academy windows were extinguished, until only the light of the moon above lit the square, etching the statue's shadow onto the pavement.

"Well," Alistair said heavily, "let's begin."

A petite girl with copper-colored skin and short, boyish hair stepped forward, spun gracefully around, and addressed the group.

"Alistair and I will do this first one," Inez explained. "If it works, we'll go on from there. If it doesn't, well, we'll just have to try something new."

"Wait," one of the students said. "I want to know why we're doing this in the first place."

Inez raised an annoyed eyebrow, but the student continued.

"I mean, I'm here—and I'll bet I'm in the majority—but I'm here because, let's face it, I'm not so great at magic, and this seems like the next biggest thing, and I intend to ride its coattails to the top."

"Your point, Olivia?"

"My point is, I've been led to believe that we're doing some groundbreaking new magic tonight that will make us all famous, and yet we're scurrying around like criminals. We even sent Professor Leech away, when he could have witnessed and approved of the event."

"He wouldn't have approved it," Alistair said solemnly, and looked at the ground beneath him. "What we are about to do *is* groundbreaking. No one, human or goblin, has ever done what we're about to do: create an immortal beast."

"About that," Olivia continued, unimpressed by this speech. "Why an immortal beast? They're just legends, right?"

"Which is why we need to make our own," Inez said.

"But why? I mean, we can conjure birds and flowers out of nothing. What's so special about bringing something else to life?"

"Birds and flowers aren't out of 'nothing'; When we conjure a bird, it comes from the potential existence of any real bird. Professor Hollyhock explained that in year one."

"It's been a while," Olivia mumbled, smoothing down the purple underskirt that signified she was in her final year of school.

"And anyway," Alistair said, "birds and flowers die."

"Don't tell me you're seeking some secret to immortality," a tall, serious-looking student named Jurek asked.

"No," Alistair said. "'I'm almost certain that immortality is linked to a creature's form. The legends about immortal beasts suggest that their immortality, as well as their shape-shifting ability, is due to their fluid, changing form. Humans have always had a mortal form. The only way to be immortal would be to start out that way.

"Which brings us here tonight. I think, if we could create an immortal beast, we could at least learn more about healing magic. As it stands now, we have to stick with healing people inside of boxes, which is not only unreliable under the best conditions, but completely impractical in real-world emergencies. If we could find a new way of healing, think of the lives we would save."

Most of the students nodded, but Olivia looked up at the statue, its cavalier grin seeming out of place in the dark courtyard.

"So..." Olivia said, "why do we need to do this... shadow thing?"

"Since we can't take something that's mortal and make it immortal, we have to make something immortal from scratch, specifically, from starting with nothing."

"How exactly is this 'something from nothing'? A shadow is still something, isn't it?"

"No," Inez said, sounding offended by the suggestion. "A shadow is a privation. An absence. It's like if you have dirt, and then you have a place without dirt, you call it a hole, right? We all know what a hole is. We can identify it or draw it or even make one, but technically speaking, a hole doesn't exist. It's just a place where there isn't any earth. But a hole is too abstract a thing to cast a spell on, so we chose a different privation, namely this shadow," she said, pointing to the pavement at their feet. "A shadow is an absence of light. It exists, to use the term loosely, as a nothingness. So, to test our theory, we're going to try to bring it to life."

"And this living shadow will be immortal because…?"

"Because a shadow is on the edge of existence and nonexistence, I believe it will have a similar form to that of the mythical immortal beasts."

"If you say so," Olivia muttered, sounding unconvinced.

"If there are no more questions," Alistair said pointedly, "then let's begin."

He and Inez knelt on either side of the shadow.

"Now remember," Inez said, "magic is an act of the will. We really have to mean it. Ready?"

They placed their hands on the shadow and began to speak together in low voices.

> "Empty shadow, nothingness,
> a hole in the light in which we stand,
> listen with the mind which is absent,
> obey my will's command."

"Why are they reciting poetry?" Olivia whispered.

"I've heard that the K'nic-k'nack goblins say their spells out loud to aid in concentration," Jurek answered, then muttered, "but this spell sounds… dark."

Inez silenced them with a stare while Alistair continued, unperturbed.

> "Take on shape and substance,
> like dew forms from a mist.
> Like breath brought forth from a corpse,
> Defy your form: exist!"

The courtyard became utterly silent. Not a single student dared to breathe. Only the faint fluttering of birds on the academy roof could be heard, and some footsteps out on the street. Each student waited, and willed, for something to happen.

Then, the shadow began to move.

One

Chaos is Calculated

"We're lost," Bostwick said.

He, Delilah, and Emmaline had been wandering around the cobblestone streets of Catawampus for hours. They had walked far from Castle Styx, through crowded streets and down filthy alleyways in an attempt to find the library. Heather B. Monsters believed the map of Catawampus, and consequently a piece of the map of Styx, was housed inside this library, and ordered them to find it at all costs. Now the group found itself in a busy marketplace full of goblins hawking their wares—and shooting Delilah and Bostwick dirty looks.

"We'll be fine," Delilah said. "I have an excellent sense of direction. For example, Lesse's Moor is that way!"

She pointed to her right, towards a stall of turnips.

"But where's the library?" Emmaline said, from her perch on Bostwick's shoulder. "I thought you said you knew."

"Of course I know. It'll be in the last place we look, but—"

"Do you not care about the situation at all?" Bostwick asked. "While we're wandering around wasting time, Millicent is… Well, she's in trouble. Don't you think we should make finding her a priority?"

"It is a priority. But in order to find her, we must first find all of Styx. Because she may very well be in the Forest or in town as we speak."

"Why would Sebastian take her there? He obviously had other plans."

"Oh, really?" she said, raising an eyebrow. Without the Domino of Nonpareil, her face looked more human, while at the same time more dangerous and wild. "Perhaps, since you and he were on such friendly terms, you could fill me in on the details of his plan. I'm sure you two discussed it over tea and crumpets after you gave him my Domino. So, what's he plotting?"

Bostwick lowered his head and walked away from her, taking Emmaline with him. The crowd of shopping goblins jostled them about, and Emmaline heard several grumbles about "obnoxious humans" as they went. Bostwick finally stopped beside a stall selling ladles.

"Bostwick, please go back. We're going to get separated. Ignore what she said."

"She's right, though. This is all my fault."

"Well, technically yes…"

"Why did I trust him? How could I have been so stupid?"

"You were trying to get us all to safety…"

Bostwick sank to the ground and put Emmaline down next to him, saying nothing.

"Maybe it didn't work out right," Emmaline went on, putting her front paws on his arm, "but right now, your gloomy attitude isn't helping either. We need to keep our heads on straight and stick together if we're going to find Millicent. I know it may be hard to trust Delilah, but you just have to try."

"You're right," Bostwick said with a sigh. He stood up and put Emmaline on his shoulder.

When they made their way back to Delilah, they found her speaking to a wrinkled, blue-gray goblin, who looked extremely put out.

"Excuse me," she said, "do you know the way to the library?"

"Humans aren't even allowed in to the library," he snorted.

Delilah glanced over her shoulder and saw Bostwick.

"Oh, they're with me," she said, but the goblin had already hobbled away. "The nerve of some people! So…" She looked sideways at Bostwick, "Mopey Bostwick has decided to return."

"What's that supposed to mean?"

"Well, you certainly aren't Regular Bostwick, because Regular Bostwick would have defended himself or argued with me instead of slinking away into the crowd like a—"

"Move aside, humans," a tusked goblin said, pushing Delilah roughly out of the way before she could finish.

"I'm not a human!"

"Well, you look like a human, talk like a human, and smell like a human, so what are you then?" he responded, and disappeared into the crowd before Delilah could retort.

"Insults!" Delilah seethed. "How dare they!"

"How is it an insult?" Bostwick asked. "I thought you liked humans."

"Well I do, see, but… it's like this. You like pigs, right?"

"No."

"Oh," Delilah said, shocked. "Well, you like dogs."

"Not really."

Delilah squinted in concentration and looked around the murky sky as if she'd find a suitable example there. Finally, she snapped her fingers.

"You like girls!"

"Yeah…"

"And you respect them."

He nodded.

"But if I called you a girl, or said you were acting like one, or that you look like a girl…"

"Yeah, I get the picture."

"So you'd be insulted, because you're *not* a girl. And in this same way, I am insulted because I'm not a human, see? But I still *like* humans."

"That may be so," Bostwick said, "but in the course of this past discussion, you just compared us to pigs and dogs."

"I like piggies!"

"That's not the point," he said through gritted teeth. "You still think of us as lesser beings."

"I don't. I just think of you as less than goblinical, shall we say? Although," she said, taking Emmaline from Bostwick, "I must say replacing the real Domino with a fake was pretty goblinical in its own way, right, Emmaline?"

"Delilah!" she said, as Bostwick once again stormed away. "Why do you keep bringing that up?"

"Because Bostwick needs to snap out of his gloomified state and be properly sorry."

"He is sorry! Why do you think he keeps running away from you? He feels terrible!"

"Why doesn't he apologize, then? Why does he keep acting like I don't care as much as he does about Millie? Why," she said, looking truly troubled, "why did he give Sebastian my Domino?"

"*Why* don't you ask him," Emmaline said, "so he can stop moping and we can actually do something constructive?"

Delilah nodded and marched into the sea of goblins in the direction Bostwick had gone. She found him sitting on a large crate in the opening of an alley.

"So, Bostwick," Delilah said, leaning on the crate. He looked at his feet instead of meeting her eye. "Won't you tell me what's the matter? Even if our relationship is servant and employer, we're friends, aren't we?"

"That's just it. I don't know what to think of you, Delilah. Are you a friend, a villain, some sort of puppet master? I just don't know."

Delilah smiled, but hastily wiped her grin away and took Bostwick's hand.

"I am the Queen of Styx, and you are my butler. I torment you, and you act put-upon in an amusing fashion. That's who we are. That's all. Why did you give Sebastian my Domino, Bostwick? Did you actually think he'd help you?"

Bostwick turned his head again, ashamed.

"I wanted to escape from you. I wanted all of us to escape. Sebastian said he would help us do that. I thought..." He struggled, finally looking at Delilah, whose snake eyes were, for once, full of concern. "I thought you were just toying with us, like we were your playthings. I even thought that maybe you collected magicians or something, and I figured you'd trapped Millicent in the same way you had me—"

Delilah burst out laughing, attracting much attention from the goblins in the street.

"Oh, Bostwick, you're delightful! It worked just how I wanted. Well, not the Millie-being-kidnapped-and-my-country-being-destroyed part, but as far as humorous assumptions go, I couldn't have asked for better."

"You're laughing?" Emmaline asked, looking up at her.

"Oh, yes. It feels so good to laugh. Bostwick, you really should try it. Ah, but let me explain. When you first came to Styx there were so many things you didn't know, and I thought, instead of just telling you, why not let you figure it out on your own and come to some misguided conclusion that would be good for a laugh. I must say, you exceeded my expectations. Bravo."

Emmaline was at a loss for words, but Bostwick seemed to be slowly returning to his usual self.

"What didn't you tell me?"

"Oh, the reason Millie was in Styx. I'll never forget that day. A shiny letter came to our castle from the president of Melieh's Academy, asking if I would be willing to accept a pupil in the magical arts. I went to Melieh's to inspect my prospective charge, and when I got there," she said, with a winsome expression, "there was Millie, all in yellow with green hair on top. Just like a living, breathing pineapple. I had never seen someone who loved a fruit so much that they'd dress like one, and I knew right then and there that we were kindred spirits."

"She wasn't dressed like a pineapple," Bostwick said. "She just likes yellow."

"Hush, I'm not finished. So the president speechified about the alliance with Styx, and owing favors and this and that. His intention in having Millie live in Styx was to allow her to learn magic without endangering the rest of the student body, and if she did turn out to be some sort of evil overlord type, she would be in good hands. So anyway, I agreed to teach Millie, and she has been under my tutelage ever since."

Neither Bostwick nor Emmaline spoke for a moment.

"But," Emmaline finally said, "Millicent barely knew any magic when we arrived. She was your maid."

"Ah, well, when I brought her to Castle Styx, she couldn't stand it. Goblins and humans have very different ideas of how much filth is acceptable in a building. Not wanting to offend my guest and pupil, I suggested that we begin cleaning first, and then learn magic a little at a time as we went."

"You were cleaning the entire castle? For how long?"

"Three years. It was very filthy before she came, I assure you, unfit for human habitation. And even with both of us cleaning together, it still took that long to make it as nice as it was when you two showed up. So, that's my deep dark secret. How about that?"

They both looked at Bostwick to see if his mood had improved at all. Unfortunately, he appeared almost frightened, like he didn't want to ask what he knew he must.

"Why… why would President Wilfrock want *you* to teach Millicent? Goblin magic and human magic aren't the same, are they?"

Delilah threw her head back in another great guffaw.

"I knew it! I knew you didn't know. Oh, Bostwick, you're priceless. Well, it's time I told you, although you really should have learned it at the Academy. This is a history lesson for both of you, so pay attention. Ahem. There was once a man named Marco Melieh, an explorer employed by the empress herself. You see, the Empire had only just formed, and it was his job, and that of those like him, to draw a unified map of what had once been a plethora of countries. But this was a simple task, too simple for one such as Melieh, so at the empress's request he was sent to Ataxia to try and learn the secret behind our magic, since humans, even as a unified empire, were no match for goblin magic. This proved simple as well, for as soon as he crossed the border between the Empire and Ataxia, he came into my lovely country, Styx."

Bostwick was silent, for he had already guessed the end.

"Any other goblin family would have barred the way or had him thrown out, but we goblins of Styx, out of kindness, good will, and capricious whim, let him have his say. Ah, but he wasn't stupid and knew that goblins wouldn't give out magical secrets for free, so he brought us an offering: a pineapple. Pineapples grew nowhere in Ataxia, as our countries lack the climate for them, so of course, we were enchanted by its peculiar shape, its pointy hide, and most of all, its magical, sunshiny taste. My ancestors loved it, so much so that they drew up a peace treaty right then and there. The Empire would supply Styx, and Styx only, with pineapples and in exchange, the Styx goblins would teach Melieh how to perform magic. And that is how Melieh learned it, and that is why any human since can do magic with any sort of skill."

"But that means," Bostwick said, gradually coming out of

his shock, "that means that every trick I've ever done, my very way of life is all thanks to—"

"Me!" Delilah said with an ear-to-ear grin. "Well, my family at least."

Bostwick looked for a moment like he wanted to scream, but then he smothered his face in his hands.

"I'm sorry it came as such a shock," the queen said, "but you really should've known. They teach all of that in history class at the Academy."

"It wasn't required," Bostwick said miserably.

"Oh, Bostwick! Well, anyway, I should have told you all this at the beginning. Therefore, one might, if they were so inclined, conclude that the fault for your silly assumptions about my motivations might actually lie with me."

"Especially considering the fact that you stole Millicent's memory and then gloated about it," Emmaline pointed out.

"I said you *could* conclude that it's my fault, not that you should! The point is, I can completely understand why you may have thought of me as some evil magician-collecting mastermind, and I don't hold it against you one bit."

Bostwick squinted at her, his usual distrustful expression back on his face.

"There's no catch, Bostwick, not this time. I just can't have you so gloomy when my country is on the line."

"So what you're saying is," Emmaline said brightly, "it doesn't matter whose fault it is for what happened, all that matters now is getting Styx and Millicent back, and to do that we have to work together and trust one another."

"Ugh, you completely missed my point," Delilah said, feigning exasperation, "but enough talk. Bostwick, now that you're back to normal, let's find that library."

She headed for the end of the alley, but Bostwick laid a hand on her arm.

"I'll trust you, this time," he said. It was unclear whether he was being accusatory or apologetic.

"Oh great, now we have the Super-Serious Bostwick. Are all my efforts in vain?"

"All right, now we're lost," Bostwick said.

They were surrounded by tall, twisting black buildings that blocked the fading afternoon sunlight, which was already fighting a losing battle to reach earth through the smoggy sky. The streets here wound endlessly, with no sort of grid to keep them from stopping at dead ends or simply going in circles.

"Why would anyone build such a huge city anyway?" Delilah asked. "Emmaline, haven't you been here before? Why don't you know the way around?"

"I've only been to the gates. When we came through this area last year, they said no humans were allowed in the city. Apparently, we're more reviled here than anywhere else in Ataxia."

"You didn't even try to get in? Not very resourceful."

"We figured that if they couldn't even stand humans in close proximity, then they probably wouldn't be the sort to go into the Empire and wander around a human garden."

"Hmm. I suppose that makes sense. Maybe we should ask for directions again."

"No one wants to talk with us," Bostwick said. "Where are we supposed to get directions?"

"There," she said, indicating a tall building with a huge metal plaque over the door that said *Central Hall of Bureaucracy.* "If anyone will know the way around, I'm sure they will. It looks very official."

They went inside, finding a vast room with a small, octagonal desk in the center. There was a single, horny-toad-like goblin sitting behind it, cutting a snowflake out of a piece of paper. When Delilah approached him, he tossed the paper away, straightened his pince-nez, and plunked a large name plate in front of him, which read *Havoc Narishkeit: Minister of Officialdom, Vice Minister of Red Tape, and Under Secretary of Loquacity, Verbosity, and Redundancy.*

"Ah, I see we have a few humans with us. How ever did you get in?"

"Our map was dropped onto yours," Delilah said. "And for the record, I'm not a human. Now, if you would be so kind as to tell us where the library is."

Havoc spun around on his stool and proceeded to open a number of drawers behind the desk, whipping colored forms out of each before slamming them shut. When he was done, the desktop had disappeared under a layer of paper. He proceeded to shuffle the forms as he spoke, indicating boxes and paragraphs on each form before shuffling to the next and doing likewise.

"You have to fill out this pink form explaining how you got into the city undetected, take it to the Captain of the Guard three blocks east of here, and have yourselves arrested for unlawful entry. Then post bail, and take the goldenrod, orange, and tangerine forms to the Northern Hall of Bureaucracy and drop them off in the Offices of

Identification, Sports and Leisure, and Point-Record Keeping, respectively, so they can officially recognize you as non-human entities and erase any points anyone may have gotten for tormenting you. Then, take this white paper across town to the Cartography Building so they can stamp it for approval, then bring it back here so I can sign it, then take it to the Information Desk on the third floor of the Western Hall of Bureaucracy so they can tell you where the library is. Then go back to jail because humans aren't allowed in there anyway."

Delilah, Bostwick, and Emmaline were silent while Havoc straightened the forms into a stack.

"Thank you," Havoc said, "and have a nice day."

"I'm confused," Delilah began.

"I can repeat it, if you want."

"Please don't."

"Isn't all of this organization a little non-goblinical?" Emmaline asked.

"On the contrary," Havoc replied. "It's as goblinical as can be."

"But I thought goblins thrived on chaos?"

"We thrive on chaos, confusion, and discord, and that is just what we provide. 'Here at the Central Hall of Bureaucracy, where Administration and Organization—blackest of the black arts—are practiced, we constantly and consistently require our clientele to do so many tedious and useless tasks that they are at least frustrated, and at most, run screaming into our sister Bureaucracies, brandishing weapons and holding hostages. If you really want absolute anarchy, you've got to follow the rules'. That's our mission statement."

"But that…" Delilah muttered. "How can you say… Rules?"

"See, you're already losing the ability to speak. Once you fill these forms out, you'll be foaming at the mouth."

"But you can't calculate chaos," Emmaline said.

Havoc pointed to a sign hanging high above his head: *Chaos is Calculated.*

"It's our motto," he said. "I even have it on a coffee mug."

"Maybe we should just leave," she said, glancing at Delilah, who had a glazed expression.

"I'm not taking another step," Bostwick said. "Come on, Emmaline. He obviously knows where the library is; we just have to get him to tell us. Didn't you deal with this kind of thing back in Camellia?"

"My brothers and sisters dealt with the bureaucratic things. I'm the youngest, so I basically watched what Mr. Charles would do."

"Well, how would he handle this?"

Emmaline thought about it. Mr. Charles, the Tea Inspector of Camellia, was famous for being a ruthless negotiator, but he had had many more years of this sort of thing under his belt than she did. No matter how many forms he was presented with or regulations he had to remember, he never seemed to mind. He had once told her that the rules would never just go away. One had to know how to use them for one's own advantage while abiding by them at the same time.

"Well," she began tentatively, "what if we don't turn in the form saying Delilah isn't human, but we wander around the city anyway?"

The goblin squinted at her suspiciously.

"If everyone thought she was a human, then they would… what was it you said? Get points for bothering her or something? Well, wouldn't that skew the total, so that, in the end, you and the rest of the bureaucrats would be the ones who had to fix the points, and fill out all the forms having to do with the incident?"

Havoc blinked once, then replied in a panicky voice, "All right, I suppose, if that is the case, then you only have to fill out the orange and tangerine forms, and then, I suppose, I can tell you where the library is. That way, everyone's happy, right?"

"That's all right, I'm sure we'll find it on our own eventually. It might take a few days, but once we've talked to everyone in the city, and explain that *humans* have a very poor sense of direction…"

Upon hearing this, the goblin dove under the desk and brought back a folded paper.

"Here's a map, all right? I'll even circle the library for you. There. Just don't go talking to people and acting like you're human when you're not."

"Actually, I am a human," Bostwick said.

"Whatever. Just make sure you don't mess up our point total, okay? The king'll banish me faster than you can say…"

"You didn't say anything."

"Exactly!"

"Why does tormenting humans matter so much, anyway?" Delilah asked, finally coming out of her stupor.

"It's our national pastime, of course. The more you

torment a human, the more points you get, and the person with the most points is appointed king. And the current king keeps very close watch over the points, so I don't want you messing them up! He's such a jerk."

"If he's so bad, why don't you just have someone torment a human more and become the new king?" Delilah asked, as if causing humans trouble was the most natural thing in the world.

"Oh, sure, back in the day, that would've worked, but not now. See, there was once a golden age, where everyone would compete for points, and we'd have bimonthly parades to celebrate the new king, because you can't not celebrate a new king, you know."

"Well, of course," Delilah agreed.

"I used to love making everyone file for parade permits," Havoc continued nostalgically, "but the new king got so many points that he's been ruling for over a year, and he's no fun at all. And that's coming from me, the Vice Minister of Red Tape! Not only do we never get parades anymore, but he's stopped the monthly tap dance festival, and banned scissor races, and don't even think of owning a rocking chair. He's a downright tyrant, but there's no one in Catawampus who can dethrone him."

"But why?" Emmaline asked. "How did he get so many points in the first place?"

"The way I heard it, he snuck into a royal garden and cursed a human princess. Turned her into a rabbit." Havoc folded his arms, as if that was that, then did a double take. "There's no way…"

"Oh, yes there is," Emmaline said, then turned to

Bostwick and Delilah. "I think we should pay this king a visit."

"Are you planning on overthrowing him?" Havoc asked excitedly. "You said you weren't a human. Maybe that means there was a mistake with the points. Yes, we'll go with that. Maybe they'll buy it? I've so been hoping for a parade. Here, the palace is right here!"

He circled another spot on the map and shoved it into Delilah's hands, then whipped out an official looking document.

"I've got to get these parade permits ready and tell the other Halls of Bureaucracy the news. Hurry, go! I don't want you suspiciously standing around here should your plan fail. Good luck, usurpers!"

They left him to giggle manically over his work and made their way out of the building.

"So, are we really planning on overthrowing him?" Delilah asked hopefully.

"Let me think," Emmaline said.

"Because I'm so sick of everyone calling me human that I'm willing to direct my fury solely at him. We could take him away and put him in the dungeon, after he changes you back, of course. And maybe we can ask Balder Spleenbeck to pull his tail for us. He seems like he would enjoy that kind of thing."

"That's it!" Emmaline said. "We're going to see the king, but first, let's go back to Castle Styx."

Two

Awake in Chiaroscuro

Millicent woke up, but did not open her eyes. The last thing she remembered was Sebastian, in a strange new goblin form, holding a sword to her throat, then darkness. She wished it had all been a dream and that she would find herself safe in her own bedroom, but she knew it couldn't be so. Wherever she was now, it was much colder than Styx, and she was not wrapped in her quilts and cozy pajamas, but was instead lying on top of smooth sheets, clothed in the yellow dress and apron she had been wearing when she was taken to wherever "here" was. After contemplating where that might be and not thinking of a single answer, she opened her eyes.

A pale face surrounded by white hair was staring sideways down at her. Her gut reaction was to curl into a ball, which she did, and accidentally kneed the man in the nose. He yelled and turned away from her in one swift, fluid motion.

She sat up and observed the man who was now standing next the bed, covering his nose with his hand. He pulled his hand away and examined it, as it was now wet with dark blue blood. Millicent was slightly alarmed at the strange color, but was more startled when she saw the man properly. He did not have a long braid or yellow eyes. Instead, he had a black stripe running up each of his cheeks to just below his eyes, which were a soft, light blue. His hair hung loose and only down to his jawline, and his arms and hands were blue-black. In short, he was not Sebastian.

"I'm sorry!" she said.

"Don't worry," the man said gently. "It's not broken."

"I thought you were someone else. Um, but, who are you, anyway, and where am I?"

She looked around the room, which was as large as Delilah's bedroom in Styx yet seemed to contain the trappings of a living-, bed-, and bathroom; there were chairs and a table, several chests, a dressing table, a washbasin, and an armchair and sofa. Everything, including the large bed she sat on, was designed with beautiful spirals, curves, and floral patterns, but with no color. Absolutely everything, including the man's tunic and pants, was black and white.

"I'm Misha," the man said. "And you're in the Empyreal Palace in the city of Chiaroscuro."

"And where is that?"

Misha looked down at his black fingers.

"I'm not supposed to tell you," he said apologetically.

"Do you know Sebastian?"

He nodded, then exhaled.

"I work for him, though I'm not entirely sure why. You see, I'm a memory merchant—I sell fabricated memories," he explained when Millicent looked at him blankly. "But I can also take memories people have had. And recently, I think I removed a bunch of my own."

"Why?" Millicent asked, wrapping the sheet around

herself. It really was cold.

"I don't remember."

"Oh. Sorry… So, is Sebastian around? Did he tell you who I am?"

"He's, um, busy dealing with some things. He said I'm just supposed to refer to you as 'the guest of the king,' so…"

"King?"

"Yeah. I just call him Sebastian, but he's technically a king, so…"

"What?"

"Of Chiaroscuro… You didn't know?"

"No! No, I didn't. I thought he was just some cat. Well, I knew he was a goblin, but not a king. Tell me everything."

"Everything is an awful lot of thing. Well, we all knew Sebastian as a cat, too, but we made him our king when he came here years ago, because… well, I probably shouldn't tell you. I've been told I was the one who brought him here, but of course I don't remember that."

"But how can that be? Delilah said she found him in her dungeon, and he was locked in there after becoming a cat, so when did you…?"

Misha shrugged.

"Anyway, he was our king for a while, and then he announced he was going to go to Styx to get his true form back, and he was there for a while, and then he came back with you earlier today."

Millicent was still thoroughly confused—and freezing.

"Um," she said, "do you have some heavier blankets than these? I just seem to be getting colder and colder."

Misha looked her over and nodded.

"Of course! It's probably raining right now," he said, though Millicent couldn't hear any sound coming from outside. "I'll get you some blankets right away, and some warmer clothes."

He rushed out of the room, leaving Millicent alone. The first thing she wanted to know was where she really was. She went to one of the arched windows and looked out. Below her, she could see the rooftops of a city, but the buildings seemed crammed together and stacked on top of one another, as if a vast metropolis had been confined to an area no larger than the town of Styx. The buildings were all made of white, gray, and black stone, intricately carved. She could see people moving below on something that looked like walkways running between buildings, but the room she was in was so high up that it was impossible to discern any of their features. When she looked up at the sky, she saw nothing. It was dark, but not like a moonless night. Instead, it was simply blackness going on forever, and now she noticed, when she looked to the edge of the city for a horizon, there was darkness also.

"Cold and dark," she said out loud. "Maybe I'm in a cave, like a huge cavern that's so deep I can't see the top."

"Not exactly," Misha said behind her. He'd come into the room as silently as a ghost. "Here you go."

He handed her a thick quilt and a pile of clothing. Millicent spread them out on the bed. There was a thick black dress with a high collar, short sleeves, and a slit down one side of the skirt, a pair of white pants to wear underneath, and two elbow-length gloves.

"Am I dreaming?" Millicent asked.

"No, I don't think so."

"But these look a lot like the clothes girl magicians wear, and for that matter, your tunic is just like the boys' uniform."

He shrugged again, unhelpfully.

"It's just what we wear. It's much warmer than what you've got on right now, I assure you. There's a changing screen right over there."

While Millicent got the pseudo-magician outfit on, she continued to question Misha, who sat on the bed.

"So earlier, you said we aren't in a big cave. Where are we, then?"

"Sorry, I really can't tell you. Sebastian would be mad."

"Well, what if I guess?"

Misha thought it over, then said, "I suppose if you figure it out, then I wouldn't have been the one to tell you. Yes, that sounds good."

"Are we underground?"

"No."

"Is it nighttime?"

"I don't remember."

Millicent sighed. Getting information from a man who had lost his memory was going to be harder than she'd thought. She came out from behind the screen, smoothing down the skirt, then sat on the bed next to him and wrapped the quilt around her shoulders. There was so much she wanted to know—not simply about their location—that she was afraid he wouldn't be able to tell her.

"This city, Kurasuro?"

"Chiaroscuro."

"Where is it in relation to Styx?"

"Um, currently?" he asked nervously. "Well, um, mostly to the south, a bit to the south east, and um…"

Suddenly, Millicent remembered everything else that had happened before she blacked out. Sebastian had threatened her to get to Delilah, who had torn apart the map of Styx. And now, Styx was…

"Oh no!" Millicent cried. "Styx has been destroyed. How could I have forgotten that. Delilah and Emmaline and—"

She could not go on, thinking of everyone and everything she loved being ripped apart.

"Are they dead?" she asked miserably.

"No no no! Styx isn't destroyed. No. Sebastian told me when he dropped you off here that he was going to scatter the map to the four corners of the globe, although I don't really see how a globe can have corners… but that's not the point, no. He said to tell you, when you woke up, not to worry, because your friends are all right. See? Sebastian is a good king; he wouldn't kill people."

Millicent wanted to tell him he was wrong, to tell him all of the horrible things Sebastian had done, but the more she thought, the more unsure she became. He had attacked Delilah and herself, and had apparently tricked Bostwick into giving him the Domino of Nonpareil, but on the other hand, hadn't they all spent months of time together, as friends, studying magic and living happily in the castle? Hadn't he helped them when they were stumbling through a burning hedge maze, and then again when they crossed the Forest of Infinite Horrors? That couldn't have all just been a ruse to get closer to the map; at least, that's what she wanted to believe.

"I'm so confused," she said at last, starting to cry.

Misha looked around the room, searching for a way to help. At last, he ran to the dressing table and picked up several handkerchiefs, which he handed her to dry her eyes. But, try as she might, the tears would not stop coming.

"Please don't cry. Maybe you should go to sleep again. I can get you more blankets, or food if you're hungry. I'm sure someone will tell you everything you need to know soon," he said, wiping away a tear from her cheek, "and I'll do whatever you need me to do. Please don't worry about anything.

"Why are you being so nice to me?" she asked, finally drying her eyes. "We're perfect strangers."

"Everyone's perfect strangers to me." For the first time, there was sadness in his voice. "I don't remember much of my childhood, or why I live in the palace. I can't even remember who my family is, though one woman keeps claiming to be my sister. I don't have my memories anymore, so I understand what it's like to be confused."

Millicent's self-pity was instantly transformed into sympathy for Misha, and with it came new resolve.

"Don't give up, Misha! I'm sure your memories are somewhere. And I shouldn't give up either! Delilah and Emmaline and Bostwick are all right. Now I just have to find a way to get back to them, and then, we can find your memories, and find out what Sebastian wants."

When she thought about what it would entail to accomplish all this, her resolve vanished as quickly as it had come.

"It might be a little harder than I made it sound. Let's go back to location. Where in relation to the Empire are we?"

"To the north."

The only thing Millicent knew north of the Empire was Styx, and now that that was scattered everywhere, she had no idea where they were. At least she knew they were in Ataxia, somewhere.

"Can"t you give me more of a hint, please?"

"How about this: What do you see when you block out the light?"

"…Nothing?" She had never been good at riddles.

"Sort of. But it's a nothing that's shaped like something… well, a bunch of somethings that make one big thing in Chiaroscuro's case," said Misha cryptically, then rapped his knuckles on his head. "Sorry, now I've probably made it worse. I wish I could just tell you. Maybe Sebastian will say it's all right. He should be getting back soon. In the meantime, are you hungry? You haven't eaten since he brought you here."

Millicent realized that she was very hungry, so Misha hurried away to get some food. She looked out the door after him, which he'd left ajar. Beyond her room was a balcony bordered by a stone rail, and beyond that, an open atrium. As far as she could tell, the building kept going up—even though this floor was quite high already—to a domed roof. She saw, coming toward her, three of the strange black and white goblins speaking in low voices, so she ducked her head back in. This palace was huge, and full of people, Millicent thought, unlike Castle Styx, which was empty except for her dearest friends.

She closed the door and sat, again wrapped in the quilt, on the sofa to wait for the memory merchant's return. Several minutes later, she heard the door open, but it was not Misha.

Standing in the room, in the same white and blue military coat that he had worn when he kidnapped her, was Sebastian. His expression was slightly surprised, as if he'd expected her to be fast asleep when he came in, but now that she was sitting on the sofa starring at him, he had no idea what to do. Millicent herself didn't know how to respond to his sudden appearance, so she simply stared back at him.

"Ah, so you're awake," Sebastian said, shutting the door behind him. "Where's Misha?"

"He went to get me something to eat," she said, bringing her legs up to her chest. She was still not used to Sebastian in his goblin form, and felt most secure with her legs up and her arms wrapped around herself. It was a habit she had learned from Delilah.

"And he told you that Bostwick and Emmaline are safe?"

"And Delilah."

"Yes," he said, almost regretfully. He came closer to the chair next to her, though he didn't sit down. "Are *you* feeling well? I didn't expect you to pass out when we went through the hat. I suppose humans aren't meant to travel that way."

"I'm fine."

"Good," he said, and smiled in what seemed to be genuine relief. Yet it was eerie that he would speak to her so casually, as if he had taken her on a vacation instead of kidnapping her to a strange, unknown place.

"Where are we?" she asked, for the seemingly hundredth time that day, "and please don't just say Chiaroscuro."

"So Misha told you that much, did he? Nothing else, I hope?"

"He said you're a king. Is that true?"

"Technically, yes," he said, sitting down at last. "When I first came here, the Chiaroscurans realized who I was and declared me their king, though it's a fairly honorary title."

"So who are you? Delilah said you were in the dungeon, but if you were here the whole time…"

"I was imprisoned, as Delilah said, but I suppose she also told you that I ran away a short time later. That was because Misha discovered me, or rather, I discovered him and had him bring me to this place. I only returned to Styx a few days before I met you."

"Just to ruin it," Millicent said, speaking into the quilt.

Sebastian bit the side of his index finger and looked away, reminding Millicent of how he used to lick his paw. Even in his goblin form, he still had this nervous habit.

"I'm sorry, Millicent, but it had to be done. You don't know the kind of damage they've caused, that they still cause. Now that Styx is no longer a unified country, the world is a much safer place."

"Delilah never caused any damage. I can't vouch for the other Styx goblins, but Delilah's a good person."

Sebastian made an extremely disdainful sound, and turned back to Millicent.

"Delilah is the epitome of what is wrong with Styx. She's cruel, egotistical, and manipulative."

"She is not!" she said, for the first time getting angry.

"Oh, no? You don't know this, Millicent, but Delilah took something from you. A memory. I don't know if Misha told you his trade, but he captures and sells memories. And he—at least I assume it was him—gave some of his stock to Delilah, who used it on you."

"She wouldn't do something like that," Millicent said adamantly, though doubt was creeping into her mind. "She's my friend."

"You still think so? Even after she made you clean her castle from top to bottom?"

"I like cleaning! She paid me, too, and was teaching me magic, the way her ancestors did."

"Her ancestors? The Styx goblins didn't teach Melieh magic to benefit humanity; they just wanted to cause more havoc and confusion. If humans could retaliate against goblins, things would be so much more 'goblinical', as they say. And if humans had access to the sort of research the Styx goblins had done..." He trailed off, then sighed. "Your situation is no different. To Delilah, you're nothing but a toy, an amusement to be tossed away when she gets bored with you. And if you aren't just who she wants you to be, she can simply take away your memory and start over."

"Stop it!" Millicent said, burying her face deep in the quilt. She wanted to argue with him, but there was nothing she could think to say. She told herself it was a lie, but at the same time, a part of her wanted to know why he would choose to lie about something like that. When she looked up at him, he seemed sadder than ever.

"I'm sorry, Millicent, but it's true," he said quietly. "But never mind Delilah. She's safe, as are the others, and so are you. I apologize for threatening you back in the throne room, but you should know I would never have hurt you."

"Then why did you kidnap me? Why didn't you let me stay in Styx?"

Sebastian said nothing, but bit his finger again. After what seemed like ages, he spoke.

"I want to continue teaching you magic."

"Why?" she asked suspiciously.

"It doesn't matter right now—"

"If you won't tell me, then I won't do it. I'm not going to let you manipulate me the way I did before. You tricked us all just to get the Domino. You have it, don't you, so why do you need me?"

"It's... complicated."

"Then explain it to me. You and Bostwick always found a way to make me understand magic lessons. We used to talk about all kinds of things together, or... or was that just so you could get closer to the Domino? Did you tell Bostwick what you were going to use it for?"

"I didn't lie to him, if that's what you mean. He realized Delilah was just toying with you and he wanted me to help you escape. He did it for you, not for me."

She hid her face in her skirt. Delilah stealing her memory? Bostwick once again pilfering the queen's mask, but for *her*, Millicent's, sake? None of it made sense.

"Millicent," Sebastian began, reaching his hand out to her. She cringed away from him and into a tighter ball, and he withdrew his hand back to his chest.

"You have every right to hate me," he said. "You would have done so when you first met me, if you knew what kind of person I am, and after what I did in Styx..." His eyes traveled to her throat, then darted away. "...I have no right to ask you anything, but there's no one else. If you help me, I promise I won't bother you again."

Millicent looked him over. He was strange, completely

alien from the cat whom she had spent countless afternoons with. But the cadence of his voice was the same, exactly the same as when he'd told her back in the forest, so many months ago, that her magic was impressive, or when he seemed surprised to receive a gift of baked goods as a thank you for teaching her magic.

"I don't hate you," she said at last, which seemed to catch him off guard. "I hate what you did, but… well, I… I thought we were friends."

His jaw tightened, but Millicent couldn't tell what he was thinking. After a moment he swallowed and said, "Like I said, if you knew the truth about me, you wouldn't even want to believe such a thing."

"Well, then, tell me the truth. Tell me why you're doing… whatever it is you're doing. If you explain what's going on, I'll listen. But I want to know everything."

"I'd prefer you didn't," he said, almost to himself. "Then again, it's probably for the best. I think, in the end, you will be only too eager to learn what I have to teach you. Do you know that the clothes you wear now were based on the uniform of Melieh's Academy, hundreds of years ago? They suit you."

"Is that how old you are? Hundreds of years? Emmaline said you were an immortal beast."

"I can't be killed, if that's what you mean, and yes, I can remember life at the Academy over two hundred years ago."

He rose and went to the door.

"Wait," Millicent cried, running to stop him. She grabbed his hand, which was eerily cold. "I have more questions. Where are we? Where is Styx?"

"I'll explain later." He stepped out of the room. "Right now you should eat."

Misha entered the open door, carrying a tray of food, and looked back at Sebastian as he left, then set the tray down on one of the tables.

"Sorry it took so long. All the restaurants and food stalls are outside the palace or in the lower levels, so…"

"Misha," she asked tentatively, "did you ever sell something to Delilah, the Queen of Styx?"

"Um, yes," he said, sounding sheepish. "I sold her a big basket of memories, and, well, some of the daft stalks that I use to take memories."

"Why?" she asked, feeling as if she couldn't breathe.

"Well, the stocks I threw in just to get her to buy the rest. See, there's one thing I do remember, shortly after I forgot pretty much everything else. I was taking inventory of my merchandise, when I saw a bunch of bottles set apart, in a box, and on the box was a note that said, 'Urgent: Sell to Queen Delilah of Styx at all costs'. So I did."

"But why trust some note?"

"It was written in my handwriting. If you can't trust yourself, who can you trust?"

Millicent thought about this. If what he had said was true, then Delilah did have the capability of taking her memory. Millicent was forced to believe what Sebastian had said, but with one addendum. Whatever reason Delilah had for taking her memory had to have been a good one, because Delilah was her best friend. Millicent knew this for certain, and she did trust herself. With this reassurance, and many unanswered questions filling her head, she sat at the table to eat.

The tray had a cooked fish of some kind, as well as a bowl of soup and a peach. Best of all, even better than the smell, was that all the food had deep, vibrant hues. It was the first real color that Millicent had seen here, and color was the only reminder of Styx and the world she had left behind before coming to this endless sea of black and white.

Three

A Hick from Styx

"I don't see why we had to bring him along," Bostwick said.

Between him and Delilah, held captive by two long ropes, walked Balder Spleenbeck, the Gremlin who had attempted to blow up the entire country of Styx. He still wore his goggled hat and leather jacket, and did not look much worse for wear since spending two weeks in the castle dungeon.

"That's what I'd like to know," Balder said, turning his big canine mouth into a frown. "I was all set to tunnel my way out when you had to come down and interrupt me!"

"You were taking a nap," Emmaline replied, stopping in her tracks as they rounded the corner. The king's palace was just across the street, and she wanted to make sure there would be no foul-ups in her plan.

"I don't have time to explain. I don't trust that bureaucrat to keep quiet about this, so we'll have to act fast before anyone in the palace gets suspicious. Delilah, Bostwick, follow my lead. You may have to improvise, but just go with it. Balder, you don't say a word."

The Gremlin snorted defiantly.

"As if I'd listen to a human, especially a human who is actually a rabbit."

"I won't be a rabbit for long, if everything works out as planned. And if you play along, things could go pretty nicely for you, too."

He grunted, as if to say he'd see about that.

They crossed the street and entered the palace without incident. The entrance hall, much like the Hall of Bureaucracy, was needlessly large and empty, with a single goblin guarding a spiral staircase that, presumably, led to the top floor and throne room.

"Hold on there," he said, barring their way with a long halberd. "You can't see the king right now. He's talking to his court. And, as you've most likely heard, he hates humans."

"We want to challenge his right to the crown," Emmaline said.

"Is that so?" he asked with mild curiosity, then leaned down to whisper, though there was no one else around. "To tell the truth, I'd welcome a new king. This guy's a total control freak."

He straightened up and looked around, then moved his halberd aside.

"You can go up and try, though I doubt you'll oust him. The lousy, point-hoarding tyrant."

They hurried up the stairs and down a long hall that led to the throne room, which was dimly lit by the smoggy sky outside and a few candelabras around the room. The space was full of goblins, most of whom stood in small clusters, talking in low voices, though when any of them walked across the floor, they stared at the ground as they went. Emmaline at first assumed this was some sort of Catawampian show of decorum, but then she saw it, that horrible tail. Mostly bald with small tufts of gray fur, it wound all around the room. It was bandaged in several places, most likely where it had been trampled by unsuspecting courtiers. From where Delilah and Bostwick stood, the latter holding Emmaline so she could get a better view, there was no sign of the king himself. Then they heard a shout from somewhere in the crowd.

"Garrulous!"

The crowd rushed to the edges of the room, revealing a tall, plump goblin quivering before a squat, gray goblin with large ears and squashed face. The long tail was connected to the short one's backside.

"It wasn't me, King Drollery. I know it wasn't," the big one said in a meek voice.

"Do you think I'm stupid, Garrulous? Do you think I can't feel when someone steps on my tail with their great hippo feet?"

Garrulous wiggled his feet, which were wide and toeless.

"It didn't feel like I stepped on your tail, honest."

"Of course not," Drollery continued nastily. "Your head's so high up it doesn't know what your feet are doing. But *I* know. And *you* know what that means."

"No, please! I'll be more careful. I'll slide my feet around instead of taking steps. Yeah, that's what I'll do!"

"So my tail can be rolled flat instead of pressed to death in one fell swoop? I don't think so. You are banished!" Drollery said with a wave of his hand.

Emmaline expected guards to storm in and drag

Garrulous away, but instead he simply hung his head and began to walk out of the room. As he walked past her toward the door, Emmaline saw a large tear splash on the floor.

"How dare you treat your subjects this way!" she said.

All eyes fell on Bostwick and Delilah, and even Garrulous turned to see who had dared to speak out against their king.

"Humans!" Drollery growled. "How'd humans get in here? Who let them in?"

"We came in of our own accord."

He finally realized it was Emmaline who had spoken. At first he looked shocked, but then a self-satisfied sneer spread across his face.

"Come to beg for forgiveness, eh? Well, you aren't getting any. Take a good look, everyone. That rabbit there is actually the princess I cursed. It seems she hasn't changed back yet."

The goblins laughed half-heartedly.

"You should all be thanking her," Drollery continued. "She's the one who sealed my role as King of Catawampus."

No one spoke until the king growled angrily.

"Thank you so much!" a scaly goblin said. "We wouldn't have our beloved king without you."

"He's terrifically wonderful and kind," another continued.

"And a snappy dresser."

"And it's all thanks to you!"

"Yeah, it's all your fault," Garrulous said, then added, when everyone shot him disapproving looks, "Hey, I'm banished anyway."

"Not if I have anything to say about it," said Emmaline.

"Oh? And what exactly are you going to do?" Drollery asked.

"I want to challenge your kingship."

The room went silent.

"Only goblins can rule Catawampus," Drollery said.

"Of course," the rabbit agreed, "that's why we brought a goblin to do the job."

Delilah pushed Spleenbeck forward. He didn't look particularly regal, dressed in his scruffy jacket and standing only two feet tall. He was even dwarfed by Drollery, who was six inches higher than him.

"Why's he tied up?" one of the goblins asked.

"So he can't escape and do any more harm," Emmaline explained. "The Gremlin standing before you is Balder 'Dash' Spleenbeck, a notorious criminal, enemy to humans and goblins alike. And he wants your throne."

"Preposterous," Drollery said. "Aimless, tell her why."

A tall, skinny goblin that resembled a secretary bird, only with spectacles and a waistcoat, stepped out of the crowd. He held an abacus in his wing-like hands and began to furiously slide its beads back and forth. Emmaline assumed this was more for show than anything else, because she knew how to use an abacus properly, and Aimless was not doing it.

"Ah, yes, yes," the flustered goblin said. "Well, you see, Miss, because our fantastic and radiant ruler turned a human princess into a rabbit, unprovoked, he garnered himself, let's see, eight thousand four hundred and fifty-three points, and since we now know that you've remained that way for, let's see, one year, six months, and twelve days, that brings his total up to nine thousand six hundred and six."

Many of the goblins in the crowd hissed and muttered. Now it would only be harder to dethrone him.

"He was not unprovoked!" Emmaline said. "I stepped on his tail, the same as Garrulous. He was just mad, so he cursed me."

"Ah, well, that changes things." Aimless slid a few more beads to the right. "He's down to an even nine thousand."

"So you see," Drollery said, walking to a short throne that sat against the back wall. "Your little Gremlin—Spleenbeck, was it?—has no hope of defeating me."

"None whatsoever," someone in the crowd said.

"We'll see about that," Emmaline countered. "Goblins and… female goblins, allow me to tell you of the many atrocities that Spleenbeck has performed against this woman's country." She indicated Delilah with her paw. "He first attempted to bomb the entire area within our borders, and finding that this was impossible, took it upon himself to cause as much havoc as he could. He bombed buildings individually, completely burnt down our center of commerce, and attempted to murder several members of law enforcement, all the while distracting us from the real danger. Because of his efforts, an immortal beast was allowed to slip in and kidnap a girl named Millicent, who held the second highest post in the land, as the magician of the woman who stands before you now. Furthermore, all of his actions were completely unprovoked, done out of malice for our kind and no other reason. If that isn't the most goblinical mischief one can do, I don't know what is."

The courtiers looked back and forth between Emmaline and their king, wondering who would win.

"Ha," Drollery scoffed. "Even if he did all that you claim, that's hardly impressive. Messing around with a few hicks in an uncultured human backwater is child's play. I cursed a princess. Beat that."

There was a murmur of agreement from the crowd, but before Emmaline could respond, Delilah exploded into the fury she had been holding back the entire time they were in Catawampus.

"UNCULTURED HUMAN BACKWATER? How dare you, you mincing, bloated, pathetic excuse for a tail-rack! My country is comprised of only the best artisans and scientists from across the continent. Statues from our black stone mountains grace the halls of kings! Our fruit, ours only, has the beauty and spikiness of the goblin heart, and the taste of the sun, glowing overhead! And that's all going to be lost if you sit here on your long-tailed rear, gorging yourself on cheap praise from these idiots you call a court, who will no doubt be punished if they fail to do so. As we speak, my poor country is scattered across the world, imperiled by the carelessness of people like you. And for the last time, I am not a stinking hum—"

But Bostwick hastily covered her mouth before she could say anything more. The goblins stared at her in awe, while Drollery turned green with worry.

"Did you hear that?" someone in the crowd said. "A country spread across the world, the most supreme in all the land! Blimey, do you know who she is? She's the blinkin' empress of the humans!"

Delilah spasmed and clawed at whoever had said it, but Bostwick held her back.

"She's the empress, all right," a rotund goblin agreed in a deep baritone. "I seen her two years ago with me own eyes."

"Yes, yes, we remember you distinctly," Emmaline concurred, though it was an absolute lie.

"Then that means," Garrulous said, sounding thoroughly relieved, "that Mr. Spleenbeck tried to destroy the Empire!"

Aimless hastily pushed the beads of his abacus around, as the crowd and Drollery held their breath.

"Then that gives Spleenbeck," he said at last, "five million twenty-four thousand six hundred and eighty-four points! Spleenbeck wins!"

The crowd erupted in a cheer, and those standing closest to the throne picked Drollery up and threw him off it. The rest surrounded Balder and hoisted him above their heads. His grin was so big that they couldn't even see the rest of his face.

"We must have a parade immediately!" Aimless squawked.

"In a moment," Balder said. "I'd like to speak to the humans alone, but first," he called to Drollery, who was hastily gathering up his tail so none of the celebrating goblins would step on it, "change the rabbit back."

"You want to help a human? That doesn't sound very goblinical to me," Drollery sneered, clearly sore that he'd lost the throne to such a bleeding heart.

"The definition of goblinical is as follows," Aimless provided, "chaotic, unexpected, trivial, and goblin-like. All else aside, Spleenbeck is asking you to change the princess back, and he is a goblin, so we can accurately say that his request is goblin-like. Besides, kindness to humans is unexpected on its own."

"The humans did free us from a horrible tyrant," the scaly

goblin said, as if Drollery wasn't perfectly able to hear. "Perhaps they aren't as bad as we thought."

"And this one here's almost what you might call attractive, for a human," another one said, indicating Bostwick, who recoiled in disgust.

"Perhaps I shall usher in a new age of harmony between the humans and goblins," Balder said, sounding exceedingly self-important, "or perhaps not. But for now, change the rabbit."

Drollery glared at Emmaline with loathing, and was about to clap his hands when Emmaline hopped out of Bostwick's arms.

"Um, just before we continue," she said, "does anyone have a spare dress or something? My clothes fell off when I first transformed, so…"

One of the goblins ran to get something for her to wear while Bostwick conjured a curtain for her to change behind. Drollery made a show of yawning and stretching. The goblin finally returned, threw a bundle of clothes behind the curtain to Emmaline, and ran back into the crowd. Drollery clapped his hands with a bored expression and smoke puffed out from behind the curtain. After a minute, Emmaline emerged, human once again, with long, curly blonde hair, brown eyes, and a blue frock and bloomers the goblin had provided.

"Good, then," Balder said. "Now put me down and be off with the lot of you. Prepare my parade. I want lots of confetti."

The goblins streamed out, the last of which was Drollery, who dragged his feet in an act of civil disobedience. When the door shut, Balder turned to the humans, plus Delilah.

"I may have been wrong about you," he said. "I thought humans were thick-headed fools who understood little about the goings-on of the universe, but I see now that I was mistaken. That just now! Goblinical! Oh, the lies you told, monstrous they were!"

"They were mostly the truth, just stated accordingly," Emmaline said.

"Oh, you humans, lying even to yourselves! And then taking the situation with all the trouble I caused and using it to your advantage. Devious! So devious that I doubt we goblins have a word for such a thing."

"It's called 'diplomacy'," Bostwick said. Emmaline elbowed him.

"Ah," Delilah said, composing herself. "I'm glad we have your approval, Spleenbeck, though we never needed it."

"'We' nothing," he said, turning his face into a grimace. "I said I liked the humans, not you. I've always despised Styx and always will."

"What?"

"You gave the humans goblin magic, and for that, I will never forgive you."

"But if you like humans now, why does it matter if we taught them magic? You just talked about a new age of human and goblin friendliness. That's what we've been doing all along."

"I wish you could hear yourself. Sad. You really could be mistaken for a human, until you open your mouth."

Delilah lunged at him, ready to wring his stout neck. It was fortunate that Emmaline was human now, as it took both her and Bostwick to hold Delilah back.

♠ ♦ ♣ ♥ ♣ ♦ ♠

Emmaline could not stop moving. As they made their way to the library, she swung her arms, skipped, and wheeled around lampposts. Having her real body back was nothing like wearing the Domino. Somehow, she felt freer, less constricted. She wondered if this was due to some flaw in the magic of the mask, or simply the knowledge that this time she would not have to say goodbye to her human features. She would never have to be a rabbit again.

"Would you come down from there?" Bostwick said. "You're gonna fall".

Emmaline had just hopped onto a wall that gradually rose. Now, her feet were well above the magician's head.

"Calm down, Bostwick. I know what I'm doing."

"I don't want to bring you home to your family just to tell them that you broke your neck right after becoming human again."

"You can catch me, then" she said, and continued on.

By the time they reached the library, the sky had turned a dark rust color, and streetlights came on of their own accord throughout the city. Emmaline bounded up the steps of the library and threw open the door as Bostwick and Delilah trailed behind her. The inside of the building was a dark, cavernous room with hundreds of tall bookshelves that rose to the ceiling and ran in every direction. A few paces in was a circular desk of polished wood with a green reading lamp. They approached this, looking around them at the enormity of the room. A figure rose up from behind the desk, tall and spidery, but with an almost human face. Its features, however, were exaggerated. Its nose was too big, as were its drooping eyes, and its mouth was spread in a slack frown.

"And what do you think you're doing?" the librarian asked, disdainfully.

"We need to get to your map room," Delilah said.

"Well, you can't."

"Can't?"

"Can't. The map room is on the top floor, and you can't go there."

"Why on earth not?"

The librarian frowned even more.

"No humans allowed. Technically, you shouldn't even be in the library."

"I'm not human! And I certainly can go to the top floor! Now which way is it?"

The librarian pointed a long, gloved finger behind him and to the left.

"But you still can't go there. You probably haven't heard," he said, in a hideously condescending way, "but the library of Catawampus is known as the Labyrinth of Infinite Knowledge. If you go into those shelves without a guide, you'll be lost for eternity, or more likely, you'll starve and it will be up to me to haul your carcass away. Which I don't feel like doing at present. So you can't go in."

"But we're allowed in now," Emmaline pointed out. "There's a new king, you know."

"So?"

"He's a… an acquaintance of ours, and he likes humans."

The librarian rolled his eyes and made an exceedingly put-upon expression.

"I really should wait until the king fills out the proper forms, but I despise the bureaucrats almost as much as everyone else."

"As much as everyone else… does?"

"No. Now follow me, so you can look at the map and get out."

The librarian led them through rows and rows of bookshelves, all set at strange angles. It was obvious why the place was called a labyrinth. By the time they stopped walking, Emmaline was certain she could never have found her way out again. She looked around for a staircase.

"Aren't we going up?"

"We are," the librarian responded, sounding disdainful once again, "in here."

He gestured to a cage-like room that was set into the wall of books. When they were all inside, he shut the door of the cage and pulled a shiny brass lever downward. The cage immediately started to go up. Emmaline looked above them, and saw a long rope going around a pulley, as layers and layers of shelves slid past them.

"Amazing!"

"Isn't it just," the librarian said, though his voice made it sound as if he would've preferred watching mold grow.

The cage stopped abruptly, and the librarian opened the door, revealing a brightly-lit, circular room with windows looking out from every angle. There were metal devices scattered around the floor and hanging from the ceiling, and a strange, froglike creature sat in the center of the room facing them. Its stomach was the color of parchment, and on its back was an enormous brown birthmark.

"Visitors to see you, Shujaa," the librarian said to the creature.

"Oh joy, some more people coming here to poke and prod at me and flip me over," it said. "That's what I get for being a map."

"You're the map?" Bostwick asked.

"Yup."

"But, I thought goblin maps were created by cartographers, like Heather."

"Some are; some aren't. They're all different, you know? I've got mine on my skin."

"Legend has it," the librarian said, "that the country of Catawampus was won from the barbarians of the Gammon Coast in the Bedlam War by Duplicity Jinx. But that's just a story."

"It's not!" Shujaa said. "Duplicity was a personal friend of mine, and when she won that battle, I let her seal the map into my skin so there would be no more boundary disputes. Not a well thought out decision on my part."

"Don't listen to him," the librarian said, poking Shujaa in the stomach. "He's mad as a brush, always claiming to be an immortal beast."

"And I suppose I've been around so long because of clean living?"

"You claim to have lived thousands of years, but I've only known you for forty. You may be about to kick off for all I know."

"Yes, lovely," Delilah said, sick of their banter. "Now turn around. We need our map piece."

"Oh, this is yours?" Shujaa turned in a small circle,

revealing the map of Styx Castle stuck to his back. "Yes, would you kindly take it, please? This crazy white guy comes out of nowhere, slaps the thing onto me, and disappears. There are just no manners these days, I tell you."

Delilah pulled the map piece away from the creature's skin, which was covered in a sticky solution.

"So, did Styx Castle go back to its location?" Emmaline asked.

"Whatever's on that map isn't moving till you put that scrap of paper onto some other poor country's map," Shujaa said. "But please, ask permission first."

They thanked Shujaa, and the librarian led them back down and out to the street.

"Do you think he really was an immortal beast?" Emmaline asked.

"I don't suppose it matters one way or the other," Delilah said. "As long as he isn't Sebastian, he can live as long as he wants. Here, Emmaline, you hold the map piece."

"Why me?"

"You're responsible," Delilah said, handing her the scrap of paper.

"How are we going to find the other pieces?" Bostwick asked. "They could be anywhere."

"We're going to someone who can give us a better look around."

"But even if we know where to go," Emmaline said, as Delilah led the way back to the castle, "how are we going to get there? Ataxia is huge. Believe me; we had to walk across the whole thing."

"We won't be walking," she said sagely. "It just so

happens that the people who can show us where Styx is can also, hopefully, help us get there. We just have to make a brief stop in Lesse's Moor first."

Bostwick and Emmaline glanced at each other. The goblins of Lesse's Moor were the ones who had told them about the Domino of Nonpareil in the first place. If Delilah ever found out it was them, there was no telling what she might do. As such, Lesse's Moor was the last place either of the two humans wanted to be.

Four

Lesse's Moor

"It seems like just this afternoon our quest began," Delilah said when they reached the castle door.

"It *was* this afternoon," Bostwick said, as Emmaline bounded past him. "Where are you running off to?"

"Well, shouldn't we get going? We've still got to find three more pieces of the map. Delilah, do you have any spare clothes that would fit me?"

"On the third story there's a whole dressing room, last door on the ceiling."

With that, Emmaline was off.

"I guess turning back into a human gives you a lot of energy, eh Bostwick? We'll still wait till tomorrow to head out of the city, though. In the meantime, you should get ready to go. We won't be returning to Castle Styx," she said, placing a hand affectionately on the door frame, "until we gather up the rest of the country. So pack whatever you might need for our journey, and get a good night's sleep. I'm going to see Heather."

Bostwick went to his room, and saw on his bed the bag of Millicent's belongings he had hastily packed that morning.

He felt sick just looking at it. Why on earth had he trusted Sebastian? It seemed obvious what his plan had been now. He'd only told Bostwick to gather Millicent's things to buy time, and here they sat, useless to the girl who might need them, wherever she was. He pictured her, alone and imprisoned, in the blackness of wherever a hat led to. They would find her; he knew they would. Delilah seemed determined, and for some reason, that gave him hope.

He picked up the bag, which was full to the brim, and found that it was virtually weightless. No doubt Millicent had bought this from the Rare and Priceless Counterfeit Shop. He smiled, in spite of the awful situation. Millicent really did have remarkably good sense when it came money.

The next morning, Emmaline came downstairs in a pair of jodhpurs, tall boots, and a leather jacket. As she had been a rabbit for over a year, she had few possessions, but she did put the map piece and the fake wishing stone that Millicent had given her into one of her pockets. Bostwick dressed in a plain shirt and vest and packed the rest of his belongings—as well as Emmaline's extra clothing—inside of his hat. He tucked his lone book of poetry into his vest pocket, donned his hat, and picked up the bag of Millicent's belongings, just in case they found her in the next part of Styx. And who knew, some of the items from Rare and Priceless might prove useful.

He and Emmaline waited on the front steps of the castle to wait for Delilah. Several passing goblins waved hello to them or even wished them good morning. When Delilah finally came down, she was not dressed in one of her many form-fitting gowns, but instead wore a beige leather tunic that bore some resemblance to a towel wrapped around her body, though it was more tailored and had a line of buttons keeping it together. Under this she wore cream colored leggings, and had long boots and gloves that matched her tunic.

"What is that supposed to be?" Bostwick asked, indicating her clothes.

"These happen to be traditional Lesserian garments. But you should know that. Now, where is Heather?"

She looked around expectantly. Without warning, a large carpetbag dropped from the sky. Delilah caught it in both arms.

"Is that everything?" Heather called from a second story window.

"Yep. Well then, I suppose we'll be off. Take good care of my castle. Make sure the garden is in good shape, and that the pineapples don't die!"

"Will do," Heather called.

Delilah led the way down the street, heading south. Emmaline looked back after they had gone three blocks.

"Delilah, don't you want a last look at your castle?"

"I'll see it again," she said, glancing back at it nonchalantly. "I think it looks nicer against a blue sky."

They arrived at the southern gate of Catawampus around noon, but the sky beyond the spiked city walls was already dark with storm clouds and haze. A short goblin in steel-studded armor turned a large metal wheel which opened the gate. Slowly and with a great amount of creaking, the doors opened outward onto a flat expanse of rock, bracken, and gray grass: the moor.

They walked out and did not turn around to see the gate shut behind them. Not having much to talk about, they went silently at first. The way was fairly easy going, though the clouds soon started to drizzle.

"So how far away is the town?" Emmaline asked, more to make conversation than anything else.

"It's really more of a hamlet," Delilah said. "We should be there in maybe an hour or two."

Emmaline looked at Bostwick, who returned her glance. If they were going to tell Delilah, it would be better for everyone if they did it when the hamlet was still far away.

"You know," Emmaline began, "Bostwick and I have been here before, to Lesse's Moor, I mean."

"Hmm?"

"The people who live out here are very nice. Much more hospitable than the Catawampians. They would never mistake you for a human."

"I should hope not," she said simply, and shifted her carpetbag to the other hand.

"And they helped us immensely," Emmaline continued, trying to find a delicate way to put it.

"They told you about the Domino of Nonpareil and where to find it. I know."

"And you aren't angry?" Bostwick asked.

"Of course not. They were just trying to be helpful. Of course, they should have known I'd never give it up. What were they thinking?"

"So, you aren't going to curse them, or burn their houses down or anything?"

"What do you take me for, some sort of monster? For such silliness, you must carry my bag," she said, shoving it into Bostwick's hand. "It's raining harder, now, isn't it?"

She stopped for a moment to conjure a large, glowing circle above all of their heads. The raindrops hissed and sizzled as they hit it.

"That should keep us dry."

"Seems like a waste," Bostwick said. "Isn't that supposed to be ancient Styx magic?"

"Why not cast a spell when it's most useful?"

"I agree," said Emmaline. "There's no point in saving magic for a rainy day. Or, well, you know what I mean."

"Exactly. Now, to make the time pass faster, I shall recite some traditional goblin poetry for you. Have you ever heard 'My Love is Like a Stripy Scarf?'"

They continued on, listening to poem after poem, and when Delilah had exhausted her store of memorized verse, Emmaline offered a sonnet and several *shi* poems. Finally, in the distance, they could see a faint glow through the downpour. Soon, they came to houses made of weathered wood that stood on stilts. Every building had a covered porch, with nets and lanterns hanging from the roof. On these porches sat a few goblins that had terra cotta colored skin and dark hair in hues of purple and pink. They were more humanoid than any of the Catawampians, though they had large bat ears. None of them spoke, though a couple waved to Delilah as she strode forward and stopped before one of the houses. She climbed the steps and knocked on the door as Emmaline and Bostwick tried to stomp as much mud off their shoes as they could.

A female goblin with a cane answered the door. She was the very goblin who had told Bostwick where to find the Domino, and looked just as she had the first time he had seen her, dressed in gray leather, with straight, gray-green hair running down her back, and triangular glasses in front of almost-shut eyes.

"Delilah?" she said, opening her eyes, revealing snake pupils.

"Mom!" Delilah cried.

She rushed forward and hugged the woman as Bostwick and Emmaline exchanged confused glances.

"She's your mother?" Bostwick asked.

"Of course I am," the woman said. "Raina Cacoethes of Styx, and Lesse's Moor, now. And if I'm not mistaken, you're that magician who came around here last year. How's everything going?"

"But you told us you were a wise woman from Mount Rigmarole," Bostwick said, flabbergasted, "who came to the moor to learn medicinal secrets!"

"I lied," she said with a shrug.

"But why are you here? I always just assumed Delilah's parents had died or something."

"Silly! I just got tired of ruling Styx and Delilah was old enough, so Bedlam—that's my husband—and I came back here. He's the potentate of the moor, you know? But why I'm here isn't important. What are you doing here, and who are *you*?"

She indicated Emmaline with her cane.

"I'm the rabbit Bostwick had last time. I was the one who needed the Domino, not him."

"Ah, so you used it, then?"

"No," Emmaline began, about to explain everything, but Bostwick cut in.

"Why did you tell me about the Domino if you knew she" he said, gesturing at Delilah with his thumb, "wouldn't give it to us?"

"Well, you just said you wanted to find something to break curses or let someone change shape; you never said you wanted to use it. I assumed you were doing research for the Academy or something."

"Then why didn't you at least tell me who you were, so I could tell Delilah you sent me?"

"I thought a magician would recognize a Styx goblin at once," she said with a haughty *hmph*, "but you obviously had no idea, nor appreciation, for who I was. So I thought it much more fun to invent some story about myself, and let Delilah do with you what she wished. What *did* you do, dear?"

"He tried to steal it," Delilah said, "so I forced him to become my butler."

"Lovely! Now Millicent won't have to work so hard. Where is she, anyway? Back at the castle? Or on vacation?"

She stopped at the look on their faces and ushered them inside. The living room of the house was covered in books and gadgets. Raina moved a pile of rolled up papers off the couch for Emmaline and Delilah to sit on, and directed Bostwick toward an armchair that was taken up by a large birdcage. She herself stood in front of a potbellied stove that had a cauldron of stew on top of it. She stirred this and added vegetables as Emmaline and Bostwick told her about teaching Millicent magic, Sebastian's transformation, and the map being torn apart. Emmaline downplayed Bostwick's role in giving the Domino to Sebastian and merely said that the cat "got the Domino and used it". Delilah was silent the entire time, and only spoke to thank her mother as Raina handed out bowls of stew.

"Well," Raina said at last, "that's no good. It would have been better if you'd kept that cat in the dungeon. And you've no idea where he went?"

"No," said Bostwick. "He just disappeared into my top hat."

"Well, conceivably, the hat could act like a portal, for whatever kind of goblin he was. Maybe there'll be a clue with one of the other map pieces."

"But how are we supposed to find them?" Emmaline asked.

"When it stops raining, you can use our telescope. Large bits of misplaced country shouldn't be hard to find. Bedlam can help you with getting there. But in the meantime, what are you going to do about Sebastian once you find him?"

"Well, we'll fight him, I suppose."

"That's a start, but what do you plan to do against the Domino?"

"What do you mean?" Bostwick asked. "He has his true form back, but that doesn't mean he's unstoppable."

Raina scoffed.

"The Domino doesn't just give things their true forms back. It allows the wearer to transform into anything as big as a dragon or as small as a gnat and, what's worse, gives them all powers and attributes of that thing. If he turns into a wyrm, he can breathe fire; if he turned into a diamond, no blade could harm him; and if he turned into a phantasmal jellyfish, he would be completely invisible."

"But then, wouldn't he also have all their weaknesses, too?" Emmaline asked.

"True, but don't expect him to turn into a mouse just because you ask nicely."

"There must be something we can do," said Bostwick. "Can't you give us more information about the Domino? Why was it created in the first place?"

"Ah, now there's a story. It was over four hundred years ago; Queen Stultiloquence of Gammon was throwing a masquerade ball for all of the monarchs in Ataxia. At this ball there was to be a marvelous contest to see which country had the best costume of all. As you know, the family of Styx had long been scorned by the rest of the goblin nations for its closeness—in appearance and proximity—to humans, so we simply had to win. It was a matter of pride. So Louis Fustian Jasper the Third of Styx, with the help of the rest of the family, created the Domino of Nonpareil for his wife Natasha Caprice to wear. That way, she could turn herself into any of the party-goers, including whomever wore the best costume, and would thus best them all."

"Let me get this straight," said Bostwick. "You created one of the most powerful magical items ever, capable of giving the wearer all abilities of anything they can imagine, just to win a stupid contest?"

"It wasn't stupid at the time, dear. Styx's honor was at stake."

"Well, I'm so glad you imperiled the world, as long as you kept your honor."

"Oh, we didn't win. See, three princes from Bombast dressed as a set: a knife, a spoon, and a fork. We had not foreseen this, and so were unprepared to—"

"It doesn't matter if you won or not! The Domino is in the hands of an incredibly powerful goblin, and it wouldn't have happened if you hadn't made it in the first place."

"What's made is made," said Delilah at last, "but I think we should be all right for the time being. Sebastian only wanted the Domino to get his true form back. I doubt he's even considered the possibility of using it for combat. He seemed perfectly happy fighting without it."

"That's true," Emmaline said. "And even if he would use it to fight with, it must have some weakness."

"Well," Raina said, "you can't turn into yourself-not-wearing-the-Domino. As soon as you try, the Domino shows up on your face, right as rain."

"Well, that's incredibly helpful," Bostwick said disdainfully.

"Hmm," Delilah said, licking out the dregs of her bowl. "Mom, where's Dad at?"

"He's working on an invention, though I'm not sure which one. I swear, he starts a new one every month. Well, I might as well take you out to see them, but you humans should finish your stew first."

After they had done as she asked, Raina led the group out a back door and over a low rope bridge that went into an immense tent that was the exact color of the mud around it. The inside of the tent was smoky and littered with metal cogs and bits of wood, some of which resembled parts of machines. Suddenly, something exploded from within the smoke and a Lessarian goblin with short, magenta, spiked hair and a leather coat came running toward them.

"Raina!" he said coughing. "I've done it! I've finally done it!"

He grabbed Delilah's mother around the waist, spun her around and down into a dip, and kissed her.

"We have guests, dear," Raina said, floating back up.

Bedlam looked from his wife to Delilah and the humans and threw his hands up in excitement.

"Delilah! You're just in time to witness the making of history. And Millicent, you've changed your hair since the last time I saw you."

"Um, I'm not Millicent," Emmaline said.

Bedlam squinted and examined her closely, then for good measure looked Bostwick up and down, too.

"No, I guess you aren't," he mumbled. "I never could tell humans apart. So, what brings you all here?"

"Millicent got kidnapped and Styx got torn up and we have to find them both," Delilah said hastily, before anyone could give a more lengthy explanation. "Can we use the telescope?"

"Absolutely! Why didn't you say so sooner?"

He ran into the smoke once more and Delilah nodded for them all to follow. When they found him, he was sitting in a chair, under a large contraption with levers, gears, and an eyepiece.

"Ah, well, the castle's sitting right in the middle of Catawampus."

"We got that piece already," Delilah said. "We need to find the town, the forest, and the Wastes."

Bedlam pulled one of the levers and turned a large knob slowly. The tent was filled with a mechanical hum as the top part of the machine rotated above them. It slowed to a stop as Bedlam flipped the lever back up.

"Okay, there's the town in the Gammon Archipelago. Say, you wouldn't mind telling me how it got there, huh?"

"I tore the map up," Delilah said reluctantly, as her father moved the telescope again.

"Risky," he said, once the humming noise had died down. "I might be mistaken, but it looks like the Forest of Infinite Horrors is spilling out from between the Tumult Mountains. I hope the snakes will be all right."

He pulled the lever once more, and turned the knob around several times. After three more revolutions, the telescope stopped.

"Well?" Delilah asked.

"Can't find it. But don't worry, this thing can't even see as far as Din, so it's probably just out of range. Anything else?"

"We could use a vehicle of some sort."

Bedlam looked at his daughter seriously, and seemed to be having an internal struggle. At last, he stood up and clapped her on the shoulder.

"Delilah, I will let you use my new invention. Only because you are my daughter and I love you and I trust you will take care of it, and only because you need to get Styx back together, and only because you also need to find Millicent, will I let you, and not myself, have the maiden voyage of my new invention."

He dropped his hand and swept away dramatically into the smoke.

"I hope this is really all right," Emmaline said.

"Oh, don't worry," Raina replied. "He's got dozens of more inventions to work on before you get back. Besides, you can make sure it's safe to ride in."

"Out here!" Bedlam called.

They made their way to the back of the tent and through a small flap in the side. Bedlam stood next to a huge wicker contraption that vaguely resembled a very large, clawfoot-bathtub floating several feet above the murky water of the moor. It was suspended by ropes from a giant, stitched-together balloon as big as two elephants. Attached at seemingly random spots upon the device were metal and canvas fins and propellers pointing at various angles.

"I first got the idea when your mother and I were traveling through Greml," Bedlam explained. "The Gremlins have been drawing up plans for aviation devices like this for centuries, talking about 'air planes' and such, but because of their lack of thumbs, they've never managed to successfully build one. And now, after years of research, I've finally done what they couldn't! Using magic and science, I have harnessed the power of flight! I call it: a flying machine!"

"I still think it needs a better name. One that rolls off the tongue," Raina said.

"Who cares what it's called? It flies!" Delilah cried. She stared at the ship like it was made of pure gold.

"How does it stay up?" Bostwick asked.

"I'd tell you how it works, but you'd never understand it," Bedlam said, then whipped out a thin, hand-bound book.

"Now, who wants to be the pilot?"

Delilah looked expectantly at Bostwick.

"No way! If I can't drive a jaunty car or an automobile, how on earth am I supposed to fly that thing?"

"Well, I can't do it. First off, I'm a queen. I must be royal and regal and working with machines just doesn't fit the bill. And secondly, if I crashed it, my dear father would certainly disown me."

"That's right," Bedlam agreed jovially. "How about you, little blonde girl?"

Emmaline took the book and flipped through the pages.

"Well, it doesn't look too difficult. I guess if I have time to study it a bit…"

"You can study it tonight while I make supper," Raina offered. "It's mushroom and moor-eel surprise!"

"What's the surprise?" Bostwick said, compelled to ask a question he didn't want answered.

"Depends on what mushroom you use."

"I don't think I can learn to fly this in one night," Emmaline said, but Bedlam insisted that it would be fine. He proceeded to show her and Bostwick the various parts of the contraption, explaining about mechano-magical engineering, while Delilah helped her mother in the kitchen.

The rest of the evening was spent eating what turned out to be several hunks of eel meat and blue mushroom pieces skewered on a stick and roasted. Emmaline and Delilah ate hungrily, while Bostwick carefully avoided consuming any of the fungus, all the while listening to Raina and Bedlam tell the story of how they met. There was far more betrayal and piracy than Emmaline would have expected in the story of an arranged marriage, and Bostwick found the third incident involving a duel to the death to be slightly unbelievable.

The next morning, Bostwick and Delilah awoke to find Emmaline already inspecting the flying machine's balloon for holes.

"It seems all right," she said uncertainly.

"No worries," Bedlam said, coming out of the tent. "The odds of the balloon popping are… slim."

"Why did you pause?" Bostwick asked.

"Ha ha. What pause? I'm just too excited about my machine's first launch to do complicated statistics. Now, we've taken the liberty of packing you all some supplies for the journey."

"Some blankets and clothes," Raina said, handing them several large baskets, "and there're also plenty of snacks in there for when you get hungry. Make sure you tie them down, in case of gusts."

"And the ship is already outfitted for an expedition. That's what I've decided to call it: a sky ship."

"Still needs work," Raina said, laying a hand on Bedlam's arm.

"Well, I suppose we should get going," Emmaline said, hopping into the tub.

"Thanks for the ship," Bostwick added, and followed Emmaline.

Delilah hugged each of her parents, did an odd sort of salute, and fell backwards into the tub, then stood up.

"I'll take good care of it, don't worry."

"Take care of yourself, too," Raina said.

"And bring Millicent for a visit when you rescue her," Bedlam added.

"And brush your teeth, and wear clean underwear. And make sure you get enough sleep, or else horrible monsters will infest your dreams."

"It's true, you know," Delilah said, turning to her companions.

The ship climbed remarkably quickly, leaving Delilah's waving parents far below. While Emmaline was occupied with various mechanisms around the ship, Delilah pointed out interesting geographical features to Bostwick.

"Look, there's Catawampus! And let's see, the moor keeps going, until that black line there. That's the Hubbub River, which marks the southern edge of the country of Catawampus, which was named for its capital city, of course. Then over there to the west is the Gammon Coast, that grim blue-gray sort of area. To the east is—"

"We've been through here before, you know?"

"All right then, Mr. Know-It-All, what's to the north of Catawampus?"

Bostwick looked over the edge of the ship and past the black spires of the city. The morning light shining through the smog made it difficult to see very far, but he thought he saw the gray outline of mountains away to the north.

"We never went that far," he said. "It's some country called Pandemonium, right?"

"Oh Bostwick, I wouldn't expect you to know. Perhaps you could never afford a map." She patted his hand, which he withdrew immediately. "Pandemonium is the name of the continent, or, well, a sub-continent. A dwarf continent, really."

"Yes. I get it."

"So anyway, that's where the next piece of the map is. My dad said that it's in Tumult, that-a-way."

She pointed to the left of the city. Emmaline turned a brass wheel, and the ship spun violently, sending Bostwick and Delilah to the floor

"What are you doing? My parents can still see us!"

"Sorry," Emmaline said, steadying the craft. "This is my first time piloting an air ship, you know?"

Delilah sprung up and grabbed Emmaline by the shoulders, then ran to the side of the ship and leaned over.

"Hey, Dad, how about calling this an airship?" she called.

"Brilliant!" came the distant reply.

"All right, then, Emmaline. You have dubbed this an airship. Set course for Pandemonium!"

Five

Keeping Up Appearances

Sebastian nodded to one of the many goblins working in the palace as he traveled up the southern staircase. He had already attended that morning's council meeting in an effort to acclimate everyone to his new appearance, but most of the other goblins continued to stare at him in fascination.

He was eager to be alone in his room, where he could finally look at himself properly. Though a full day had passed since he had brought Millicent here, he had spent most of his time dealing with the map pieces of Styx and meeting various Chiaroscurans in his true form. The most irritating task was getting Misha to remember who Millicent was and what he could and could not tell her about the city.

Finally, he reached the king's chambers, which were on the top floor of the palace and had been offered to him when the Chiaroscurans first learned who he was. He entered his room, which had seemed comically large for a cat and was still too big for one person. Ignoring the beautifully carved furniture and woven tapestries, he went to a vanity that sat, unused, since he had taken up residence in this room. He looked at the face in the mirror—his true face—and felt awakened from a long dream. Long ago, deep in the dungeons of Styx, that man had put him into a trance which muted his senses and allowed him to pass the centuries of his imprisonment without going mad. This dreamlike haze was interrupted only when Delilah found him, but even then, he knew he was not himself. In his true body, everything was clear. He felt the skin on his face and breathed in, finally having a chance to focus on existence itself without having to worry about Styx. He was almost happy, but whatever form he was in, his mind was the same, and the events of hundreds of years ago were still at the forefront of his thoughts.

Those events would soon be rectified. Styx was taken care of, but there was more to be done. He stood up, only to sit down again to think. Millicent had begged for an explanation, and he planned to give her one, but that was easier said than done. Remembering everything himself was one thing, but talking about it with someone else was something he could never bring himself to do, not even with the Council or Misha. Then again, Millicent was easier to talk to…

He glanced back at the mirror and noticed movement from the other side of the room. Turning, he saw a petite Chiaroscuran woman sitting on one of the couches brushing her silky white hair. She turned her blue eyes—one of which had a diamond shaped marking around it—towards him and smiled.

"I see you finally made it up here," she said in a sultry voice.

"Alcea," Sebastian said stiffly, "I wasn't expecting to see you here."

"I wanted to get another look at your pretty goblin face.

You left so abruptly yesterday… But you don't look too happy to see me."

"It's been a long day," he said simply.

"Every day is long," she said, running the brush through her hair again. "I've spent *this* day thinking about your proposition."

"If I remember correctly, you were the one who approached me."

"Perhaps," she said, still smiling. "But it really doesn't matter. We both get what we want, after all." Sebastian nodded, saying nothing. "You'll be glad to know that I'm already working on a way to save Chiaroscuro."

"And?"

"I haven't worked out the specifics yet. But we've still got time."

"*We* don't. Remember, Alcea, if you don't keep your part of the bargain, then neither do I."

She stood up and walked to a table that had an upturned top hat on it.

"I thought you would be happy for the delay. You're quite the conundrum." She was about to say something else, but stopped when someone knocked on the door.

"It must be Misha."

"We'll talk later," she said quietly, then turned into black smoke and left through the hat.

"Come in," Sebastian called.

Misha entered and gazed around the room in awe.

"Wow! You sleep in here?"

"Yes. You've been in here hundreds of times, so don't act so impressed."

"Sorry."

Sebastian had no idea why Misha had removed his own memories. He had always been somewhat foolish, but this latest development seemed to have no reason behind it at all. Sebastian had expected to come home to find Misha ready to tell him of any developments since he left, as well as help him with the rest of his plan. Instead, he was greeted by a confused, infantile buffoon who was lucky to remember his own name. Sebastian had never liked the idea of manufacturing memories, either artificially or by taking them from a person, but he'd never imagined that anyone could lose so many in one sitting.

"Have you spoken to Millicent yet today?" Sebastian asked, and Misha nodded. "How is she?"

"She still seems sad, and she's still asking about where we are."

"And you haven't told her?"

"Right. But I don't think it's fair to just keep her in her room. She has nothing to do."

"Didn't you say that when you brought her dinner yesterday, she was practicing magic tricks?"

"Magic tricks? She's a magician?"

"Yes," Sebastian said in annoyance. "As we've discussed. *Three times.*"

"Then she already knows about us."

"She doesn't know anything about us, and you're not going to tell her anything, either."

"Oh… well… Why is she here then?"

Sebastian groaned and brushed a strand of hair out of his face before answering.

"As I told you before, I need to her to perform a spell for me. And why she needs to do it is something you will know when the time comes."

He could tell Misha was unsatisfied, so he changed the subject.

"I have a question for you. You deal in the workings of the mind, so tell me, if I wanted to show somebody an event that had happened in the past without taking any memories, how would I do it?"

Misha thought, twirling his index fingers around each other.

"Well, you could just tell them, but if you wanted a fairly accurate visual representation, you'd have to be able to do a sort of illusion. Will-o-wisps are pretty good at that. Or if you had an immortal beast…"

"What do you mean?" Sebastian said, attempting to react calmly to the mention of immortal beasts.

"Legend has it that they have the ability to show other creatures their thoughts. I'm not sure how it works exactly."

If you had an immortal beast, Sebastian thought, *or maybe if you had the powers of one…* For the first time, he realized the Domino he was wearing might be used to give him more than just his goblin form. If it had returned his ability to use his shadow-magic, then why should it not also allow him the powers of an immortal beast?

"What do they look like, Misha, in their true form? If you could find me some more information about them…"

Misha nodded and looked somewhat lost, not knowing if he was supposed to do this immediately or not. Sebastian continued.

"Take this to be laundered as well," he said, handing Misha the coat he had taken from Styx's treasure room. It was dusty from years of being on display. "And then bring back several changes of clothes. These are technically an effect of the Domino," he said, pulling at his shirt sleeve. "I'm not sure if they are part of my overall form, or if they are a construction of magic."

Misha assumed that he was finally free to go and turned towards the door, but Sebastian called him back once more.

"And also," he began, somewhat sheepishly, "could you bring me something to eat?"

Misha went over the list of things to do in his head: get a book about immortal beasts, give coat to laundry maids, get food, don't tell Millicent about anything. *Wait,* he thought, *if I'm not supposed to tell Millicent anything right now, was I supposed to tell her something before?* After he had purged so many of his memories, he found it harder to remember ordinary things, almost like all his thoughts were slowly leaking out of his head.

"Stay in there," he said, patting the side of his head, garnering a strange look from a passing goblin. He thought he might have recognized her, with her short stature, black complexion, and surly demeanor.

"Um, do I know you?"

"For the millionth time, Misha! I'm Heidi! Heidi! Cleans the palace? Hates her job? You and Danika—that's your sister, which I'm sure you forgot—used to take me on trips to the Fields of Umber. Any of this ringing a bell?"

"Oh… that's right."

"Don't act like you remember. You didn't have a clue who I was."

"Um. I guess not. Anyway, um…"

Heidi let out a breath and lost some of her coldness.

"So, what's the matter? You look a little more lost than usual."

"Well, you know Sebastian?"

"No."

"Oh."

"I'm joking! Of course I know Sebastian. Everyone does. Of course I have yet to see him in his non-cat form, but I've heard he looks quite dashing."

Misha looked a little lost, then continued.

"He told me not to tell Millicent, who is this girl he, um, brought here, anything about anything, which I think means I was supposed to tell her something, along with three other things I was supposed to do, but I don't remember if I really was supposed to tell her something, or if I just made that up."

"For what it's worth, I didn't understand any of that. But I will tell you this: you should probably do the things Sebastian told you specifically to do, before wondering about whatever it was you were talking about."

"That sounds like a good idea," he said, as Heidi smiled self-importantly. "I have to get this coat washed and bring some new clothes, and get Sebastian some food."

"What? Since when?"

"Since… now?"

"You don't get it, Misha. Sebastian doesn't eat. Anything."

"Nothing?"

"Nope. Chalk it up to him being immortal, I guess. Are you sure he asked for food?"

"I thought so. Maybe I made that part up, too. And the third thing was, um, something."

He must have looked utterly helpless, because Heidi sighed once more and took the coat from his arms.

"Look, I'll take care of this and the food. Why don't you go talk to this Millicent person, since you seem to remember that? Maybe the other thing will come to you?"

"Thank you!" he said, relieved.

"Eh, what can I say? I'm a generous person. Plus, it's better than cleaning."

With that, she continued past him down the hall, and Misha went to Millicent's room. He found her gazing at the window, flicking a playing card against her palm—it appeared to change from a club to a diamond, though all its markings remained red.

"What are you looking at?" he asked her, following the rhythm of her card with his eyes.

"Just that blackness beyond the city. How do you get past it?"

"You don't. It goes on forever, or, well, maybe it sort of never goes anywhere. I guess it all depends on the time of day."

"So you can only leave the city at certain times?"

"No, you can leave whenever, but you shouldn't go near the edge of the city unless it's night."

Millicent thought this over for a moment, but couldn't make heads or tails of it. She was sure a day had passed since she came here, but the sky—or whatever the darkness around Chiaroscuro would be called—never changed.

"Then how *do* you get out of the city?" she finally asked.

"You have to get permission to use a ha—hey, wait, you're not thinking of leaving, are you?"

"Of course I am," she mumbled.

"But Sebastian said he has things to show you. Oh, that's what I was supposed to get! The immortal beast thing. Yeah, he said I was supposed to get a book with a picture of an immortal beast so he can show you something," he said, then slapped his hand over his mouth. "Which I probably wasn't supposed to tell you. Well, I'm sure you'll find out anyway. But back to the matter at hand, please don't try to leave."

Millicent considered this, slipping her cards back into her pocket.

"Do *you* think Sebastian's a good person?" she asked. Misha nodded resolutely. "Then I'll stay… Besides, it doesn't sound like I would be able to escape on my own."

"You really couldn't."

"I guess this is how Bostwick must have felt."

"Who's Bostwick?"

"He's a friend of mine, and, well, a prisoner of Delilah's. I always told him to trust her, though he didn't want to. Of course, Delilah's schemes pretty much revolved around making Bostwick fall in love with me. I think Sebastian wants something more sinister. But still, I have to stay here to find out, right?"

"Right," Misha said, though he didn't sound as if he completely understood. "Now, let's see. What was I supposed to do with you?"

"You said Sebastian wanted to show me something."

"Oh, right! Well, I guess you can come with me to get the book about immortal beasts, and then we can go to Sebastian. That'll save us a trip."

"You're taking me with you?"

Misha nodded again and ushered Millicent out of the room before she could question why.

The rest of the palace was immense, at least as large as some of the buildings in the Capital. Misha took her directly to a large library full of scrolls, paintings, sculptures, and books housed in silver frames or on gleaming white shelves. Misha took his time looking through these while several Chiaroscurans who worked in the library stared at Millicent.

"Um, Misha, are you sure I should be out here?" she asked. "I'm sort of conspicuous."

"Sebastian told me to," he said confidently, though Millicent had started to suspect that he had done no such thing.

At last, Misha plucked a greenish yellow book off the shelf and brought it to one of the librarians, who wrote the title down in a record book, all the while glancing at Millicent.

"Who is *she?*" he asked Misha, whose smile faltered. It seemed he was beginning to doubt whether his recollections of Sebastian's instructions were real.

"She's just, um…"

"I've never seen hair like that. Is she some kind of goblin from *out there?*" the librarian asked, though it sounded more like an accusation.

"I'm a Chiaroscuran!" Millicent said hastily. "What else would I be? I just dyed my hair, is all."

"Ah, my daughter and her friends have started doing that. Yellow or bright blue, but I've never heard of green."

"I mixed them," she said. He continued staring—at her face, not her hair—and she realized that the white parts of the Chiaroscurans' skin was significantly lighter than her own, and had that blue tint to it. "The, um, dye had some unintended side effects. It turned me all pinkish."

The librarian took a cautionary step back and handed the book back to Misha.

"Well, that's the end of my daughter's hair changing escapades. Enjoy your book."

Millicent grabbed Misha's arm and led him out of the library and behind a sculpture of two fighting wyrms that took up part of the ambulatory.

"Misha, what did he mean 'out there'? Are you not supposed to bring other goblins and humans here?"

"Absolutely not! That's the most forbidden of all forbidden things! We can't even tell outsiders about Chiaroscuro!"

"Why not?

"I can't tell you," he said miserably. "I guess it was a bad idea to drag you all over the palace. But Sebastian told me to!"

"I don't think he did."

"Me neither. Well, now what? If the others find out about you, I might get in trouble, and then... I don't know exactly, but I'm sure something bad will happen, to both of us probably."

Millicent looked down at herself. Her clothing suited the palace perfectly, but nothing else about her matched. Her ears were not pointed, her skin was too dark, or too light, and it lacked any marking either way. All the Chiaroscurans she had seen had white hair and yellow or blue eyes. Her problem, it seemed, was almost entirely a matter of color.

"That's it, Misha!" she said suddenly. "I practiced it with Bostwick, so it shouldn't be too hard on my own… Well, good-bye, first spell."

She concentrated hard, willing every hair on her head to change. She held a strand in front of her eyes, and watched it turn from green to white. Misha looked on in amazement.

"Is that human magic?" he asked in awe. "How do you do that? Can all humans do that?"

"Only some," Millicent said, now focusing on her skin, "and I'm not even one of the very good ones. Bostwick could probably—"

She winced in pain. Her skin had turned the same black and white as Misha's, but the change was accompanied by a slight burning sensation.

"Are you all right?" he asked.

She nodded, rubbing a spot on her arm till the pain subsided

"I've never done anything but hair or cloth before. Maybe that's normal on skin."

"Do your eyes next!" Misha said excitedly, but Millicent stepped out from behind the sculpture.

"I'd better not risk it. Besides, no one will notice as long as the rest of me looks normal. Let's go see Sebastian; he might be waiting for you to get back."

Misha led the way back towards her room, and then up to the top of the palace. Millicent could not help but comment on the beauty of the architecture. Misha explained that Chiaroscurans had been "classically educated", so they held art in high regard, but did not explain further. They found Sebastian sitting at a table out on the balcony of the king's chambers, finishing his meal. He stopped eating immediately upon their entrance, and glared at them in exasperation.

"I don't recall asking you to drag her up here," Sebastian said, turning to Millicent, "but I suppose it doesn't matter, since you saw fit to disguise yourself."

"I brought the book you wanted," Misha said, opening it and handing it to Sebastian. "I'm not sure if that's their true form, but it doesn't look like any goblin I've ever heard of."

After reading the page over several times, Sebastian stood up and transformed into a humanoid with purple skin and feathers running from his head to his back. Misha stared in amazement, but Millicent, who was used to Delilah's use of the Domino, merely wondered what creature Sebastian was supposed to be.

"So," he said, looking back at the book, "I just place my hand on her forehead? What if it doesn't work?"

"You can try it on me," Misha offered, and turned to Millicent with a shrug. "You know, to make sure it's safe."

"I'm not going to use you as a test subject," Sebastian said seriously.

"I'll be fine. My brain's already so addled, it can't get any worse. Besides, I'm volunteering."

Sebastian looked apprehensive, but placed his palm on Misha's forehead.

Millicent looked on as the two goblins stood, Sebastian with his eyes closed, concentrating, Misha with a glazed expression. It seemed as if nothing was happening. Several seconds passed, and Sebastian simply removed his hand.

"Well, did you see anything?"

"Delilah was carrying you around as a cat and pulled your tail and you tried to bite her," Misha said. "How extraordinary! It's not at all like my memories. It was distinctly third person!"

"Good. Now, if you would excuse us."

Misha turned to do so, but spun around once more.

"Is there anything I should be doing, or anywhere I should be going?"

"Not that I know of."

"Why don't you go find your sister?" Millicent suggested. "You should get to know her… again."

Misha nodded and left. Sebastian looked after him with a mild air of annoyance.

"So what is it you want to show me?" Millicent asked.

"A memory, or more properly, a visual retelling of the past. You wanted to know why you should help me, so I've changed into this form so I can show you how I began, and what I am."

He directed her to sit at the table, as he leaned against the rail of the balcony and looked out over the city.

"Long ago, there was a student at Melieh's Academy named Alistair. He did something which no one had ever done before. He might have been a great magician, if not for the influence of Styxian thinking. You see, the magic books you studied as a child were written by him."

"How do you know?" Millicent asked. She was, at last, genuinely interested in what he had to tell her.

"There was the spell you used to heal Bostwick's arm, or more accurately to make the blood flow backwards into his veins. That was a spell Alistair was working on. Some of the other spells you knew reflected his abilities. And there was the fact that you were denied admittance to the Academy."

"What do you mean?"

"Alistair, and those with him, were the reason that the entrance test was enacted. I imagine that the group of students was surveyed, and their specific personalities and tendencies were what defined someone who should be barred from the Academy. You don't strike me as their sort of person, so I assume you applied knowledge from Alistair's books on the test, and were thus deemed unsuitable."

"But I didn't think there was anything bad about the magic in those books," Millicent protested. "Some of the philosophical parts went a little over my head, but I understood most of it. It made sense."

"I suppose it would. I will never deny that what they did was wrong, but the theory behind it was logically, if not morally, sound."

"What did they do?"

He seemed to tense up at this question, looking troubled, but relaxed the next moment and walked to Millicent's chair.

"May I?"

"I suppose if there's no other way…"

He placed his palm on her forehead and shut his eyes, calling to the forefront of his mind the memories of long ago.

"These events occurred almost three hundred years ago, on a moonlit night in summer…"

Six

Shadow and Light
260 Years Ago

The silence of the night was shattered by a sound like electricity. The two students withdrew their hands as the sides of the shadow sparked with energy. The shadow itself darkened to opacity, then started to bulge slowly upward, as if there was something beneath it trying to break the surface. As it grew in height, the sides shrank inward, until it was clear that the shadow itself was becoming a solid object. Energy continued to surge around the form, which became more humanoid, until the blackness slid off the creature, revealing snow-white skin underneath. Some of the blackness settled in piebald spots on the thing's arms and back, while the rest sank to the ground beneath it, becoming a transparent shadow once more.

What lay before the awestruck students was a tall creature, indistinguishable from the goblin that the statue represented, save for coloration. While the statue's hair was braided, the creature's hair lay loosely over his unclothed body, as is if the attire and braid of the statue were never part of the shadow itself.

The students continued to stare, most with their mouths open. Alistair and Inez, for all their explanations, appeared to be in a state of shock. Jurek was the first to speak.

"Shouldn't we get him some clothes or something?"

One of the students supplied her picnic blanket, which Alistair wrapped around the unconscious creature. He sat it up and held it in his arms as the group inspected it.

"So… is it alive?" one asked.

"It's breathing. See?"

"Who knew immortal beasts would be so pretty."

"Don't ruin the moment!"

"Do you think it will be intelligent?" Inez asked.

But Alistair couldn't reply. He only looked at the creature in his arms in amazement.

"We really did it," he said at last.

"Do you think this is all right?" Jurek asked.

"Of course it is," Alistair said defensively. "Do you *realize* what we've done? We're—"

He stopped as the creature's eyes slowly opened, revealing yellow irises. At first, it seemed in a daze, but after a moment recoiled from the crowd of faces.

"Back up," Jurek said. "This is the first thing he's ever seen; give him some space."

The creature looked around from student to student, then up at the moon, and finally at Alistair, who steadily returned his gaze.

"Should we ask it a question?" Inez said. "I mean, do you think we'll have to teach it how to talk?"

Jurek knelt down beside the creature, who surveyed him with curious, unsure eyes.

"Can you talk?"

After a moment, he nodded.

Inez laughed softly and said, "Well, then, say something."

The creature seemed to be considering, then said, "What is all this?"

The crowd gasped. Some took a step back, while Inez only leaned closer.

"So you can talk! Do you know where you are? Do you know your name?"

The creature shook its head, so she explained.

"This is Marco Melieh's Academy of Magic; we're all students. And you, your name's Sebastian."

"Is it?" Jurek asked.

"It might as well be. His shadow came from the statue of Sebastian Galimatias of Styx. See, we made you," she said, addressing Sebastian once more, "out of a shadow. I really can't believe it worked. I mean, we had factors on our side, but still... And now we can make more. I don't know if they'll know how to talk, but—"

Inez was stopped short by the sound of breaking china. In the archway that led out to the street stood a tall woman with long black hair hanging down to her waist. She wore glasses and a magician's dress and held the handle of a tea cup in one gloved, trembling hand; the saucer lay broken at her feet.

Jurek attempted to hide the creature from her view, but it was obviously too late.

"Professor Hollyhock," Inez said. "It—it's not what it looks like."

"I don't even know what it looks like," the woman said,

staring past Inez to the creature. "Is that a goblin? Or…"

She walked deftly over to the creature, looking wide-eyed from Alistair to the statue, and then to the ground.

"That statue has no shadow," Professor Hollyhock said steadily, glancing at the creature once more. "I see. I always thought this was possible, but… to actually do it… I should inform the president at once."

"Please," Alistair begged, "Please don't. There's no rule against what we're doing. It's just… just an experiment."

Professor Hollyhock's mouth twitched into a smile, then she knelt down next to Alistair.

"I suppose I would ask the same in your case," she said. "And I have no doubt I'm responsible for putting the idea in your head. I have always been fascinated by immortal beasts. To see one, in reality, brought to life…"

"How does she know that's what it is?" Olivia muttered, but no one deigned to answer her.

"I won't tell the president," Hollyhock said, standing. "But you must keep this an absolute secret. I assume you have some ultimate end for this experiment?"

Inez and Alistair glanced at each other, then nodded in unison.

"You can explain it to me inside, Inez. As for the creature, Alistair, take it to the basement laboratory. No one ever goes in there anymore. For now, everyone else should go back to their rooms, immediately."

With that, she turned and walked into the academy with Inez following nervously.

"Jurek," Alistair said, "can you bring some clothes for him to wear?"

The creature stood unsteadily and followed Alistair to the laboratory. In the darkened basement the only light came from the high window that opened onto the street outside. The creature went and huddled in one corner against a shelf of dusty books while Alistair stood by the door and observed him.

"So… I'm Sebastian?" the creature said after some time. Alistair said nothing, but the creature continued to stare back at him.

"Inez decided to name you after that Styx goblin," Alistair finally said, just to fill up the silence. "Styx is the country to the north of us. They're the ones who taught us magic. Sebastian was a very generous goblin, a prince of his country, and the first to befriend Melieh. You come from the shadow of his statue, so you look like him."

"Who are you named after?"

"My grandfather," Alistair said. "Humans are often named after family members. The Styx goblins aren't your family, but I suppose we'd have to call you something."

Sebastian let this sink in, then said "So, you're…?"

"Alistair."

"Alistair," he said, and smiled. It was more gentle than the statue's manic grin.

"How is it you can talk," the boy asked, "but don't know anything about yourself or where you are?"

"Shouldn't I be able to talk?"

"You were just created tonight. Before then, you didn't exist. It takes humans a few years to learn to talk like you do."

"Am I not a human?" he asked.

"No," Alistair said, having worked all of the matter out in

his head beforehand. "You used to be a shadow of a Styx goblin. Now you are an immortal beast."

"Oh."

Alistair was spared from further explanations by Jurek, who came in carrying a boy's uniform.

"Here," he said, "you can wear these. They're mine, so they should fit."

It turned out the pants and tunic, though long enough, were too wide for Sebastian's narrow frame. He looked at his reflection in the metal laboratory table, then compared what he saw to the students who stood silently observing him.

"What is an immoral beast?" Sebastian asked, pulling his unruly hair behind his long, pointed ears.

"Something we created," Alistair said.

"Am I the only one?"

"For now. But we'll make more."

"If Professor Hollyhock doesn't tell anyone about it," Jurek said.

"She won't," Alistair said confidently. "I think she's just as fascinated by all of this as we are. I think we can trust her to keep it a secret and look the other way, at least until we're ready to unveil our research to the world."

Alistair swept out of the room, followed by Jurek, who awkwardly wished Sebastian good night, and locked the door behind him.

"So, this is what we're going for in terms of groundbreaking research, eh?" Olivia muttered, watching Inez point to various countries on a large map spread out in front of Sebastian, who looked on in interest as he finished plaiting his hair into a braid. Though all of the students had visited the laboratory at various times in the past two weeks, Inez had made a point of spending several hours a day there. She now sat across from Sebastian, explaining the difference between Ataxia, Aphasia and the continent that only a few decades ago had been called "Astasia" before it was renamed "The Empire" after the human nations formed their alliance.

"This whole region used to be considered uninhabitable because it was so close to the goblins," Inez said, gesturing to a small star just below the border of Styx, "which was why the Capital was placed here. Since no country had a claim to the land, all of the nations of the Empire felt that they could meet on the same terms here. Because we're all essentially immigrants to the Capital, we can truly feel like equals."

"But you originally came from the Nopali Desert, didn't you, Inez?" Sebastian pointed to a yellow-inked region on the center of the map.

"That's right."

"I wish I could see it. You always visit me here, but someday I would prefer to go to where you live."

His suggestion seemed to catch her off guard, and she hastily rolled the map up and scrutinized the floor as if she were searching for something lost. "Let's not get ahead of ourselves. You have to stay in this laboratory… though I wouldn't exactly say you 'live' here. Maybe… maybe someday you might be able to come outside, within the academy courtyard at least."

"I don't know," Olivia mumbled, "it seems like you two are doing just fine in here."

"To answer your earlier question, Olivia," Inez said, standing up, "I've actually been doing research this whole time. I've found that Sebastian learns at an abnormally fast rate. So far, I've taught him reading, writing, geometry, and philosophy. Now we're working on geography and history."

"And that matters… why?"

"'Why' is exactly right. I want to know why he can learn all this in so short a time. I suspect it has something to do with the fact that we created him to already be an adult, so perhaps our own expectations influenced his form. What I don't understand is why he doesn't need to eat or sleep."

"Conceivably," Sebastian offered, "it has to do with my immortality. My body probably doesn't require nutrients or rest to replenish itself."

"That's true. Hmm… but you still breathe."

"Do I?"

"You're doing it now. But I wonder if you need to. Try holding your breath, and I'll time you."

At this command, Sebastian simply stopped breathing, while Inez took out one of the pocket watches used for restoration spell practice.

"Enthralling," Olivia said, and wandered over to Alistair, who was busy writing down what he had observed in Sebastian's behavior. He had been keen to note Sebastian's sleeping and eating habits, or lack thereof, as well as his lack of pulse. In Olivia's mind, not much of it was noteworthy.

"Why are we all just sitting here?" she asked. "Aren't we supposed to be doing more experiments?"

"It's important to establish a baseline first. Immortal beasts obviously aren't human, so we need to figure out what's normal and healthy for them. Once we make more of them, then we'll begin the main part of our experiments."

"More? Are you crazy? If Hollyhock already knows about this one, then there's no way we can keep more of them a secret."

"Everything will be fine," Alistair assured her. "Inez told me that Professor Hollyhock has already agreed to look the other way no matter how many other experiments we create. And Inez had the idea that if anyone overhears anything about this, we should just tell them that we're in an existentialist theater club and that we do our rehearsals in this laboratory."

"Well, that would certainly keep *me* away. Trust Inez to come up with something like that. So how are we going to make more immortal beasts, anyway?"

"I think it's just about time we discuss that." Alistair called the room to attention as a tall boy entered. "Kibwe, here, has generously offered to supply the blocks of stone we will need for more statues. We'll commission the students from the Imperial Art Academy to sculpt them, since they're always in need of work."

"The stone will be arriving sometime next week," Kibwe said, "and should be sculpted in maybe two months."

"So, how do we go about conjuring life?" Olivia asked.

"Don't we have to know how it worked in the first place? It could have been an accident," Jurek said. "Should we just do the same thing you did before?"

"Yes," Alistair said. "The question is: why did it work? Inez is the one who figured that out."

"Well," she replied, addressing the group, "I would say

the reason is three fold. First, the stone for the statue, and consequently the stone's shadow, came from the Wastes of Styx, where a strange white grass grows which is reported to have a connection with the mind and memories. Second, the fact that we used the shadow of the image of a person helps tremendously, because of the sculptor's love of their subject matter, which brings me to the last, and I would say most important point: willed existence. Going back to ancient philosophy, to love something is to will the total good for it; for nonexistent things, existence is the greatest good there is, so to love something nonexistent is to will it to exist, and, since we as magicians can physically and actually exert our will over something, we can, with the help of certain incantations, will something into existence through love. So you all get it?"

Everyone stared back blankly at her. Only Sebastian nodded, but said nothing.

"You don't get it. Oh, boy. So Sebastian's existence is thanks partially to whoever carved the statue of Sebastian Galimatias. To spend so much time on it, to create his features so perfectly, the sculptor must have had a great love for the image he was sculpting, and that image, or rather the shadow of that image, is what we used for our raw material.

"The artist willed the image of Sebastian from stone, but Alistair and I willed an actual, real Sebastian out of the nothingness of his shadow. We willed the good for him, and that caused him to exist, because existence is the greatest, really the only, good that a non-existent person can have.

"Alistair used his love for the people he'll be helping through our research as a source, because he couldn't help them without Sebastian's existence. And I simply loved the perfection of form exhibited by Sebastian's statue."

"Meaning…?" Olivia asked.

"Meaning that each of you has to find your own reason for doing this. For example, Jurek," she said, directing Olivia's question away from herself, "you want to do something constructive, right?

Jurek stared at his left arm, which had several scars on it. His classmates knew they were from failed attempts at the healing spells they had practiced earlier that year, when the newly invented biological restoration technique—which involved healing in boxes—had been introduced to them.

"Well, I'm not very good at the nice kind of magic, like healing and making flowers. I'm good at fire conjuration and making stuff disappear."

"Oh yeah, you're just a storm of rage and destruction," Olivia said, not unkindly. "So you want to prove you can create something for once?"

Jurek nodded.

"That's almost love as an abstract concept," Inez continued, "but I believe it will still work. As for the rest of you, it could be anything: love for those who sacrificed for you to be able to attend this school, who would be proud of this new spell you'll be casting; love for those magicians who will someday follow in your footsteps because of the research you'll be performing. Whatever it is, use it as the source of your spell." The students continued to stare, and Inez groaned in exasperation. "All right, we'll work on the specifics later. Let's just say, for now, that if you want to make any more immortal beasts, you'll need statues made out of black stone from the Wastes, and you have to be perform the spell as an act of love. And we have to keep it a secret."

"Why?" Sebastian asked. Many of the students jumped, apparently forgetting that he was still there. "Why can't you let anyone know?"

"You're supposed to be a big, never-before-seen surprise," Olivia said.

"That's what I don't understand. Despite how I was created, I seem to exhibit many of the same qualities as naturally created humans. According to the philosophers—"

"You're not ready yet," Alistair said hastily, though there was something guilty about his smile.

The students left the actual design of the statues up to the sculptors, though Alistair insisted that they resemble Styx goblins so the circumstances of their creation would be as similar to Sebastian's as possible. The sculptures were finished in no time, and by the start of fall, the students had created nineteen new immortal beasts successfully.

To the student's distress, they did more than merely resemble goblins in appearance. Unlike Sebastian, they were wanton and wild, and although they sometimes occupied themselves with the books on history and art that Inez had left for Sebastian, they often wrote on the pages and argued with much of what each author said. They also found great pleasure in destroying lab equipment.

"Why are they so unruly" Kibwe asked, watching as one of the beasts painted rude caricatures of the students onto the wall with chemicals.

"Well, if we think of their original shadow forms, Sebastian spent thirty years or so in a courtyard filled with humans," Inez said, clenching her teeth as one of the creatures started to poke her repeatedly in the shoulder with a look of amusement, "whereas the others came directly from the wilds of Ataxia. It's only natural for them to act more goblinical."

"You're making that up, aren't you?" the creature asked.

Inez waved her away and counted to ten, then said, "Can't you reason with them, Sebastian?"

He looked up from where he was reading in the corner. "Why me?"

"Well, you're one of them. You know how they think."

He carefully set his book aside and approached two of the creatures who were mixing chemicals in a large beaker.

"Listen, you two…"

"Lizzie and Laura" they said together.

"What?"

"I'm Lizzie, and she's Laura. We got the names from a poem."

"He never gave us names," Laura said, pointing to Kibwe, "so we picked them out."

"All right," Sebastian said, not knowing what to do with this information. "You shouldn't be playing with those chemicals. It's dangerous."

"It's fun though," Lizzie said, dumping some purple powder into the mixture as Laura steadied the beaker. The substance foamed, turned black, and covered Laura's hands as the glass cracked. She shrieked in pain and let the beaker fall to the floor. Sebastian had no idea what to do, but Alistair pushed him aside, threw a cloth over Laura's arms and vanished the liquid.

When he lifted the cloth, the creature's arms were covered in chemical burns, which smoothed and disappeared before their eyes. Laura curiously examined her arms and, finding them healed, wandered away to find some other amusement.

"How did you do that, Alistair?" Inez asked.

"I didn't do anything. They're immortal, remember? That's why they don't need to eat or sleep. They can't be harmed by anything."

"Right," Inez said unsurely. "Right… but what if it was a fluke? I mean, we theorized that what we made are immortal beasts, but what if we're wrong?"

Alistair had already conjured a knife to test the theory. Sebastian stared at it, feeling a cold, clenching feeling in his chest. He'd never experienced such a thing in all his months of existence, so he didn't know what to do besides stare at the blade.

"Hold out your hand, Lizzie," Alistair said.

She hesitated, but did as requested, but flinched it back as Alistair cut swiftly across her palm. Unlike the wet, red blood Sebastian had read about, something like smoke ran from Lizzie's wound and clung to the knife. It floated slowly back to the cut, which healed over, leaving not even a mark.

"Amazing," Inez said. "Do you realize what this means, Alistair?"

"We really did create immortal beasts," Alistair said. "Tomorrow, the real experiments begin."

Alistair walked back to his stack of papers and wrote

something down, but Sebastian continued to stare at Lizzie, who hadn't moved an inch.

"Did it hurt?" someone asked.

The two creatures looked up to find Jurek watching them with an air of apprehension. Lizzie nodded, but wandered away after Laura without a word. Sebastian went back to his corner and picked up his book, but looked blankly at the letters on the page, unable to concentrate on reading.

"You look pensive, Sebastian," Inez said, coming over to the corner of the lab where he so often occupied himself.

"I was just thinking."

"That's what pensive means," she said, sounding amused. "*What* are you thinking?"

"Just about… all of this."

He gestured to the room around them, where the other creatures were gathered into three groups. Six sat in a circle reading the new books about music and architecture that Inez had brought to keep them less-destructively amused. Next to this group, six of the creatures were practicing what Jurek had dubbed shadow-magic. Several weeks ago, an immortal beast named Natasha had been particularly annoyed by a fly buzzing around the room. Something black had shot out from under her, slicing the fly neatly in two, while taking a chunk of the lab table with it. Inez, ever eager for more knowledge about the creatures, had asked her to do it again. Natasha did so, raising what they discovered to be her own shadow off the floor, and swiped it through the air. The other creatures tried it, and found this to be the magical power of their race. They learned that they could not only slice through things, but also pick objects up, carve their old statues into new shapes, and even turn their bodies into a smoky substance and travel from one top hat to another.

"You are a most impressive set of creatures," Inez said. "We might even show you to the faculty at the end of this semester."

The students had all been busily talking about graduating to the next level. Some of the students were moving from green to blue uniforms, while most, like Inez and Alistair, were eagerly awaiting purple garments, signifying their last year. Olivia and Kibwe alone in the group were hoping to graduate on New Year's Day, though they would only be looking forward to a life as lowly door-to-door magicians. The research done on the immortal beasts was their only hope of a better life.

"I was thinking more about *that*," Sebastian said, pointing to the group of students and creatures at the far end of the room.

Ever since the incident with Lizzie and Laura, Alistair had insisted that they find out how, exactly, the creatures' healing ability worked and what it entailed. He claimed that the knowledge learned from the experiments could vastly increase all magicians' abilities to heal the sick and wounded.

Still, Sebastian wondered if all of that could justify the experiments, which involved the use of scalpels, acids, and matches. One of the students had even fingered a canister of arsenic briefly, but Jurek slapped it away; he was squeamish about the experiments, even though, as Alistair said, the smoky substance always returned to or settled back on the creatures' bodies and they were always all right in the end. Only Sebastian was spared from these procedures, since—as Inez explained to him after bringing him a book on scientific theory—a proper experiment needed both an experimental group and a control.

"There's something wrong about it," Sebastian continued.

"We told you already, it's for the sake of magical and scientific knowledge."

"Not just the experiments. There's something wrong about all of this. Why did you bother to bring us books to read if you're just going to slice away at us? You all seem a lot more interested in what our bodies can do than our minds. And why is it you don't want anyone to know about us?"

"We've discussed this," Inez began, but Sebastian cut her off.

"Is it the way we were created, or maybe the *reason* we were created? Humans have their own reasons for creating life, reasons which are fundamentally different from pulling a shadow out of thin air for the sake of 'magical knowledge'."

He seemed incensed, and for once the talkative Inez had nothing to say.

"Long ago, you said that the willing of existence is the same as love, Inez, but there was something different about the kind of love you used to make us, isn't there? Otherwise, we would be treated the same as human children."

"Well, you aren't human."

"No, but we're still rational creatures, and yet somehow, because of the way we entered the world, we are less to you than the creatures which naturally exist. This must be the case, or else you would not be justified in experimenting on us, which Alistair has assured me that you are."

Inez didn't meet his eye. "What's your point?"

"I simply want you to tell me if my assumptions are correct."

Inez was about to answer, but stopped to watch as one of the creatures threw down the book he had been studying and crossed the room to where the students stood clustered around their test subjects. Alistair was standing with a scalpel poised over the wrist of a creature named Midori, but looked up as the other approached.

"Go back to your studies, Petri."

"I'll do the experiment," Petri said.

"You've already gone today."

"Midori doesn't like the experiments. I'll go for her. I don't mind."

It was an obviously lie; his arm shook even as he held it out to take the place of Midori's.

"It won't hurt her," Alistair said, and raised the scalpel.

"But it *does* hurt. We've told you it hurts. I'll go instead. Please—"

But Alistair had already swung the scalpel down, cutting cleanly across Midori's wrist, where blue blood welled. Alistair dropped the scalpel and gasped, but regained his composure, held his hands over her wound and mumbled something. The blood returned to the wound as quickly as it had come out, but the cut did not heal over. Alistair snatched up a box that was sitting under one of the lab tables and quickly cast a healing spell, but was not experienced enough to do it perfectly; a blue-black scab was left on Midori's pale arm.

"We're done for today," Alistair said, sounding panicky. The students gathered their things and left, all with looks of worry and apprehension. When they were gone, the creatures clustered around Midori, who was more shocked than upset.

"It still hurts," she said softly, as Petri put his arm around her shoulder and looked at the scab. "Thank you, Petri. But you know that was a pretty stupid thing to do."

"I hate it when they hurt you," he said. "I hate how they treat us. They told me, when I first woke up, that we were a brand new thing, the most amazing creatures ever created. But they treat us worse than dogs."

"Maybe we are," Sebastian said quietly. "We were created through an experiment, so why should the experiment end now that we're here?"

The creatures all looked at one another, some huddling together as if a sudden chill had come over the lab.

"I'm hungry," Lizzie said at last.

In the next three days, seven more creatures had confessed to wanting food, and several, including Midori, spent their nights sleeping. These developments only increased the students' curiosity, and despite the incident that had occurred with the scalpel, the experiments continued. By the end of the week, they discovered that twelve of the creatures would no longer heal if cut or burned. Kibwe theorized that, for whatever reason, the more the creatures were injured, the more mortal tendencies they displayed, especially considering that Sebastian, the control, had shown no changes. Inez remained skeptical of this theory, though she could offer no better explanation. Before leaving that night, one of the students questioned if this meant the creatures were no longer immortal. Alistair simply said that they would find out tomorrow.

The creatures sat in darkness, many holding each other, dreading what the next day would bring. Alone in the corner, Sebastian ruminated over whether or not they should defend themselves—he felt that all of them were ignoring the fact that they obviously *could*—until they heard footsteps outside the door. Jurek entered the lab and asked them all to listen.

"We don't have much time," he said in a low voice, "but I think you should all leave this place."

The creatures gasped and looked around at each other. How could they leave? That was the one thing Alistair had expressly forbidden.

"I think Alistair… Well, he's gotten some pretty weird ideas lately. I'm worried about all of you."

"Where will we go, Jurek?" Natasha asked; she was the creature he had brought to life.

"To Ataxia." This was met with more gasping. "I don't think you really are immortal beasts; I don't think you ever were. You all act like goblins, and you look Styxian, so it's possible that you're actually some new kind of goblin… shadow goblins or something. If you go to Ataxia, you won't be so conspicuous. And if you stay here…"

He did not elaborate.

The newly christened shadow goblins gathered what few possessions they had, which consisted almost entirely of cast-off students' uniforms and Inez's books, and followed Jurek out of the laboratory, through the darkened halls of the academy that had for so many months been forbidden territory. They could see their breath in the cold air as they made it to the inner courtyard, where a figure with folded arms blocked their path.

"Leaving, are you?"

"Let us pass, Inez."

"Or what? You wouldn't hurt a soul, Jurek. And you'll never get twenty black-and-white immortal beasts out of the Capital unnoticed. Didn't you think that through?"

The way Jurek's shoulders sagged showed he hadn't, but he straightened up with new resolve.

"I'm not just going to leave them, Inez. This is getting too dangerous."

"If you're going to be heroic, you should come prepared."

With that, she clapped her hands and three men ran forward. They looked extremely confused by the proceedings, but stood obediently in a line behind her.

"My uncle happens to own the only hired carriage company in the Capital," she said, gesturing to the men. "He's a bit eccentric, so he let me have three cabs for the night, no questions asked. We wouldn't want our *actors* to get too tired walking to Ataxia."

The overjoyed goblins ran to the carriages that sat just beyond the academy gates while one of the drivers mumbled something about "wild make-up". Jurek, Inez, and Sebastian shared a carriage with Lizzie and Laura, who sat on either side of Inez, each hugging her arms, and Natasha, who watched the buildings of the Capital go by out the window.

"Thank you, Inez," Jurek said. "I'm sorry I thought you were trying to stop us."

"Well, I played up the part a little, didn't I?" She smiled.

"Why did you do it?" Sebastian asked.

"Always the serious one, aren't you? To tell the truth, something you said got me thinking." She looked down at a bundle she had folded in her hands before continuing. "Maybe we did something wrong when we created you, but that doesn't mean you're sub-human, or..."

"Sub-goblin?" Jurek suggested, then when Inez looked at him questioningly, explained, "I think they're goblins, Inez. That's why they aren't immortal anymore."

"Well, be that as it may, I think maybe experimenting on them... It's hurting us, also."

She didn't go on, so they rode the rest of the way in silence. Before long they came to the forest, but turned to the west and traveled along the edge of it.

"The drivers won't go through the woods," Inez explained to Jurek and Sebastian. The other goblins had fallen asleep. "We'll go as far as the Wastes, and they can make the rest of their way from there. I've heard the Gammon Coast is a lovely place to live, except for the occasional pirate attacks."

"What do you mean 'they'?" Jurek asked, "What about Sebastian?"

"Well, I just thought..." She glanced at Sebastian, then back at the bundle she held. "I mean, we never really experimented on you, so maybe you don't have to leave."

Sebastian said nothing. He had always felt somehow different from the other shadow goblins. Even now, he was one of the few who exhibited no mortal tendencies. It had never occurred to him that he, too, was escaping.

"I got you something," Inez said, unwrapping the bundle.

What she held before him was a white coat with deep blue edging and interior. The embroidery of the sleeves was exquisite, as were the silver buttons lining the front. It had a militaristic look, but somehow seemed regal as well. Sebastian pulled it on and found it fit perfectly.

"You had this made for me?"

Inez nodded. Sebastian ran his fingers over the embroidery, not knowing what to say. No one had ever given him anything that was meant for him in particular.

"Thank you," he finally managed to say, "but... why?"

Inez looked away from him, out the window. It was a while before she spoke.

"You may not know this, Sebastian, but, well, even when it was the original Sebastian Galimatias, or your statue in the courtyard, I've thought you are probably the most perfectly structured being I've ever seen."

"That's sweet, Inez," Jurek said sarcastically.

Inez glared at him, but then looked at Sebastian.

"I just thought it would look good on you, and I wanted you to have something that didn't come from that laboratory. I ordered it weeks ago, and I was going to give it to you today, but with everything happening with the other exp— shadow goblins, the timing didn't seem right... And I brought it tonight in case it turned into a going away present," she said as the carriages came to a halt.

They got out and surveyed their surroundings; the Wastes were as desolate as they had heard. Night winds swept over the dark, flat expanse before them. There were a few leafless trees, and far in the distance, a pile of broken furniture could be seen.

"I wish we could have taken them farther," Jurek said, "to a nicer place."

"I think it has a certain sublime aesthetic," Natasha said, stretching her arms. "Well, I guess this is goodbye."

"Maybe we'll visit the Styx goblins on our way out," Lizzie said. "I bet we'd confuse them, huh?"

"No," Inez said seriously. "You can't let the Styx goblins know about you. They're in alliance with the Empire. I'm sure they would tell the Academy about you, and then they might bring you back."

"So we have to stay in hiding?" Petri asked.

"Just until you get past the Wastes. The other goblin nations don't care what humans do, but you still might not want to say too much about what you are, just in case. Anyway, you better get going."

The goblins shook Jurek's hand and hugged Inez, while a few blew kisses to the baffled drivers, then turned and walked into the Wastes. Sebastian waited with the humans.

"There's still time to catch up with them," Jurek said.

"I'm staying."

"But—"

"There are still things I want to know and… some things I need to do," he said, returning to the carriage. Jurek and Inez followed suit, and signaled the coachmen to drive.

"This is a bad idea," Jurek mumbled, looking out the window.

"Well, I'm glad you're staying," Inez said, sounding relieved.

"Inez, you mentioned the Styx goblins," Sebastian said. "And Sebastian Galimatias was Styxian?"

She nodded. "He taught Melieh how to control magic, and the rest of the Styx royal family helped. Professor Hollyhock told us about some of the inventions they've created by studying different goblins from across Ataxia."

"'Studying' the same way Alistair does?" Sebastian asked coldly.

The two humans glanced at each other, and Inez continued. "Professor Hollyhock didn't go into detail, but they apparently have a mask that lets the person wearing it actualize their will to an absurd degree. In order to create it, though, the royal family stripped a dozen goblins of their powers so they could bind their magic directly into the mask."

"And it was that story that inspired Alistair to pursue his type of research?"

"I suppose. The Styx goblins can use some pretty extreme methods, but without them, we never would have learned magic."

Sebastian fell silent and watched the Wastes fade into the distance outside the window.

The humans soon went to sleep, while Sebastian contemplated what would happen when the other students found out what Inez and Jurek had done. He guessed that they would most likely make a new batch of creatures to experiment on.

By the time they got back to the Academy, the clouds above had turned from black to light gray, and small white flecks were floating down from them.

"It's snow!" Inez said, springing up and out of the carriage.

"I hope it doesn't snow in the Wastes," Jurek said.

Sebastian simply looked at the white flakes, which were coming down in more abundance as he stood watching. They made the events of the previous day seem like a distant memory.

"This is your first snow, too, isn't it, Sebastian?" Inez said, practically dancing over to him.

"Too? Have you never seen it before, either?"

"It doesn't usually snow in the desert, and in all my time in the Capital, it's never snowed before."

It seemed as if a weight had been lifted from her. Sebastian wondered if it was an effect of the weather or the fact that she had helped his fellow goblins escape. In an indescribable way, he thought she seemed more like she had when he had first awakened and they had spent so much time together, before Alistair's ideas of experimentation had begun.

"It's beautiful," she said. "Who'd have thought frozen ice crystals could be so pretty. Our first snow!"

Sebastian smiled at her, then silently gazed up at the clouds.

Seven

The Goblin Avalanche

As it turned out, traveling by air was not nearly as exciting as it had first seemed. Emmaline was busy steering the ship, but Delilah and Bostwick found themselves with hours of free time as they sailed to Pandemonium. Delilah amused herself by alphabetically listing synonyms for various attitudes, starting with *arrogant*, *boastful*, and *conceited*, while Bostwick occupied his time by figuring out what the devices in Millicent's bag were. The small music box played a short, chaotic song that Delilah knew the words to, but seemed to lack any magical properties. He then picked up one of the two matching opera glasses and looked out at the landscape.

"What do those do?" Delilah asked, pausing at *overconfident*.

"Apparently nothing. It's just black."

He handed her the glasses so she could see, then fished in the bag for the other pair. As he pulled them out, Delilah gasped.

"What do you see?" Bostwick asked, and held his pair up to his own eyes. What he saw was first the balloon above them, then himself, looking through the glasses.

"I see me!" Delilah said. "They must show what the other pair is looking at. How about this, Bostwick?"

Bostwick's vision went out of control as Delilah twirled her glasses on their stem.

"Cut that out! You're gonna make me sick." He grabbed the glasses from Delilah and put both pairs back in the bag. "These could come in handy. I don't want you dropping them over the side when you're playing with them."

"I'm not a child, Bostwick," she said. "Now where was I? Ah yes, 'P'. *Pompous.*"

Bostwick then inspected the strange, spindle-legged teapot, but finding nothing extraordinary about it, decided to look at the country below them.

The region they were flying over was fairly dismal, with little ground cover and even less in the way of landmarks. It seemed to be a vast expanse of gray rock going from a glittering line of blue far on their left, which he supposed must be the ocean, to a scrubby forest on their right. The city of Catawampus was just a dark spot on the horizon behind them by now, while a range of mountains loomed in front. He had to admit that air travel had the advantage of speed, covering as much ground in a day as would have taken weeks on foot.

"What time is it?" Emmaline asked after a while.

Bostwick checked his pocket watch and said it was about two in the afternoon, though he didn't know if that would be accurate for the area they were in, as it was set to Styx time.

"Lunch time!" Delilah said happily, pulling one of the baskets her mother had packed towards her. "Ah, my mom loves me! She gave us black jelly, dried centipede, salted cactus and beet salad, bat jerky, yum! And look, a wheel of kyo cheese!"

"What, dare I ask, is a kyo?" Bostwick said.

"They sort of resemble cats, only they're much slower and they fall down a lot."

"I see. So, is there anything fit for human consumption?"

"This is all perfectly good, Bostwick. The salad might be a little questionable, though. Here, I'll make you a black jelly sandwich."

"No thanks."

"So picky! You know, starving Gremlins would be happy to eat food like this."

"Then mail it to them; I'll get by on bat jerky."

"I'll try some of the salad," said Emmaline, who'd eaten a similar dish quite frequently at home, and had gotten used to a heavily vegetable diet during her time traveling the wilds of Ataxia. Delilah handed her the bowl with a look of revulsion, apparently being just as picky as Bostwick.

A day later, they came to the mountain range, which Delilah instructed Emmaline to fly through. The journey was breathtaking, partially because of the rugged beauty of the peaks, but also because of their close proximity to the ship. There were several times when the trees and boulders they flew past were close enough to touch, and once they exchanged a few sentences with a bewildered giant-dodo herder before sailing away.

"We are now officially in Tumult," Delilah said, gazing over the side of the ship.

"I don't think I'll be able to land down there. There are too many trees."

"No need," Delilah said. "The regions of Pandemonium are unincorporated. That means, Bostwick, that they aren't part of any country."

"I know what it means!"

"Of course you do," she said patronizingly. "So anyway, it is common knowledge that the artifacts of the various goblin peoples in Pandemonium are protected by the K'nic-k'nack Tribe. They keep these precious articles on Mount Tumult in some sort of temple. That's probably where the map of Pandemonium is, as well as the map of our forest."

"So you want me to land on top of a mountain?" Emmaline asked, turning the ship just in time to avoid colliding with a passing dodo.

"Don't be absurd! We'll land on the side of a mountain. That way, we won't have too far to climb, up or down."

"Down?"

"Well of course. One of us will have to wander around the forest and see if Millicent is there."

"I'll do that," Bostwick said. Emmaline gave him a surprised look. "I've been in there before, so I'll know what I'm dealing with. That, and I can use magic."

"This is true," Delilah said. "It'll be just us girls, eh, Emmaline?"

"Right. So, about landing..." she said nervously.

"Don't worry, I'm sure you'll be just fine. Try for that grassy ledge on that mountain over there, the one sandwiched between those jagged rock formations."

♠ ♦ ♣ ♥ ♣ ♦ ♠

Emmaline landed the ship, much to her credit, exactly where Delilah had indicated. The ledge was wide enough for the tub-like ship to sit on, but Emmaline still had misgivings.

"Do you think we're stable? It's a very long way down if we're not."

"It's a long way down anyway," Bostwick said, peering into the gorge below them. "So are those tree tops from the Forest of Infinite Horrors?"

"Indeed they are," Delilah said. "They're different from those trees over there, which are native to Tumult."

"How do you know so much about this place, anyway?"

"It's a queen's job to know a bit about everything, you know? I especially learned about this continent when I was a child and there was talk of going to war with all of Pandemonium. Here you go, Bostwick."

She handed him a length of rope with a grappling hook at one end, which he took with a quizzical stare.

"My parents packed it, of course. I don't just lug these things around for fun."

Bostwick secured the rope to a nearby rock and tugged it several times, mumbled something about trees breaking his fall, and began the climb down.

"I guess it's our turn," Emmaline said, taking the rope Delilah held out for her. "But don't you think we should bring coats or something, if we have some?"

It turned out they had three scarves, a woolen coat, and four and a half pairs of elbow length mittens, which Delilah insisted would be fine. Emmaline wore the coat, while Delilah wrapped the scarves around herself with some success, and wore a glove on each ear.

Their journey was easy going at first, as the rocks of the mountain formed a natural path, but by evening it began to snow heavily. They came to a narrow ledge which forced them to hug the edge of the mountain, hoping that the ledge would lead up to the peak and not to a sudden drop off.

"We'll be fine," Delilah shouted, as the wind picked up. "I'll go first, so if I fall off, I can maybe float back up."

"Can you float from this high?"

"I don't know. It's not the sort of thing you try out."

Delilah said something else, but Emmaline could barely hear over the wind, and all she could see was blinding snow on her right and the black rock of the mountain on her left. Her gloved hands were losing feeling and her face, which moments ago had ached with cold was now numb. To make matters worse, the path along the ledge abruptly stopped. They would have to go vertically.

She looked up to the top of the cliff, where the cloudy sky was barely visible through the flurry of snow.

"So what kind of temple is this?" Emmaline asked, beginning to doubt if even goblins would build in such a ridiculous place.

"One for people who are very good at climbing, apparently," Delilah responded, unwrapping some of the rope. "I hope this is enough. We really should have had Bostwick enchant it to make it longer."

"It'll just have to do."

Emmaline took one end of it while Delilah held the other and floated to a narrow outcropping above them.

"I'm going to try to make it to the top."

Emmaline waited below, letting more and more rope unravel, and focused on trying to warm herself up by breathing on her mittens and holding them to her face.

Minutes passed. Suddenly, Delilah called out, "I think I see it!"

Emmaline waited, watching more and more of the rope disappear up the cliff, until it stopped.

"Is that it?" she called, but received no answer. "Delilah?"

There was a faint yell, and then silence. Emmaline tugged on the rope, which held fast, and started to climb. The journey was slow going, as footholds were difficult to find, but thankfully, Emmaline thought, her year of hopping around on all fours had strengthened her arms enough so that climbing was not totally impossible. Looking up, she breathed a sigh of relief when she saw more sky than mountain, signifying the edge of the cliff. Finally, she managed to drag herself over the edge, roll over, and lay flat on the snow-covered ground and stare up into the dark sky.

"Wait a minute," she said to herself, and looked around. The rope she had climbed up was tied to a boulder, but Delilah was nowhere to be seen. At first Emmaline panicked, imagining all sorts of Pandemonian snow monsters, then noticed a large structure several yards away which lit up the night around it.

She walked to the building, which was carved out of the mountain itself, pulled open its huge wooden door, and dashed inside.

♠ ♦ ♣ ♥ ♣ ♦ ♠

"Millicent!" Bostwick called, though by now he knew it was useless. He had traveled halfway down the length of the valley, wandering back and forth between the two mountain bases that formed its sides, but had seen no sign of Millicent. He had expected this, but even stranger was the fact that he hadn't encountered any snakes, wyrms, or other animals. He wondered if they had all gone dormant as he passed a carnivorous mushroom with its cap tucked low to the ground; it seemed to be snoring. He supposed that the animals might be sleeping away somewhere, as the climate in Tumult was much colder than in Styx, but still found it a little odd that he did not see even one nocturnal creature crawling out of its nest as the sun went down.

The forest was as dense as ever, but Bostwick kept stumbling through it even in the dark, using only a flame spell for light. He half-heartedly hoped that, if Millicent was here, she too would use the spell, even though he knew the odds of her being in the area were slim at best. He considered giving up, but then he saw something which gave his heart a jolt.

It was light, far off, and he assumed it was one of the forest will-o-wisps, but called out to it anyway. To his surprise, a male voice called back.

"Hello?" Bostwick said again, to make sure he wasn't hearing things.

As the light came closer, the voice said, "Hey there! Is this your forest?"

"Sort of," Bostwick replied, approaching the light, which was cast by a lantern that swung from a long pole held by someone that appeared to be a cross between a human and a goat. "I know the owner."

"Ah, well, that'll make things a bit easier," the man said. "Hey, Bramble, come here."

Another goat man with an unruly mass of hair between his two short horns ran up to them. He, too, held a pole; his had a lantern on one end and a cage holding several snakes on the other.

"This guy says he knows the owner. So what, are you a snake herder or something?"

"Technically, I'm a butler," Bostwick said, "but actually I'm a magician."

The two men made impressed noises, then bleated something to each other.

"We don't get many humans this far north. The last one must have been a couple generations ago," the one called Bramble said. "So what's a human forest doing here?"

"It's a long story."

"Well, you can tell us back at the village. A forest is no place for a human to be at night, even if you are a magician."

"Um, thanks," Bostwick said, not used to goblin hospitality. "But first, have you seen a woman with green hair?"

"We haven't seen anybody in here," the other one said. "Only snakes and things like that. See, we were collecting them into a barn we built at that end of the forest. That way, they won't wander into our territory and get mixed up with our dodos. Also, they won't freeze if there's an avalanche."

"Do you have a lot of avalanches?" Bostwick asked, worried about Emmaline, Delilah, and the airship.

The two goblins gave each other knowing looks.

"You might say that."

♠♦♣♥♣♦♠

Emmaline found herself in a long corridor lit by fires in notches along the wall. Proceeding down this, she came to a wide, high-ceilinged room with a fire burning in the center of it. Around this was a circle of floor cushions, one of which was occupied by Delilah.

"Are you all right?" Emmaline asked, running over to her.

"I'm fine."

"I thought you got eaten by something! Why didn't you wait for me?"

"I figured that my being out there wouldn't have gotten you in here any sooner."

"What ever happened to camaraderie?"

"I imagine it froze outside waiting for its friends. Now, if you'll just sit down by the fire here…"

"There she is!" someone cried. "And she's frozen solid!"

A woman came hurrying into the room carrying a pile of blankets. She threw most of them down on the cushions, then rushed over and wrapped Emmaline in one. The woman had a humanoid figure, but with cloven hooves for feet and long, floppy ears hanging behind her blonde bangs. At first glance, Emmaline thought that her skin had a dark tan, but then saw that it was actually covered with short brown fur. To top it all off, her pupils, like a goat's, were bean-shaped.

The woman threw a blanket around Delilah as well, then hurried away down another corridor, returning with a tray of cups, dried herbs, and a small pot and brazier.

"So, I'm sure your friend told you who I am," she said, crushing the herbs into the pot.

"She's the guardian of this place," Delilah said matter-of-factly.

"I prefer to think of myself more as a curator, protecting knowledge and displaying it for any curious minds that come here. Not that very many do. I suppose the terrain is sort of harsh, but that's what keeps this place safe from thieves and pot hunters."

"What do you keep here?" Emmaline asked, realizing that they really had no idea what sort of building they were in.

"Ah, well, let's see. This place is sort of a cross between a repository and a museum. I call it a reposeum, though the name hasn't caught on. We keep art and artifacts here, to be preserved for future generations."

"Are there a lot of you?"

The goat woman blushed, pushing her bubbling tray of herbs behind her.

"How silly of me! I completely forgot to introduce myself. I'm Thistle Dolores Inanity, of the K'nic-k'nack Tribe, but you can call me Dolly. My specialty is naturalistic magic and herbalism." Here she paused, as if trying to remember the next part of a memorized introduction. Something seemed to click, and she continued on. "Ah, yes, but now I am the Guardian of the Gifts of Tumult. See, there's a lottery every year, and whoever wins has to be in charge of this place, although I keep getting picked. Must be five years in a row by now. I wonder if it's not just a coincidence?"

She leaned back and knocked the pot over, somehow catching both the pot's contents and part of her robe on fire.

"Blast!" she said, patting the flames out. "This always

happens! Oh well. It looks like your tea is ready."

She handed them each a cup filled with colored water and topped with singed twigs and leaves.

The village of the K'nic-k'nack Tribe was on the side of the mountain opposite the Forest of Infinite Horrors, built beneath the overhang of a large cliff. The two goblins brought Bostwick into a large room with a fire in the center, where many other goat goblins were seated, eating stew. They insisted Bostwick sit and eat with them and tell what had brought him and his forest to their mountains. He was brief, but his story seemed to satisfy their curiosity.

"How utterly bizarre," one of them remarked. "Magicians certainly lead crazy lives. That might even put Dolores's story to shame."

"Dolores?" Bostwick asked.

"Dolores was a magician explorer," a goblin with large spiraling horns said. "Came here I don't know how long ago. She told us of some adventures that we only half-believe are true, then went back to the Empire to teach at the Academy."

"'Course she's not as interesting as our Dolly," Bramble said.

"Your Dolly?" Bostwick asked, taking another helping of stew which he assumed might be his last bit of decent food until they found Millicent.

"See, since Dolores was so impressive, there was a real human-name trend a while back. My name's Bramble José, for example, but there is one among us known as Thistle Dolores Inanity."

"A name that strikes fear into the hearts of all," said Bramble's friend, who was named Thorn.

"See, she's also known as The Goblin Avalanche, as causing them, and other lesser disasters, is her specialty. The first time was when she was out herding dodos. She sneezed, and the whole mountain gave way."

"Then there was the time she was collecting wild flowers for some potion or other," another goblin chipped in. "She found a patch of herbs that wouldn't come loose, tugged and tugged, and ended up dislodging the boulder the herbs were keeping up, which rolled down and hit a bigger boulder, which started a rockslide and destroyed the bridge to Mount Palaver."

"I believe," said the big goblin, "there have been five avalanches, one rock slide, one forest fire, and three broken pots."

"The problem is," Thorn continued, "we can't just banish her. She's a sweet kid, just a bit mixed up."

"But surely you have to do something about her?" Bostwick said.

"We have. See, every year, there's a lottery to see who's supposed to be the guardian of our temple, up there on the mountain."

"Dolly won it one time," the big goblin said, "and caused two avalanches that year alone. However, because of the temple's location, the avalanches were on the opposite side of the mountain from the village, so everyone was safe. We have since rigged the lottery."

"So you're saying she could cause an avalanche at any time?" Bostwick asked, springing to his feet.

"Don't worry. We constructed the barn holding your reptiles as far from the avalanche path as we could manage."

"That's not it! Two of my friends are up in those mountains, and so is our airship."

"So it was you I saw flying around," a gray-haired goblin said. "I saw where you landed. I can take you up there straight away. We'll use the wagon road."

"Wagon road? I didn't see any… Of course I didn't. That would have been too easy. All right, let's go. Um, thanks for your hospitality and everything," he said, waving, and followed the goblin out the door.

"So, what brings you here?" Dolly asked as they sipped their tea. "Are you doing research?"

"Actually," Delilah said, "we think a bit of our country's map has stumbled into your reposeum, or rather, been brought here by a… Oh, how would you describe him, Emmaline?"

"He's a very tall, pale goblin with long white hair. He was probably wearing a fancy coat. And he can also turn into gray smoke and move things with his shadow."

Dolly raised an eyebrow suspiciously.

"I haven't seen anyone with such a peculiar appearance. In fact, you're the first visitors I've had up here, well, ever. What was it you were looking for again?"

"Our map. It would probably be amongst your artifacts, on the map of Pandemonium. If we could just see that…"

"Sure," Dolly said, but there was something strange in the way she said it. "Right this way."

She brought them down a hallway that led to a room full of items in glass display cases. Most everything looked ancient, from pottery to woven mats to paintings.

"So, where's the map of the realm?" Delilah asked. "I don't see any parchment or paper around here. I suppose it could be anywhere, carved into a wall, or maybe painted. Have you found anything yet, Emmaline?"

"Here, Delilah. It's on this table."

One of the biggest cases held a diorama of a furnished room including a frock coat on a mannequin and a table with scientific instruments, an upturned top hat, and an open journal. On one of the journal's handwritten pages lay the map of the Forest of Infinite Horrors.

"Well, that was easy. But why is the map in a book?"

"Dolores Shrimper, a human explorer, drew that map during her expedition," Dolly supplied. "It's the only complete map of Pandemonium, and takes up the entire book. Rumor has it, it took her three years to draw the entire thing."

"That's lovely," Delilah said. "Now if you could open the case for us, we'll take it off your hands."

"Aha!" Dolly said. "So you admit it?"

"What?"

"You admit that you intend to steal one of the precious treasures of the K'nic-k'nack Tribe!"

"Um, no. We want to take back what is rightfully ours."

"Dolores drew that map! It's been here for generations."

"Not the book, just that little scrap of paper."

"That must have been in the book the entire time! You don't honestly expect me to believe some white-haired smoke-and-shadow man sneaked in here and left it for you. Don't you think I would have seen him?"

"We don't exactly know how he did it," Emmaline said. "He might very well have come out of the top hat on the table for all we know."

"Such audacity!" Dolly said. "I've been waiting to stop a couple of thieves for a long time, but I at least thought they would come up with a better story than that."

Delilah ignored this and instead walked over to the display case and attempted to open it.

"It's locked, of course," Dolly said, grabbing a wooden staff that hung on the wall. She stepped in front of the display, holding her staff out beside her to block Delilah.

"You should know, I've been trained in naturalistic magic, and I'm not afraid to use it! I suggest you leave now, while you still have the chance."

"Not without my map."

"You'll have to get through me first!"

"Fine," Delilah said, shoving Dolly backwards into the case. When her staff hit the glass, the entire panel shattered, and Delilah floated up, whipped the map piece up between two fingers, and floated back down.

"How dare… with my own staff!" Dolly sputtered from the ground.

"This is all we wanted," Delilah said, handing the map to Emmaline. "Come now, let us away."

Emmaline glanced back at Dolly, uttered an awkward apology, and followed Delilah out of the reposeum. They were almost to the edge of the cliff when the door burst open and Dolly charged out, pointing her staff at them.

"I warned you!" she cried over the howling wind. "Those who steal from the K'nic-k'nack Tribe for their own profit must face the wrath of the Guardian of Mount Tumult!"

"This sounds serious, Delilah. What should we do?"

"Well, we tried to explain nicely," Delilah said innocently. "There're just some folks who won't listen to reason."

"You didn't have to shove her!"

"She was in the way."

"It's no use begging for mercy!" Dolly continued. "Hear me, oh Guardian, I summon you! Rain down your punishment on these thieves!"

The top of her staff began to glow green and emitted a low hum, and suddenly, the wind died down. Apparently, Dolly's threats were more than empty words.

"Come forth, Roc of Tumult!"

Out of the silence, they could hear a flapping of wings. Over the top of the peak, a black shape flew and circled down, getting larger as it came. When it finally landed in front of Dolly, they saw that it was a black bird about the size of a small cat.

"Is this the roc?" Dolly asked, bending down to inspect the bird.

"It's a pebble!" Delilah said excitedly.

"It's a raven," Emmaline said. "The spell obviously didn't work."

Dolly looked more than a little disappointed, but pointed her staff at them resolutely.

"Go, my raven! Teach them not to tamper with the treasures of the K'nic-k'nack Tribe!"

The bird obediently flew at Delilah, who swiped at it

several times with her arm. The terrified creature flew away from the attack and landed on a large boulder higher up the mountain. The weight of the bird, though certainly not equal to a roc's, was enough to upset the boulder from its upright position and send it rolling down the slope towards Dolly, who barely managed to dive out of its way before it plunged over the edge of the cliff.

"Th-that could've been you," she said shakily. "You better give the map back before I really show my power!"

Before Delilah could think of a snappy comeback, the boulder hit a ledge far below, sending tremors all up the mountain. The ground beneath them shook, and the snow on the peak above began to rumble.

"I say, at this time, the discussion of who stole what or if they did is purely academic," Delilah said. "Let's run for our lives."

"To where?" Emmaline cried. "If there's an avalanche, it'll push us right off the mountain if we're clinging to the rope, and if we stay here or go into the reposeum, we'll be buried alive."

"The airship!" Delilah said.

"We'll never make it in time!"

"No, I mean, there's the airship!"

Emmaline turned just in time to see the tub of the airship crash against the ground, tipping the entire thing sideways, spilling much of the contents of the baskets onto the ground. Bostwick was clinging onto one of the ropes tied to the balloon for dear life. Delilah and Emmaline ran to the ship and managed to climb in as it righted itself, pulling Delilah's and Millicent's bags back in with them.

"How did you manage to fly it up here?" Emmaline asked Bostwick, who was detaching himself from the rope.

"Purely by accident."

"Well, it's a good thing you're such a lousy flyer," Delilah said. "You saved us from a snowy death. Ascend, Emmaline, or at least get us as far from the mountain as you can."

"I take it you met Dolly the Goblin Avalanche?" said Bostwick.

"Indeed. She's a lovely person, really, but a bit touched in the head."

"Where is she anyway?" Emmaline said, looking over the side. Dolly was nowhere to be seen as a wave of snow and rocks barreled down the slope, engulfing the reposeum and everything else in its path. "You don't think…"

"She's fine," Delilah said, "Wackadoos always find a way of surviving even the most unlikely of situations. It's part of their job."

"I hope so," Emmaline said doubtfully.

"If she could survive five other avalanches, I don't see why the sixth would do her in," Bostwick said, and was met by looks of curiosity. "It's a long story; I'll tell you when we get going. For now, did you get the next map piece?"

"We did. And I take it you didn't find Millicent, unless you were extremely absentminded and left her in the forest."

"She wasn't there."

"Well, no worries. At least we know where the next map piece is. I would say the safest route is that way," she said, pointing west between two mountain peaks. "Emmaline, if you would be so kind?"

♠ ♦ ♣ ♥ ♣ ♦ ♠

Far below, from out of the top-most window of the reposeum, Dolly dug her way out of the snow. She had managed to dash inside just before the avalanche hit, and was safe within the carved stone walls. She hastily gathered some herbs, mortar and pestle, and enough food to last for a week, which she wrapped in a bindle and shoved out the window before her. With nothing but this and her staff, she had decided to leave the reposeum, which was safe under several feet of ice and snow, and pursue the thieves. It was her duty as the guardian.

"You haven't seen the last of me!" she cried to the flying machine as it swiftly sailed away, even though she was pretty sure they couldn't hear her.

Eight

Shadow Crisis

The vision of the snowy academy courtyard faded away and the king's chambers of Chiaroscuro returned. Sebastian stepped back and changed from an immortal beast to his true form. Placing a hand to his head, he staggered and sat on a couch behind him.

"Are you all right?" Millicent asked.

This had been the fifth time he had called her to his chambers to show her moments from his past. Whether due to emotional stress or physical fatigue, it always seemed to take a toll on him, so much so that he only showed her a handful of memories per day... at least what she assumed was a day.

"I'm fine. I just haven't remembered it this vividly for a long time."

His drained appearance belied his words, so she poured him a glass of water from a pitcher on the table, which he accepted with a word of thanks.

"I'm glad the shadow goblins got away," she said. "Do you think Alistair would really have killed them?"

"I don't know," he said darkly.

"So what happened after that?"

Sebastian shook his head, seeming exhausted.

"Anyway," Millicent continued, "I'm really impressed with the shadow goblins. They built this whole city in less than three hundred years! It's amazing."

"They used their shadows to carve the stone," he explained, "though I've never understood how they got so much of it here in the first place."

Millicent gave him a conspicuously questioning look.

"I can't tell you where we are," he said. "I'm afraid I still need your help, and if you left…"

"But I've been here for days, and you still haven't told me what exactly it is you want me to do."

"A spell," he said simply.

"But why didn't you ask Bostwick to do it? He's better at magic."

"It's a spell that *you* already know, I believe, although you may not yet know how to do it."

"But even if it is one of Alistair's spells, couldn't you have taught it to Bostwick anyway, to be sure it worked?"

"You should have more confidence in your own abilities." He stood up and returned his glass to the table, then turned to face Millicent once more. "Anyway, you won't need to cast that spell until I've made some other preparations, and of course there's more for you to see. Though I can't exactly say that showing you all this is pleasant, I'm glad you asked me to. I want you to understand what it is you'll be doing."

"Which is?"

"Something best discussed when the time comes."

As usual, he didn't elaborate, but Millicent had been forming her own ideas about what her magic practice might entail.

"I assume it has to do with not being able to live out in the open without fear of being experimented on."

"I would want nothing greater for my people, though what I want for myself is another matter."

"You don't want revenge for what happened!" she asked, jumping up out of her seat.

"Quite the opposite, in fact. You'll understand when I show you the rest of my experiences with Alistair, but we'll do that later. For now, you may return to your room, unless there's something else on your mind?"

"I have been wondering, actually… if I help you, would you let me go back to Styx?"

"I'll let you go wherever you wish. If you really want to go back to Delilah, then you can."

"But I don't know where she is. Can't you at least tell me where the parts of Styx are?"

He thought it over for a moment.

"I suppose there's no harm in telling you. Styx Castle is in the walled city of Catawampus. Emmaline and Bostwick should be safe there. Though," he said with a smirk, "Delilah will certainly not be treated like royalty."

"What about the rest of Styx. Are the townspeople all right, and all the animals in the forest?"

"The town is on an island in the Gammon Archipelago, and the forest is in the mountains. The Wastes I left, to be a buffer between Ataxia and the Empire, because humans do not need any more goblinical influence."

"So," Millicent said, grasping for more information, "will Emmaline be all right? Do they treat rabbits well in, um, that city?"

"I couldn't say, but as long as Bostwick is with her, she should be fine. You really don't have to worry about them."

"And Bostwick? Do you think he'll be all right, after what you did in Styx?"

Sebastian looked as if was about to say something, but bit his finger and turned away.

Millicent continued. "If he really got the Domino for you because he wanted me to escape, then don't you think he'd be worried about me now?"

"I never meant—"

"You held a sword to my throat! Bostwick trusted you, and you did *that*. And then you took me who-knows-where..."

"I had to," he said miserably.

Millicent could think of nothing more to say, and stood up to leave. When she was at the door, she heard his voice behind her.

"I promise, Millicent, after you help me, I'll see to it that you get back to him. I promise."

Outside the king's chambers, Millicent leaned against the wall, thinking. Misha was waiting by the stairs and bounded forward, but stopped when he saw her.

"Are you all right? Did he show you something bad?"

Millicent shook her head. "No, he showed me something good, for once. It was the night the Ancient Shadows escaped."

After seeing Sebastian's memories on the first day, she found it helpful to discuss them with Misha. She learned that most Chiaroscurans referred to the original shadow goblins, who had all died long ago, as the Ancient Shadows. There were many details of their story that Misha hadn't heard, though. Millicent wasn't sure if that was because the facts had been forgotten over the years or because Misha had lost his memories.

"Everyone knows that story," he said as they walked back to her room. "Sebastian and Inez and Jurek brought the Ancient Shadows to Ataxia, and then they built this city."

"But Sebastian didn't go with them, so what happened to him after that?"

"No one knows. Some say he went back to plead our case to the empress herself, while others say he fell in love with Inez and couldn't leave her. Who can say?"

"I think he probably wanted to confront Alistair."

"Who?"

"A magician. The one who started the experiments."

"Oh."

"Misha, how do you feel about magicians, after what happened?"

"For the most part, I think they must be pretty amazing. Look at you, for instance. You can do all kinds of magic tricks."

"Only a few."

"Yeah, but you'll learn how to do others. On the other hand, we can't ever show ourselves to magicians, in case they want to take us back and, well…"

"But that was only a group of students, not the president

of the Academy," Millicent said. "I don't know what the authorities would have done if they found out about the experiments. They probably would have stopped them, although that professor didn't seem to care about what was going on. But she might not have known entirely what was happening. Still, it does seem as if it might be dangerous out there."

"You can never be too careful when vivisection is involved."

She laughed at his choice of words, then inwardly squirmed. The topic was far from funny, and she had a sudden urge to change the subject.

"By the way, Misha, how's your sister?"

"Who?"

"Oh, Misha! You have to try to remember! She's your family."

He flinched and said, "I'll try."

"You know, I've been so preoccupied learning about Sebastian's past that I almost forgot. I said I'd help you find your memories, didn't I?"

"Did you?"

"Well, I'm saying it now. But I don't really know where to start. What does a memory look like?"

"Ah! *That* I can show you."

He brought Millicent farther downstairs and turned into a hallway Millicent had never been down before. She thought they must be going further into the interior of the palace, as there were no windows. Strangely, it seemed no more or less dark than anywhere else.

"I just noticed," she said, as Misha stopped before a black

wooden door and fiddled with a ring of keys, "there are no lights here. No lanterns or anything. How are we able to see?"

"Must be the magic of the place," Misha said, fitting the correct key into the lock. Millicent entered the small room and gazed around. Every surface—shelves, a table, and the floor—was covered in hundreds of glass bottles in deep, bright colors. Some even hung from the ceiling.

"It's like walking into a stained glass window!" she gasped. "Are these memories?"

"Mm-hmm," he said, moving a few bottles and opening a wooden drawer in the wall. He pulled out two glass jars, one full of dark leaves and another with an orange liquid and held them up for her to see.

"See, memories don't really look like anything, but I can fabricate one by combining scents and other ingredients, such as these leaves, into a substance that retains the memory— this liquid. Then I put that into an atomizer and sell it."

"Do a lot of people buy memories?"

"They do in Chiaroscuro. We live in a very beautiful city, but there are a lot of things we don't have, like trees and weather and sunsets. Some of us are only allowed outside every so often, so we miss those things. And most of the population has never been outside, so memories of rainy days and flower gardens and such are in high demand."

Millicent could understand that. This room in and of itself was like a breath of fresh air compared with the rest of the black and white city.

"You know, Misha, if you want to live, um, outside, why not talk to Delilah? I bet she would let all of you come and live in Styx."

"I couldn't possibly! We can't reveal what we are to anyone on the outside, especially the Styx royal family."

"Delilah wouldn't turn you in. And I'm sure there would be enough room for all of you. Styx is a pretty big country. I've never been to the Wastes, but I don't think anyone lives there, and Heather could add some nice trees and things."

Misha returned the jars to their drawer. "As much as I might want to live out there, I can't risk everyone else's lives. If the wrong people found us…"

He gasped and grabbed Millicent by the shoulders.

"Which reminds me!"

"What? Is there something wrong?"

"Yes! Something's really, really wrong! It's, um, something about… a machine?"

"Is it here in Chiaroscuro?"

"I don't know," he said, stepping back.

"What kind of machine is it?" she asked, but Misha shook his head. "Well, before we think about that, we better worry about getting you back to normal. Do you think maybe your memories are mixed up with these bottles?"

"No. These are all fabricated memories. I don't make a habit of leaching out real ones, and even when I do, I keep them separate from the others. But I haven't had any of that kind for a long time."

"Maybe you gave them to your sister, for safe keeping or something?"

"You think so?"

"You can always ask her. I'm sure she wants you to get your memories back as much as you do. And the rest of your family does, too."

"It's just us," he said. "Huh. That's weird. For some reason, I remember that my parents died when I was too little to remember them. Strange."

"I'm sorry, Misha."

"For what?"

"Just… you seem like you have a really tough time."

"It's all right," he said with a shrug. "I have a cushy job, live pretty high up in the palace, and have a sister who most likely loves me, even if I can't remember her. You don't have to feel sorry for me. You're the one who was kidnapped away from your home and friends."

"Oh…"

"S-sorry! I didn't mean to depress you again. It's just, well, remembering your friends and being away from them seems worse than not remembering your sister but still getting to see her, you know?"

"I do miss them."

"What are they like, anyway, your friends? What's it like out in Styx?"

"It's nice," she said with a small smile.

"Be more specific! You know, I'm very interested in memories."

Millicent laughed and leaned against the table, thinking.

"Well, Delilah's pretty stubborn, and she likes to scheme about things, but she really cares about everything, both her country and me and everyone. You met her, right?"

"I remember she had pink hair and hung around with a talking rabbit."

"That's Emmaline. She's actually a princess, and seems to think of everything, and knows how to handle things in just the right way. And then there's Bostwick. He's a magician like me, only he's really good at magic. He's a little blunt, but I think it's just because he trusts people enough to be open with his feelings. I'm not sure if he liked me very much at first, but he's helped me clean a lot, and also taught me magic and… I just liked being around him, I guess. Even if we were just scrubbing floors, being with him made me really happy."

"Are you all right?" Misha asked.

"Oh, I just… I really miss him. I miss all of them, of course, but… I wish Bostwick was here. He'd probably just respond to this whole situation with a few sarcastic remarks. Even if he wouldn't know how to solve Sebastian's problem, or if he couldn't figure out a way to escape, I'd feel better if he was with me."

Misha gave her a sympathetic frown.

"Sorry," she said. "I guess I'm being a little silly."

"Not at all. I wish I could make memories with half the feeling you have."

"I wish I was a little less emotional, actually."

"Well, maybe your emotions are your way of being honest, the same way your friend is blunt? You match!"

"Don't say that!" she said, blushing.

"Aw. As I suspected," Misha said with a grin.

"Don't… don't say embarrassing things!"

"No one can hear. Besides, you aren't sad anymore."

Millicent considered this, but only deepened in color.

"Well, that's no excuse," she said, smiling. "Still, thanks for cheering me up, Misha."

"Eh, what else are memory merchants for?"

♠ ♦ ♣ ♥ ♣ ♦ ♠

The next day, Misha came back to Millicent's room to bring her up to Sebastian's chambers once more.

"I talked to my sister," he said excitedly. "She didn't have my memories though. But she said that if I ever needed anything, I should come to her."

"That's great!" Millicent said. "So does she live in the palace, too?"

"No. She lives by the edge of the city in case something blows up." Seeing Millicent's concerned expression, he added, "I think she does something with chemicals or something. I can't remember exactly."

"Sounds exciting," she said nervously.

When they arrived at Sebastian's chambers, Millicent waved goodbye to Misha, hoping he might find some information about his past by the time she was done. She found Sebastian sitting on one of the sofas, deep in thought. He jumped slightly when she approached, but quickly regained his composure.

"Ah, hello," he said, standing up.

"Hi." She always felt awkward greeting him. He was always polite, but that didn't change the fact that she was technically his prisoner. "So, will I find out what it is you need me for today?"

"Yes. Today you'll find out everything. You'll understand… you'll understand about me." He sounded as if he was trying to talk his himself into something.

"Don't worry. I don't think anything can shock me too much, after what I've already seen."

Sebastian grimaced, then transformed once again into the purple-skinned humanoid. He placed his palm onto her forehead and closed his eyes in concentration, but before he could show her anything, a black shadow issued out of the top hat that lay on the table at the end of the room. The shadow materialized into a short Chiaroscuran in a silky lavender dress, who stared at Sebastian, open-mouthed. She tilted her head in confusion, until her eyes fell on the copy of *Flora, Fauna, and Fungi of the Goblin World* that lay open on the table.

"Well, well, well," she said, her eyes traveling over the page as Sebastian turned back into a shadow goblin. "Why the hurry to change? I've already seen what you're up to. The only question is, who is this *human*?"

"Alcea, she's not—" Sebastian began, but the woman turned into a shadow again and rematerialized in front of Millicent, staring into her eyes.

"You have human eyes, and ears, and you smell like a human, too. Honestly, Sebastian," she said, sitting in one of the chairs, "what fascination do you have for these creatures? After everything they've done, you still associate with them?"

"I was—"

"Showing her something from your past?" She studied Sebastian's face for a moment, then frowned. "At the Academy?"

Sebastian began to tremble, but Millicent couldn't tell if it was in fear or anger.

"That all happened hundreds of years ago. All of those humans are dead and gone," the woman said without emotion, as if she were explaining something simple to a child. When she received no response, she tossed her head back haughtily. "Well, you may as well relish your memories. I don't care what you do. For now," she added. "Which reminds me, I came to inform you that I have come up with a way to remove the city to safety. Unfortunately, it may be difficult, given your all too hasty destruction of Styx."

"Difficult, but not impossible?"

She tapped her fingers on the arm of the chair, and looked Millicent up and down.

"You know, I thought we could trust each other, Sebastian. Sneaking humans into Chiaroscuro is not something I would have suspected you of. Surely, you don't think I would ever go behind your back?"

"Actually, I was almost certain you would."

She raised an eyebrow, hopped up, and went once more to the hat.

"Well, in that case, saving Chiaroscuro won't be difficult at all, but you're not going to like it."

"I've told you before, as long as Chiaroscuro is safe, I'll do whatever it takes."

"I'm counting on it," she said, and went back through the hat once more.

Sebastian bit the side of his finger, then glanced sideways at Millicent.

"Who was that?" she asked.

"Her name is Alcea," he said, and walked to where she had stood a moment before.

"What did she mean about saving the city?"

Sebastian brushed hair nervously out of his face without responding.

"Sebastian, you have to talk to me. I can't help you if I don't know what's going on. If Chiaroscuro's in trouble… Is it because it's in a shadow?"

He blinked and said, "How did you…?"

"I figured it out," she said with a shrug. "That's why the city just ends in blackness, and why there aren't any lights inside the palace. Considering that all the Chiaroscurans were originally made out of shadows, it's not so strange to think you could live in one. But what could be big enough to cast a city-sized shadow? A mountain?"

"In a manner of speaking."

"So the city needs to be saved because…?"

"Technically speaking, the 'mountain' is slowly collapsing, and thus the shadow the city resides in is getting smaller. The parts of the city that were at the edge of the shadow disappeared when pieces of the mountain crumbled, and the people who lived there… It's not like when a magician vanishes an object and then re-conjures it. Even at night, when the shadow stretches out forever, the parts of the city that were destroyed never come back."

"Oh…"

"Hundreds of shadow goblins have lost their lives that way. Even Misha's parents. Every day, those that live at the edge of the city are forced to move inward, and it's only a matter of time before all of Chiaroscuro is destroyed."

Millicent stared at her shoes, remembering just yesterday that Misha had mentioned his parents. He said they died, not that they had disappeared into the blackness beyond the city, which seemed so much worse. She'd only encountered a few shadow goblins, but judging from the number of buildings she'd seen from her window, there must be thousands of them. The idea of all of them suddenly vanishing, as if they'd never even existed in the first place, hurt to think about.

"My people did nothing to deserve this precarious existence," Sebastian continued, "so I've asked Alcea to find a way to move Chiaroscuro out of the shadow, for a price."

"When you said you'd do whatever it takes, you meant *whatever* it takes?"

Sebastian nodded and picked up the hat.

"What if she asks you to do something bad?" Millicent said. "She sounds like she doesn't like humans. What if she wants revenge for what happened to the Ancient Shadows?"

"That's where you come in. Whatever happens, Alcea can't know why I brought you here." He threw the hat in the air and slashed his shadow across it.

"Is that the only way out of the city?" Millicent asked, watching the two halves of the hat fall to the ground.

"No, but destroying that hat will at least keep Alcea from coming directly into these chambers."

His shadow returned to his feet and he stood there, lost in thought. Alcea's unexpected visit had clearly unnerved him, and considering how reluctant he was to talk about himself, Millicent wondered if he wasn't even more frightened than he let on.

She fidgeted a moment before saying, "Um… I-I'll cast the spell you need."

His head jerked up in surprise.

"I know I said I wouldn't unless you told me everything first," she continued, "but I don't want anyone else to disappear."

He held her gaze, a pained look growing in his eyes, then wandered over to the table and began to absent-mindedly flip through a few pages of *Flora, Fauna, and Fungi* with shaking hands.

"You should still see the rest of my memories. They'll… help you with the spell."

"All right."

She took a step toward him, but he hunched where he sat, closing the book with a snap.

"Not right now, though," he said. "I'm too…"

"Maybe if you just told me about what happened?"

"I don't want to talk about it," he admitted "even if I can't help thinking about it. In a few days, then I'll show you."

"Sebastian…" She took his hand, which was strangely lukewarm. "Whatever happened, it won't change how I see you."

For an instant, she thought she saw relief in his face, but he turned from her and said, in a strained voice, "Just go back to your room."

She left his chambers and looked for Misha, but realized that he probably didn't wait outside the entire time. She considered searching for him in the memory room, but she didn't know the way, so she went back to her bedroom and looked out across the city. She did want to help the Chiaroscurans, but Sebastian still hadn't told her how she would do it. It was one of Alistair's spells that was needed, but she couldn't think of a single one for the situation at hand. There was a spell to make shadows disappear, but that would only make the situation worse. Then there was a spell to make blood flow backwards… With a sickening feeling, Millicent realized that that spell was the result of the experiments performed on the shadow goblins. That wouldn't help them now, Millicent thought. All that was left were numerous household spells that had made her days of cleaning Castle Styx easier, but she couldn't imagine that her skills as a maid would be called on any time soon. The only thing she could do was stare out the window and wonder about what Alcea's price entailed and hope that Sebastian wouldn't have to pay.

Nine

Love Potions and Soliloquies

"Behold, the forest of Skimble-Skamble," Delilah said. "The only forest on the planet made up entirely of fungus."

Stretching out before them from the hilly region they were flying over to the ocean beyond lay a dense growth of mushrooms. Some of the caps were several yards across, while a few puff-ball and straw mushrooms grew as tall a pine trees and overshadowed the others. From the airship, they could see smaller mushrooms growing on the stems of larger ones, while patches of yellow and black mold covered the few spots of ground visible from above. Overall, the effect of the many different colors and textures was quite picturesque.

"I thought fungus needed to feed off decaying plant and animal material," Emmaline said.

"Usually, but these are cannibal mushrooms."

"We're landing," Bostwick declared, grabbing a chain that hung from the balloon, causing them to lose altitude. Delilah pulled it back up, though the airship continued to descend.

"Don't be a baby, Bostwick."

"Cannibal mushrooms! I've already encountered one of those; I don't want a whole forest of them."

"That was a carnivorous mushroom. Cannibal mushrooms are fine, unless you're a mushroom. You're not, are you?"

"Oh, so they only feed off each other," Emmaline said, bringing the ship back up to its original elevation.

"It's no more dangerous than the Forest of Infinite Horrors."

Bostwick pulled the chain down once more.

"Why are you being so silly, Bostwick?"

"Because if we fly over that forest, then we *will* have a malfunction in the ship, we *will* crash, and we *will* have to go through that forest on foot."

"Why…?"

"Because that's the way things work, especially for me."

"Well, we could restock our supplies, and give the ship a checkup, just in case," Emmaline said, adjusting several knobs and levers.

"Fine, be that way," Delilah said. "But if bad luck follows you everywhere, Bostwick, it will certainly find you even on the ground."

"They're going down!" Dolly said, breathing heavily.

She had been following the balloon full of thieves since the previous day without catching a wink of sleep. Even though her people were skilled at climbing the steepest of ridges, that did not make the task of following a flying device—which went linearly over hill and mountain—any easier, especially when she kept taking wrong turns and falling into open mine shafts.

She was not going to allow the disgrace to her tribe to stand, and would therefore use the skills she had learned as an herbalist to retrieve the map they had stolen. From out of her bindle she pulled a bunch of herbs and cackled, catching the eye of a passing goblin that strongly resembled a walking fur cone with a tail.

"I'm going to make a potion," she explained.

"Poison?" it asked in a gruff, squeaky voice.

"I don't want to kill anyone!" she said, scandalized, then resumed a sinister smile. "It's a potion that will make the flying machine's captain— obviously the leader of the band— my slave, and then he'll bring me the map."

"And then you'll eat him?"

"I'll let him go back to his friends!" she said. "Oh, dear, I'm afraid I've fallen in among riff-raff. Not that you're riff-raff, of course."

The goblin shrugged, and went on his way.

"All right," she said to herself. "All I have to do is mix up this potion, and then sneak it to him once they land. Looks like they're heading into that village over there. Heh heh, perfect!"

The "thieves" landed without incident beside a patch of mushrooms as tall as trees and went into the village, which turned out to be populated entirely by kobolds: short, round-snouted creatures with plated scales, beady black eyes, and needlessly long tails. Delilah explained that kobolds were the miners of Pandemonium. They went deep underground to dig out gems and precious metals that other goblins used in their currency and art. The town itself was a small mining village, which they hoped would have what they needed in terms of supplies and food.

"I'll take care of inspecting the ship, if you get supplies," Emmaline said. "Here, I made a list of what we need."

She handed them a piece of paper and returned to the ship.

"So what do we use for money?" Bostwick asked.

"Kobolds accept any precious metal as tender," Delilah explained. "They just melt it down again anyway. So, Bostwick, how about I handle food?"

"No. You'll just get more inedible goblin food. You should get the rest of the supplies; I'll handle what we eat."

"Fine," she said indignantly. "I wouldn't expect a butler to know how to pick the proper sort of supplies for an adventure anyway."

"Can I just have the money?"

She threw a sack of coins at him and wandered over to a large open warehouse that sold mining equipment.

This did not have most of what they needed, so she spent the next hour going from store to store until she had gathered a large assortment of rope, grappling hooks, springs and other "necessities". When she finally brought it to Emmaline, she was greeted with an exasperated look.

"Um, I'm glad you got what we needed, but what are the springs for?"

"I just like them. So, has Bostwick come back yet?"

"I thought he was shopping with you."

"Hmph. He's getting food, supposedly, although he probably got lost or something, or eaten by kobolds."

"Do they eat people?"

"Only sometimes. Well, we better go rescue him."

They went to the town's small food market, but Bostwick was nowhere to be seen. They inquired about him from the various food vendors until they found one who had seen him.

"Tall fella? Human looking? Yeah, he came through here," a kobold selling pastries told them.

"Do you know where he went?" Emmaline asked.

"After I sold him a few sweet rolls, he wandered away, probably to die."

"Die?"

"Well, yeah, die. A lady give me twenty silver to sneak somethin' into me sample pastries. I can only assume it was poison."

"Y-you what? You just put something into your food because someone told you to?"

"Gotta make a living," the kobold said. "Care for some sticky buns?"

"Which way did he go? We have to find him!"

"Hold your dodos. He's coming right here. Apparently the poison wasn't strong enough. Oh well, not my job to care one way or the other."

Bostwick was, sure enough, quite alive and came bounding toward them, waving hello as he went.

"There you are! I guess I must have missed you at the airship."

"Bostwick, are you all right?" Emmaline asked. "Do you feel faint? Maybe you should lie down or something."

"Feel faint? I should think not. How could I feel anything but wonderful in the presence of you two angels."

Emmaline and Delilah looked at each other, the former grabbing Bostwick's wrist to take his pulse, the latter feeling his forehead.

"What's gotten into you?" he continued. "I'm not sick. In fact, I feel better than ever!"

"No, no, no," Emmaline said. "There is definitely something wrong here."

"That there is," Bostwick said, pulling away from them, "for at this very moment, there is a distressed young woman, and you know I can't stand to see a woman in distress. So, Emmaline, if you could just give me the map piece…"

"What does that have to do with this?"

"If you give me the map piece, I can give it to Dolly, and we can all live in harmony."

"Dolly the guardian goat girl?" Delilah asked.

"The same. Ah, her name is like the sounding of a bell. Dolly!"

Emmaline and Delilah turned from him to converse with each other.

"This is bad," Emmaline said. "It's like she put some kind of mind control drug in that pastry."

"Oh, I think it's worse than that," Delilah said, pointing back to Bostwick, who appeared to be reciting a sonnet to a female kobold. "It must have been a love potion she gave him. It's not as bad as poison, I suppose…"

Bostwick ran up to her, took her hand, and kissed it.

"Ah, but I almost forgot to tell you, Delilah, how lovely your yellow eyes are in this light, like a glistening jar of honey in the setting sun on a summer evening. How they enchant me, my love, my dove, my only!"

Delilah whipped her hand away like it had been burned.

"No! Poison would be better! Definitely better! Ugh! The Lovey-dovey Bostwick is even worse than Mopey Bostwick. How many Bostwick's are there? A whole herd?"

By this time, the magician was dancing away down the street.

"Shouldn't we stop him?" Emmaline said.

"Although he wouldn't really be a herd animal I suppose. Well, then he would be… a grumble? Yes! A grumble of Bostwicks!"

"Stop making up weird phrases and come on. Who knows what he'll do if he's let loose in the town!"

They caught up to him as he knelt to propose marriage to another kobold, who tittered bashfully and ran off.

"Listen, Bostwick," Emmaline said. "Where did you see Dolly? Is she here somewhere?"

"Ah, yes. It was in an alley not too far from here."

"We have to find her."

"Of course! If she's here then we can simply work out this silly misunderstanding. Dolly? Oh Dolly, my love?"

Dolly appeared from behind one of the buildings. "Um, hi, you guys," she said sheepishly.

"There you are! Now, why don't you ask Emmaline yourself. I'm sure you can work something out. Meanwhile, I must compose a ballad about your beautiful bean-shaped pupils!"

"Yes," Emmaline said seriously, "Let's talk."

They went a little away from Bostwick, leaving him in the care of Delilah, who looked repulsed.

"So," Emmaline began, "a love potion?"

"Well, it was supposed to be a love potion, only I think it sort of made him in love with the whole world, instead of just me."

"How on earth did you make that mistake?"

"Well, I never really made a love potion before, but I'd read about them and they seemed simple enough. But, um, I guess it was more complicated than I thought."

"And this was all to get some stupid map piece, that isn't even yours in the first place?"

"But it is mine! Dolores drew that map and bequeathed it to all of Pandemonium. It's a national treasure!"

Emmaline pulled the map piece from her pocket.

"Does this look like a national treasure to you? First off, it isn't even finished, which the rest of the pages in Dolores's book certainly were. Secondly, you can see the 'The Forest of Infinite Horrors' written quite clearly. Do you know of any place in Pandemonium with that name?"

"Well… no."

"Furthermore, this paper, aside from a few coffee stains, is clean and white. If Dolores had drawn it, don't you think it would be yellowed with age?"

Dolly nodded reluctantly and said, "But if the map really was yours to begin with, why not just say so?"

"We did!"

"Oh, come now. You don't expect me to believe all that about that shadow-wielding man. It's simply too farfetched."

"I spent the last year and a half as a rabbit. Nothing is too far-fetched for me. Now, do you believe that you were wrong about the map or not?"

"I… I suppose so. I was just so excited about finally

catching thieves that I guess I got a little carried away. Um, no hard feelings?"

"That depends. Can you fix *that*?"

She gestured to Bostwick, who was now leaning on Delilah's shoulder with a dreamy expression, gesturing at cloud formations. Dolly looked downcast.

"I'm not really sure. The potion's effects should escalate until it runs its course. It shouldn't last for more than a day. Of course, that would be if it was an ordinary love potion."

"So what will happen with this one?"

Dolly shrugged, as Delilah ran toward them.

"For the love of all the goblin races, please make it stop!"

"If you wish for an end to my love," Bostwick called, "I'm afraid I cannot help you, for it shall last forever. But only death can silence my lips, if you wish it!"

Before they could stop him, he conjured a dagger and plunged it into his chest. Emmaline and Dolly screamed and Delilah stood gaping, but he pulled the dagger out. It was spotless.

"Alas, even death cannot separate me from your perfect presence."

"But how?" Emmaline asked.

From out of his pocket, right where the dagger had been, Bostwick pulled a book with a hole cut through it.

"It's a book of Ruzicka's poetry. I carry it with me always."

"Oh dear, this is getting dangerous," Dolly said. "I really would stop it if I could."

"I know!" Delilah said. "If we get him to remember that he's really in love with Millicent, that will break the spell."

"Um, I don't think that'll work," Emmaline pointed out, "for a couple of reasons."

"Bostwick," Delilah said, taking the dagger from his hands. "This isn't you. You're a sarcastic, gloomy person, but you're also my beloved butler. And right now, you're breaking my heart. Fight the love potion, Bostwick. You must!"

"But I told you, I cannot fight my feelings for you, my precious, rose-haired idol."

"You have to fight it! It's important that you do, Bostwick. Somewhere out there is a girl who needs you, grumpy and standoffish as you are!"

"Girl? What girl?"

"Millicent! Don't you remember Millicent?"

He stopped for a moment to think, and it seemed that the madness left him briefly, until he smiled and shrugged his shoulders.

"Doesn't ring a bell."

Delilah gave a primal yell and punched him right then and there. He lifted a foot off the ground and went flying back. She was about to go after him again, but Emmaline blocked her path.

"He doesn't know what he's saying, Delilah. It's the potion's fault."

"Yes," Delilah said in a deep, furious voice, "the potion's fault." She turned her head slowly toward Dolly, fixing her with an icy stare.

"I didn't intend this!" Dolly told her, shaking her hands out in front of her. "I'm really, really sorry!"

"Worry not," Bostwick said, brushing himself off. "It's not your fault. We may fight and have our differences, but in the end, love will find a way. For the world, in all its wonder, through all the discord and disunity, is a beautiful place. Why, take Emmaline for instance." He seemed to have chosen her for no other reason than proximity. "So brave and true. Always there with a kind word, the voice of reason in this world of chaos.

'White and golden Emmaline stood,
Like a lily in a flood,
Like a rock of blue-veined stone
Lashed by tides obstreperously,
Like a beacon left alone
In a hoary roaring sea.'

Ah, your flaxen hair like fields of wheat, and your eyes! Eyes as brown as…"

He stopped, as if searching for a proper comparison.

"Eyes as brown as… you know, there just aren't a lot of nice things to compare brown to."

With that, he collapsed on the ground.

"Bostwick!" Emmaline cried, running over to him.

"I apologize, but my verbal skills are not up to par with your beauty. If I could simply… But really, brown?"

He then passed out.

"I know I shouldn't be insulted by that," Emmaline said, "but still…"

"This is horrible!" Dolly said. "I just wanted the map. I never wanted to hurt him! And now that I realize you were all innocent, that makes it worse, doesn't it?"

"Indeed," Delilah said. "Well, let's take him to the airship. At least he can lie down there and we can decide what to do with him."

Dolly attempted to summon a beast of burden for the task of carrying the unconscious Bostwick, but all she managed to bring were several rats, a beetle, and a hedgehog. Emmaline and Dolly ended up carrying him themselves, as Delilah kept up a running commentary about how all poetry was ruined forever after today.

When they got to the airship, Emmaline spread out some blankets for Bostwick while Dolly gathered herbs that might come in handy. Delilah declared that she might as well get the food Bostwick had failed to procure and went back toward the town.

"Any luck?" Emmaline asked Dolly, who had a small pile of twigs and leaves in front of her.

"Not really. I can make a sleeping potion for him, if he wakes up again, but that's about it. How is he?"

"He's developed a fever, and he keeps mumbling about flowers and the firmament."

"Oh dear. He hasn't said anything about being no good for you, has he?"

Emmaline nodded.

"Oh dear! Well, that means that this potion is almost to its final stages. The good news is, in a few more hours, he may be back to normal."

"And the bad news?"

"Well... the shock of coming back to reality... It might kill him."

"What?"

"I've heard of it before. Whether it was a potion overdose, or if the person had just been under the influence too long, sometimes it's too much for the system."

Emmaline shook with anger, but went back to Bostwick, who was saying something about "beauty like the night".

"This is all my fault," Dolly said to herself as she boiled water for the herbs

"Yup." It was Delilah, returning with two sacks full of food, one of which was carried by a young kobold porter. "But worry not, I think I've come up with a solution. All we need to break the spell is true love's kiss which, according to several human fairytales, is the most powerful panacea in the world! In this case, we'll settle for some random kiss from whoever draws the shortest straw."

"He's really sick, Delilah," Emmaline said from the airship. "He's pale, and his breathing's shallow. We have to try something that will actually work."

"The kiss will work. I wouldn't have suggested it otherwise. Now, I have here three straws. Who wants to draw first?"

"Did someone say kiss?" Bostwick said groggily, stumbling from the airship. "Why, only if it's on the cheek. Otherwise, it would be too bold of me."

"Quiet, you. Here Dolly, pick a straw."

Dolly picked a straw, one of the long ones, and went back to stirring her pot.

"Now you, Emmaline."

"I really must protest," Bostwick said. "A girl's first kiss is supposed to be special. I'd be an absolute cad if I used that up, willy-nilly. Besides, I'm happy. Really very, very happy."

Emmaline pulled her straw, looking grim, and visibly relaxed when she saw it was quite long. Delilah opened her own hand to reveal the last, shortest straw, and shuddered.

"It's not that Bostwick isn't attractive or anything, but I mean, are we even the same species? Maybe a kiss won't work after all."

"I think I finally realize what I've been missing in life…" Bostwick went on, ignoring the rest of the proceedings.

"Well, we have to do something!" Dolly said.

"…I feel like a new man. The clouds of sarcasm have lifted away…"

"But what if he dies?" Emmaline said.

"…revealing the bright sun of human compassion…"

"Of embarrassment?" Delilah asked.

"…and friendship. In fact, so elated am I that I feel like, nay, I declare that I shall, without further ado, break into song!"

Delilah threw her straw into the fire, grabbed the kobold porter by the back of the collar, and lifted it up to touch Bostwick's lips. For a brief moment, time seemed to stop, as Emmaline and Dolly looked on, mouths agape. The kobold looked vaguely shocked, while Bostwick's face went from a blissful smile to a horrified expression that seemed to bring everything back to normal time.

"My first kiss," the kobold said, sounding theatrically bashful.

"You don't even have lips! I'm sure it doesn't count," Delilah said, and chased the snickering creature away.

"Bostwick?" Emmaline asked, approaching him slowly. "Did the love potion wear off? Do you remember what happened?" The look on his face was enough to confirm this. "Oh, Bostwick, it wasn't your fault. You had no control over your actions. We don't have to mention this ever again if—"

"Don't even talk to me," Bostwick said, burying his face in his hands.

"I'm so sorry," Dolly said, "I really—"

The look he gave her made it impossible to go on; it was a cross between the face of a man betrayed and that of a wounded animal.

"Oh dear," she said to Delilah. "What if the potion's side effects were to make him miserable forevermore?"

"Pshaw, he's only slightly gloomier than usual. He'll be back to normal soon."

"Gee, thanks," he said.

"See, the healing has already begun. I think, aside from the horror of it all, and the deep psychological scars we will all have, it turned out all right."

"Easy for you to say."

"You didn't die."

"I would have liked to."

"And, looking back, I think we shall all have a good laugh."

"And now that you know that we aren't thieves," Emmaline said to Dolly, only a little accusingly, "you can go back to Tumult."

"But I can't!" Dolly said miserably. "I've completely disgraced my tribe. First with my magical ineptitude, then by causing an avalanche—well, a lot of avalanches, to be honest—and now by soiling our herbal traditions by making a shoddy potion with the ill intention of controlling another person. I'm starting to think my tribe stuck me up in the reposeum on purpose." It was true, but sounded especially pathetic when she said it all together. "I'll have to wander the world alone, purposeless and destitute. I don't even have any marketable skills."

"You could always sell potions," Emmaline suggested.

"Because that worked so well last time," Bostwick said, though the look from Emmaline made him regret his comment immediately.

"Can't we just say that nothing too bad happened this time and sweep it under the rug?" Delilah asked.

Dolly shook her head, sending her ears into her face. "Even if you forgave me, I would have the stain of my actions forever on my soul. Plus, a snow-covered reposeum will be sort of hard to explain to the tribe elders."

She bowed to them dramatically, picked up her staff and bindle, and started to leave.

"Wait!" Bostwick called. "Since I'm the person you did the most damage to, I think I should be allowed to have some say in your punishment."

Emmaline began to protest, but Dolly said she would hear him out.

"You may not be able to go back to your tribe," Bostwick said, "but that doesn't mean you can't get your honor back. You're going to travel the world, right? Then you can keep your eyes open for a friend of ours. She's a human, a little shorter than me, with green hair. She shouldn't be too hard to spot. Her name is Millicent. And she'll probably be with a tall Styxian-looking goblin, only with white hair and black and white skin."

"The smoke-and-shadow man? So he's actually real?"

"Yes. Real and dangerous, so be careful."

"So, you're saying that by finding this girl, you would

overlook all my past misdeeds?"

"If you found Millicent, I would forgive you *even* for slipping me a love potion."

"Great green globs! He's serious!" Delilah said. "You better take him up on the offer. Forgiving, Sensible Bostwicks rarely make an appearance this time of year. They usually hibernate."

Ignoring Delilah's peculiar dehumanization, Dolly put her hand over heart and bowed, yet again, to Bostwick.

"I shall never rest until the green-haired girl is found. I swear it! But, well, how am I supposed to tell you if I find her?"

Bostwick thought it over, went to the airship, and came back with one pair of opera glasses, which he handed to Dolly.

"These work with another pair that we have. If you find Millicent, write down where you are on a piece of paper and point the glasses at it, for at least a day, so we can check and see where you are. Then stay put until we get there."

"Wow, Bostwick," Emmaline said, "that's pretty clever!"

"Don't patronize me."

"I wasn't."

"Oh. Well, thanks."

Dolly bowed to them once again and walked toward a path that led into the mountains. Though her newfound friends had already turned away, she waved goodbye as she went, and went pitching backwards into an open mineshaft.

♠ ♦ ♣ ♥ ♣ ♦ ♠

"Now that my life has taken the next step in its cavalcade of misery," Bostwick said, "we might as well get back to work. We're going to the ocean, right? Let's find out what humiliations await."

"On the bright side," Emmaline said, "it's very likely that this was the worst possible thing that could happen to you, so it can only get better from here."

"No. If there's one thing I've learned in life, it's that it can always get worse."

"It's true," Delilah said. "You could have kissed *me* instead of the kobold."

Bostwick looked relieved. "True. I feel better already."

"And so the matter was ended."

She began walking back to the airship, but then spun around and wrapped one arm around Bostwick's shoulder. She looked left and right suspiciously, then reached into his pocket and removed the book of poetry.

"Although there is still something I'm unclear about. If you had this book in your pocket, doesn't that mean you had it before you drank the love potion?"

Bostwick grabbed it back from her and glared.

"Your point?"

"I just think it's cute, is all. Who knew you liked poetry?"

"It is surprising," Emmaline agreed. "All this time, you never told me."

"Yeah," he said, and walked sullenly to the ship. "I don't tell a lot of people. Clarence knows. There's a story about that."

They looked at him expectantly.

"But you will never hear it. Never, ever, ever."

Delilah kept prying, then added a few threats at the end, but Bostwick remained tight-lipped.

Emmaline sailed the ship around the edge of Skimble-Skamble and then headed south-west, towards the Gammon Archipelago. Delilah estimated the journey would take them several days, and that they might as well amuse themselves.

"We could take long naps, or play twenty questions, or Bostwick, we could read from your poetry book. Bostwick? Bostwick, don't look sullenly into the distance when I'm talking to you. Whatever is the matter?"

He showed them the small book of poems and flipped through the pages, which stuck together where the knife had cut through them. A few had even torn all the way across.

"I told you terrible things always happen to me."

Ten

Scales and Archipelagos

Bostwick looked through the opera glasses and, once again, saw nothing. They had been flying over the Gammon Sea for a day, and he had checked the glasses every hour on the hour. Now the sun was setting, turning the ocean the color of fire, and all he could think was that they had lost another day in their search for Millicent.

"Nothing," he informed Emmaline, as Delilah was sleeping, curled, in one corner of the ship.

"Do you actually think Dolly will find her?" Emmaline asked. Since there were no mountains or trees in their path, she did not have to attend the steering as much and was free to relax and talk with Bostwick.

"It couldn't hurt, and we need someone to look for her since she's not in Styx, despite what Delilah might think."

He was certain of this, and had declared to Delilah earlier that they would not find her there. Delilah had responded by saying, "Not with that attitude we won't," and had haughtily gone to bed.

"She's probably just worried," Emmaline said, glancing at the queen's mass of pink hair.

"That's no reason to live in denial. If we face the problem head on, maybe we can figure out where Sebastian went."

"I was thinking about that, actually. A few months ago, Delilah had me investigate him. He said his people lived somewhere to the west of Styx."

"His people? I thought he was that old Styx goblin."

"I don't know. It's just what he said."

"So what's to the west of Styx?" he asked, looking out over the sea.

"I think the Gammon Archipelago is to the northwest. But directly west is just open ocean."

"And beyond that?"

"Some islands, and then the Aphasian continent, and then more ocean, but by that time you're back to Styx. Maybe he's from Aphasia?"

"But he couldn't possibly have gone that far, even by magic. I was thinking about how you said there was a top hat in the reposeum. I didn't see one in the library at Catawampus, but a few goblins on the street were wearing some. Sebastian can obviously travel through them, but all magic is limited by distance to some extent. I don't think he could make it to the other side of the world, at least not carrying a hostage," he finished quietly.

Bostwick had seemed exceedingly depressed since the love potion had worn off, and at first Emmaline assumed it was due to the humiliation. Now she was starting to think that he was dwelling on what had happened with Sebastian again. She'd done her best to take his mind off it, and now that he was staring out across the darkening ocean, she felt the need to step in once more. She asked if he was hungry, and he sullenly said yes, so she handed him a roll and a pink apple. Delilah had surprised them both when they realized the food she had purchased from the kobolds was almost normal. According to Bostwick, she really did have something like a heart.

"These apples are weird," Emmaline said, more to make conversation than anything else. "They're good, but I can't really describe the flavor; you know what I mean?"

Bostwick nodded.

"I wish humans were on better terms with goblins. I've actually grown accustomed to some of their food, and it would be nice if we could trade with them."

"Yeah," he said, without much heart.

"Plus, this airship is wonderful. I'm sure someone could market it. It's a very relaxing way to travel. Sort of like a train, but more refreshing. And you can pack your own food, like a picnic."

Bostwick put his apple down, uneaten.

"What's wrong, Bostwick?"

"I was thinking about Millicent. She would've loved all of this: riding in an airship, having a picnic in the sky. But without her here, it's just…"

"There's no reason to talk about her like she's deceased," Emmaline said.

He gave her a look that made all her airy, carefree words evaporate.

"Bostwick! Be sensible. Sebastian wouldn't have kidnapped her just to kill her."

"How can you be so sure?"

"Because I can think logically. He could have killed her

right then and there, in front of us, but he took her with him. Why? I don't know, but I'm sure that whatever his reason was, it requires her to be quite alive. And you know, Bostwick, since Millicent is alive, and we *will* find her; it doesn't do her any good for you to be so upset about everything. If I were her, I'd want to see you happy and safe, not wasting away worrying."

"I can't help it. I just want to see her again, to know that she's all right, but all I can think of is her being alone, trapped somewhere, or worse. Even when she was serving Delilah, she was happy... I should have realized that she wasn't in danger before. I should have trusted her when she told me that Delilah wasn't so bad. It's all my fault."

"Bostwick, I don't mean to sound impertinent, but..."

"What?"

"I think you love her. I really do."

"Not that that would make any difference," he mumbled.

"Yes, it does. You made a mistake trusting Sebastian, but you were trying to do what was best for Millicent. You even told me you didn't care if you got cursed, as long as she and I were safe. That doesn't sound like a fault to me. Under the circumstances, anyone would have thought Delilah was evil."

"Did you?"

Emmaline coughed demurely.

"Not exactly, but I've had more experience dealing with manipulative people than you have. Mr. Charles used to do the most devious things."

"So I was a chump."

"No. You did the best you could with the information you had, and you didn't do it to free yourself, but to help

Millicent, which is extremely admirable. Sebastian's the one at fault for using your concern for Millicent against you. Can't you blame him for once, instead of yourself?"

Bostwick looked at the apple in his hands, still not eating it.

"Do you think she would think of it like that?" he asked after a while.

"Well, she did seem rather fond of you."

"She's had a bit on her mind since then," he said irritably. "I don't think a little crush is high on her list of priorities right now."

"We'll see."

"Don't sound so sure of yourself," Bostwick said, annoyed, and finally started eating the apple. Content that annoyance was closer to his usual demeanor than sadness, Emmaline considered her work done for the evening, wished him a good night, and went to sleep next to Delilah, who was purring as she slept.

By the second day, they could see some islands far off on the horizon, and by the morning of the third, they flew over what Delilah guessed was the largest island in the archipelago. Though most of the land was overgrown with coniferous forests and low bushes, a fishing village sat at one end. The gray, weathered, wooden buildings soon gave way to the mishmash of the town of Styx. The market, which had been blown to pieces by Balder Spleenbeck, had been rebuilt, and the fountain in the middle of town still flowed. Delilah told Emmaline to land in the town square, where several members of the Roly Police had already gathered after spotting the airship.

"Hello there, Chief!" Delilah said, hopping out of the ship once it landed.

"Your Majesty!" the chief said. "I was wondering when you were going to show up. I gather something happened with the map?"

"Precisely. Perceptive, aren't they?" she said over her shoulder to Bostwick.

"Actually, it was because one of the natives informed us that he had seen a small map with this town drawn on it."

"Ah, well, that would do it."

"They've been incredibly helpful, actually. Because, well…" He leaned toward her and whispered, "they think we're pirates."

"How did they make that mistake?" Emmaline asked, tying the ship to the fountain.

"You see, about seven or eight generations ago, a band of Armored Bugbears did, in fact, pillage these shores frequently. As those pirates were our ancestors, it's only natural that the islanders would mistake us for them."

"And letting them believe that makes crowd control a bit easier," said the big bugbear.

"So where exactly did you see this map?" Delilah asked. "We'd like to get it as soon as possible."

"It's in a cave on the next island over."

"See, round about the same time our ancestors were pirating," the chief said, "a strange woman came to these islands and offered to protect the people's valuables from the pirates, in exchange for whatever she asked. So the people brought their treasures to her cave, and she kept the pirates away, though they didn't know how at the time.

"The only catch was, the fee she charged for her services was the treasure she'd sworn to protect. So the gold and jewels were all safe from pirates, but the islanders still lost them."

"Depressing," Delilah said. "But why didn't they just wait for her to die and then take it back?"

"They did wait, but she didn't die. It was about the hundredth year since she came to the island that the people realized just what she was: an immortal beast. That was why she was able to ward off pirates, see? Well, even if they couldn't get their riches back, a few of the townspeople went to see if they couldn't bargain with her."

"And they were never seen again," Delilah said, and when they all stared at her, added, "What? That's the way these stories always end."

"But they were seen again," the chief continued, "and how! Those that went in carrying carved sea shells and worn out clothing came out with fine jewels and gold. It seemed the creature, for that's what the islanders said they saw, had a taste for barter. She would sometimes trade for gold, but if there was something of sentimental value, that's what she liked best of all. Every so often, townspeople still go in seeking their fortune."

"How do you know all this?" Emmaline asked.

"This town's lousy with informational plaques and brochures. It's a major tourist attraction, you see."

"So one of the people doing a trade saw the map piece in the cave?"

"Indeed. And we've been gathering up payment for it since we found out."

"What do you mean gathering payment?" Bostwick asked. "Can't you just trade something in town for it?"

"The beast won't accept just anything. See, she has a mermaid's scale, a magical device that weighs a thing's worth based on the value that the two parties hold for it. So far, we've cleared out half of Rare and Priceless trying to balance the darn thing, and the beast has finally said she's through with counterfeits. Polkory bristled at that, of course, but what can you do?"

"I say we see this creature personally," Delilah said, "and see if we can't reach an agreement. As for the people of Styx, Chief, see that they stay inside the city limits and that the islanders stay out. We're going to be bringing Styx back home by the end of the week!"

They took the airship to the next island, which was rocky and barren, and landed on the flattest spot they could find, then wandered the coastline, eventually coming across the cave. It tunneled naturally into the rocks, though the ground looked like it had been smoothed down with wear. They had just gotten to the darkest part of the tunnel when they saw light ahead of them, and the path opened into a large cave full of treasure. Sunlight from cracks in the ceiling spilled down onto heaps of gold coins and clay statues. Some fires burned in braziers throughout the room, flooding the chasm with light that reflected off of pools of water, standing mirrors, and precious metal.

Emmaline and Bostwick stared in awe, but Delilah glanced quickly around the room and said, "Well, it doesn't look like she's here."

"Oh, no?" said a low female voice from the only dark corner of the room. Out of the shadows walked a Gremlin in a long leather coat. "So you've come to trade with me?"

"We want the piece of the map of Styx that you have," Delilah explained. "It's part of my country, you know?"

"You mean this?"

She transformed in one fluid motion into a tall, dark-skinned Lesserian goblin and walked to a stone platform that was covered in paper scrolls, an ornate knife, and what looked like half of an ancient tea set. Carefully clearing these items away, she revealed not only a map of the Gammon coast, but the entire continent of Ataxia carved onto the stone. The map piece lay on the left side of the platform, but the woman delicately picked it up and held it out for Delilah to see.

"This little piece of paper is in high demand; I've had people coming in every day trying to get it. But they just don't have enough."

"Can't we at least see how much more you need for it?" Emmaline asked. "We've been told there's a scale."

The woman pointed behind them. Above the opening to the tunnel they had just come through was an enormous scale with stone steps leading up to each side. The golden bowl on the left was full of swords, sculptures, and a grandfather clock that Bostwick vaguely recalled seeing in Rare and Priceless. The objects in the bowl weighed it down all the way to the ground, while the other side of the scale hung high in the air.

"It's a mermaid's scale," the creature said. Now she had transformed into a squat, scaly goblin. "Once, it belonged to the Queen of the Sea, but now it belongs to me. Underwater, regular scales can be a bother, so they invented this one. That side is yours."

She indicated the heavier side, which Delilah floated up to.

"It measures the worth that *I* put on those items. And this side is mine," she said, dropping the map lightly onto her golden bowl. Though it was empty except for the piece of paper, the bowl sank to the ground, lifting the other side of the scale a foot above it.

"This weighs the value you've placed on this map. If the two sides are level, we trade. But I don't want any more counterfeits, no matter what that Polkory thinks of them."

"So we just have to add something to make the two sides match up," Emmaline continued. "Something that you value?"

The creature nodded.

"What do you want, exactly?"

"I never know until it's been offered. Maybe gold, or a treasured love letter. Maybe a first-born son."

She swirled again, this time into the form of wispy-looking white bird.

"Can you not do that shape shifting thing?" Delilah asked. "It's kind of creepy."

"Now, now, if I stay in one form too long, I'm liable to stick that way. I've heard of immortal beasts who get so attached to the animals they associate with that they go around looking like them all the time."

"So you really are an immortal beast!" Emmaline said excitedly.

"Well," the bird said, "it's not often I meet someone who is properly impressed to see what I am. And a human, too? I thought you stopped believing we existed."

"A friend of mine told me about you, and I think we've met another one of your kind."

"Is that so?" she smirked, transforming once more into a purple-skinned humanoid with a crest of feathers running down her back, "and what did that one look like?"

"He's tall, with long white hair and white skin, with some black spots. He looks sort of like a Styx goblin."

"Ah, yes, he traded this map to me."

"He was here?" Bostwick asked. "Did he have anyone with him?"

"Is that information precious to you? I'll tell you, but it'll cost you extra on your side of the scale."

"We'll pay," Bostwick said immediately, thinking this might be the only lead they would get on Millicent's location.

"Just what I like to hear. Well, then, he came through that hat down there." She pointed to a tattered tricorn hat that sat on a stone table. "Alone. He wanted a hiding place for the map piece, and in exchange, it became my property. It was a simple trade. Then he whisked away though that hat again."

"And he didn't say where he was going? He didn't mention… anyone else?"

"Why would he? It was strictly business."

"Then that information is completely worthless!"

"Apparently so," the creature said, looking at the motionless scale with an air of annoyance. "But we're getting off topic."

"I don't know what we'll be able to trade," Emmaline said, "because the map is more important to us than anything we could give you."

"Now you're getting the idea," the creature said. "But it's not totally impossible. This map represents people's lives, it's true, but I feed off more important things: curiosities, hopes, desires. I have life; I want those things, too."

"Maybe if you got out more," Delilah suggested.

"But then I wouldn't have all this." She gestured around her with a thin purple hand. "Now, show me what you want to trade."

"Ah," Delilah said, "how about this, then?"

She produced a small jar, which contained a satchel.

"Millicent's memory!" Emmaline gasped.

The creature leaned forward hungrily, but calmed itself.

"Now that is something. I can feel such a bittersweet feeling coming from it. That could prove to be quite valuable."

She reached her long hand out for the jar, and Delilah went to place it on her side of the scale.

"Wait!" Bostwick said. "Delilah, that's not yours to give."

Both the queen and the creature turned to look at Bostwick, who had bounded half way up the steps. The beast's face was placid as Delilah turned her outstretched arm, offering the jar to Bostwick.

"You're right," she said. "It's yours."

"What?"

"A memory is a thing that can be shared and experienced by more than one person. This is yours and Millicent's memory. If you both hadn't shared it, it wouldn't be precious."

Bostwick walked up the last few steps and took the jar, not knowing what to do with it.

"But," he said, "this couldn't possibly make up the difference in weight we need."

"Maybe it could," Emmaline said, getting a shrewd expression. "Consider what that memory means, Miss Immortal Beast."

The creature once again transformed, this time into a Styxian woman and leaned forward. Emmaline took this as a cue to continue.

"I assume you already know what that memory is about?"

"I can feel a vague idea of it," the woman replied.

"Right, but you don't know what happened next. She," Emmaline said, gesturing to Delilah, "took this memory without permission."

"I don't care if it's stolen property or not," the beast said. "That does nothing to change its value."

"No, no, that's not my point. See, the theft of the memory is what finally convinced Bostwick to try and escape with the help of that immortal man we told you about earlier, the one who had Delilah tear up her map. So if you think about it, Bostwick basically *already* traded the map of Styx for that memory."

"Emmaline!" Bostwick gasped, looking hurt.

"You valued it that much?" the beast asked, intrigued.

Bostwick was about to explain that he hadn't even thought about the map at the time, but Emmaline caught his eye and shook her head almost imperceptibly. So it was one of her schemes. He was glad that she hadn't meant what she'd said, but he worried about what her time with goblins was doing to her upbringing.

"Well, that *is* something," the beast muttered to itself, and changed into a huge, white spider with a blue hourglass on its abdomen. "A most interesting story. I suggest you weigh it now, before I change my mind."

Bostwick didn't move, but examined the jar in his hands.

"But it's still hers," he said, and the beast leaned forward hungrily. Apparently, his reluctance to give it up only increased its value in her eight eyes.

"Well, Bostwick," Delilah said, placing her hand gently on his shoulder, then grabbed him by lapels, "if this stupid jar is more important to you than getting back the map piece, and fixing Styx, and finding Millie in the process, then keep it. Then we'll never find Millie, and all you'll have are memories."

She released him and sat on the scale. It didn't budge.

"How very rude!" she said to the immortal beast, and floated down to where Emmaline stood.

"Millicent isn't even in Styx," Bostwick said, and the spider clambered across the ceiling and dropped down, right in front of him, leaning its fangs into his face.

"Then you won't give up that memory? Not for anything?"

"Millicent isn't here," he said, turning from the creature, "but... that doesn't matter. The rest of Styx is. It's like Emmaline said, I traded the whole country for this memory, even if that wasn't my intention. Well, now I'm trading it back."

He placed the jar onto the pile of artifacts from Rare and Priceless, and the scale shifted. First, the sides evened out, then Delilah's displaced the balance, lowering by half an inch.

"Bostwick!" Emmaline said, running up to him, "You did it! I'm sorry I said all that about you trading the map for the memory."

"It all worked out. I figured you were trying to be diplomatic."

"Why do I get the feeling you just insulted me?"

"Anyway," he said, "let's get the map and get out of here. This place is starting to get to me."

"Not yet," the beast said, returning to her purple feathered form once more. "The scales still aren't balanced. Perhaps if I gave you some small amount of information, just enough to balance them. Perhaps you would like to know the whereabouts of the rest of your country?"

"You *could* tell us where the Wastes are," Delilah said, "though I wouldn't expect a shut-in like you to know."

"I have been known to wander the seaside near there from time to time," the creature said, looking pleased with herself. "At this very moment, the Wastes are directly to the Empire's northern border."

"Well, make me a black bird and bake me in a pie! The little weasel left it where it was! Tricky. Still, is it enough to balance the scale?"

"I think it's quite valuable," Emmaline said, as the two sides of the scale matched up perfectly. "If the Wastes are in the same spot, then we can put Styx back properly. Otherwise, we'd have to somehow put the map pieces on the map of the Empire or something. This is much better."

"Lovely!" Delilah floated over to the beast's side of the scale and snatched the map piece, upsetting the balance once more. "That about does it. Well, enjoy your memory, you creepy purple thing."

The beast picked up the jar of memories and held it up to the light, appraising it.

"There are such exquisite feelings here. Even for Styx, why would you just throw this away?"

"We can just make more memories," Bostwick said, descending the stairs.

The beast stared at him a moment, then flitted across the room, placing the jar on the stone platform where the map was carved. She then perched on top of large, round metal device in her Gremlin form again.

"You're not even going to use it?" Emmaline asked.

"*Having* it is the important thing."

"Creepy," Delilah said from the side of her mouth.

"Maybe, but it makes me feel a little better about it," Bostwick said, and went out through the tunnel.

When they got back to their ship, they flew past the town, and Delilah yelled to the chief that they had the map.

"Well, Bostwick," Delilah said, as they sailed away from the island, "all that back there certainly was noble of you. What made you do it?"

"Styx needs fixing," Bostwick said. "As much as I want to find Millicent, the pieces of Styx are also in trouble. If Dolly's avalanche didn't decimate the forest, the weather in Pandemonium probably will. It's much colder than Styx."

"Hmm, I never thought of that."

"Considering that," Emmaline said, "then the murky skies of Catawampus can't be too good for the pineapples either. They need sunlight."

"True," the queen said, raising her eyebrows. "Well, then, thanks a lot, Bostwick. Maybe I'll shorten your sentence to only eighty years."

"Thanks," he said sarcastically, "but you do realize, Delilah, that I'm going to tell Millicent everything about that memory when we find her?"

"*Everything?*"

Bostwick faltered.

"Everything that won't embarrass her, yes."

Delilah smirked. "It's your funeral."

"Millicent will understand, and she won't be angry, since…"

He trailed off. Delilah gasped and grabbed him by both hands.

"Bostwick! Is it possible that you have finally realized that you love her, and she loves you, and you love each other forever-and-ever-lovu-lovu-love?"

"I didn't even understand that last part," he said with contempt.

"Isn't love beautiful, Emmaline?"

"So we're heading southeast, right" Emmaline asked, trying to hide her smile.

"Don't change the subject so blatantly! But, yes, the southeast it is."

♠ ♦ ♣ ♥ ♣ ♦ ♠

In the day it took them to make it to the Wastes, Delilah could not stop talking about how they were victorious, and about what she would do to Sebastian when she found him. She even acted out one scenario, swinging a grappling hook around and almost puncturing the balloon. After a stern reprimand from Emmaline, she sat in the corner and talked peacefully about the many curses she would inflict on him and about which ice-cream flavor they should pick out to welcome Millicent home. She had even offered to fly the ship to let Emmaline get some rest, saying that she couldn't possibly sleep at a time like this.

When Bostwick and Emmaline woke early that morning, they saw Delilah standing at the wheel, looking grim.

"Are we at the Wastes yet?" Emmaline asked.

Delilah nodded and said, "What a bleak place."

"Have you never been here before?" Bostwick asked, looking over the side. Below them were miles and miles of flat, red earth and bare trees. This was interrupted in some places by large hills of black stone jutting out of the ground, or else by enormous piles of broken furniture, rotting fruit, and tattered clothes.

"No one goes here except for garbage collectors," Delilah said. "A queen certainly wouldn't frequent a place like this."

She seemed inordinately angry about the look of the Wastes, and Emmaline offered to take the wheel, in case she wanted to get some sleep.

"I'm not tired," Delilah said, then held one of the ropes leading to the balloon with one hand and leaned out far over the side, searching the ground. "Where is she? We've been over the Wastes for hours, so where is she?"

She called Millicent's name several times, then went to the other side of the ship and called again.

"Delilah, she's not down there," Bostwick said.

"Where is she, then? We've run out of options! She has to be there, or else… Where would she be?"

She sunk to the floor and curled her arms around her legs and rested her chin on her knees, looking utterly dejected.

"She's with Sebastian," Emmaline said. "But where's the map? If the Wastes are where they've always been, then that piece must still be in Styx somewhere, right?"

"It couldn't be in one of the parts we were in before," Bostwick said, sounding unsure.

"He wouldn't have just thrown it away, would he?"

"Check the opera glasses, Bostwick," Delilah said.

He did so, and reported that he hadn't seen anything. Delilah grabbed the glasses away and checked them herself, then threw them back to Bostwick, and curled up once more.

"We can't look through all of that," Emmaline said, staring at a massive pile of trash below them.

"We can just have Sebastian tell us," Delilah said, quite calmly, "after we keelhaul him from the airship. We'll let Millie cut the rope, if she wants to."

She leaned against the side of the ship and sniffed, letting one tear roll from her snake eye down her cheek. Bostwick felt much the same way she did, though he didn't show it, and instead conjured a handkerchief and offered it to her. She stared at Bostwick's hand as if she couldn't tell what the white thing he was holding was, then snatched it away and looked at it as if it held all the answers.

"Where did you get this?" she asked.

"I conjured it."

"From where?"

"Nowhere. I just sort of—"

"Never mind about handkerchiefs and rhetorical questions! Sebastian went into your hat, and we know he came out elsewhere, without Millie with him. Isn't it possible that there is someplace that the hats actually lead to? Like a magical hat dimension, full of white rabbits, traitorous cat goblins, and kidnapped maids?" Emmaline looked at her with concern, but Delilah continued. "It sounds a little crazy in those terms, sure, but it's possible, isn't it?"

"Maybe," Bostwick said, "but there's no way to test it."

"Can you do magic or can't you? Just try pulling a… oh, right. Sorry, I forgot. You have no hat skills."

"For your information, I keep plenty of things in this hat; I just can't use it as a portal to alternate dimensions."

"Maybe we should go to the Academy," Emmaline offered. "They can at least tell us if Delilah's theory is correct, and they also might be able to give us information about Sebastian."

"How do you figure that?" Delilah asked with a sniffle.

"Well, Sebastian at least looks like the man in that picture in the Hall of Portraits, and he may even be the same person. The human standing next to him is Marco Melieh, isn't he?"

"However did you guess?"

"Once you told us that your family taught humans magic, it was easy to figure out. And the goblin Sebastian looks like—"

"Is Sebastian Galimatias, prince of Styx, and the goblin who decided to teach Melieh first."

"Exactly. So don't you think, since Melieh and he knew each other, that the Academy might have information about him that even you don't know?"

"You speak madness, Emmaline. But since the alternate dimension theory requires it, we will indeed go the Academy. But only because it's fairly close."

Eleven

Light and Shadow
260 Years Ago

Jurek guessed that the students of the Academy would still be asleep, so it would be safe for Sebastian to walk through the halls. When they arrived at the laboratory door, however, they heard voices. Jurek gestured for them to stay silent, so they pressed themselves against the wall and listened.

"I don't know what happened," they heard Alistair say. "They're just… gone!"

"You need to calm down, Alistair," a languid voice replied.

"It's Professor Hollyhock," Inez whispered to Sebastian.

"Calm down? They're out in the Capital, probably running amok! If the president finds out about this—"

"Let me worry about the president. For now, why don't you go tell the others what's happened?"

"But we have to find the experiments. There's still time. We could catch them!"

"If they're no longer immortal, then what's the point of going after them?"

"We can still do the experiments. I have the basic idea of healing down. And with subjects that can actually get hurt, we might learn even more."

Sebastian clenched his fists, but Inez placed a hand on his shoulder, urging him to remain calm.

"What would people think if they heard you talk like that, Alistair?" Hollyhock said, her voice now right on the other side of the door.

"I don't care what people will say. Have you ever seen someone bleed to death, Professor, or watched as an infection slowly eats away at a person? Because I have. My parents are the two of the best doctors in the Empire, but there are still people that they can't save. Why should we allow so much human misery when the knowledge to combat it can be obtained so easily?"

Hollyhock let out a breath. "Whatever the case, you need to be more cautious. If you still want to catch these creatures, I suggest you wake the other students and go look for them."

She opened the door outward, which mercifully hid Jurek and Inez. Sebastian turned into his shadowy form just before Alistair walked out of the room and down the hall. Hollyhock looked after him, then turned her eyes to Sebastian.

"It looks like you didn't go too far. Don't worry, I won't rat you out," she said. Jurek and Inez said nothing as Sebastian materialized again. Hollyhock ushered all three of them into the laboratory, followed them in, and shut the door.

"So," Hollyhock said, "you helped the others escape?"

"Professor, we had to," Inez began, but Hollyhock held up a hand.

"I understand. Alistair may be taking things too far. But what is this one doing back?" she asked, glancing at Sebastian. "And where did he get the coat?" Her eyes darted briefly to Inez's flushed face, then back to Sebastian, who held an arm across his stomach. "What's wrong?"

"I think…" Sebastian began, wondering if the strange gnawing that he felt was anything like what the other shadow goblins had described. "I think I'm hungry."

"Really?" Inez asked, squinting at him in concern. He could tell that she was trying to figure out why he, the control, should be experiencing any mortal tendencies. He had the same question, but was more concerned with the immediate necessity of food. Thankfully, Jurek stepped in.

"We'll get you something," he said. "Professor Hollyhock, can you make sure Alistair doesn't find out about Sebastian being back until we get a chance to talk to him?"

Inez followed him out the door, leaving Sebastian alone with the professor.

Sebastian had not seen Hollyhock since the night he was created, and had never spoken to her. Now, she was surveying him from behind her glasses.

"You're becoming mortal," she said at last.

"What do you mean?"

"Hunger, sleep: those are the first signs, according to what Inez and Alistair told me."

"But I've never been hurt."

"Ah, you're referring to the theory that pain causes mortality. I'm afraid that's incorrect. No, I believe that whatever it is you all are—"

"Shadow goblins. That's what Jurek said."

"An acceptable description," she said, leaning against a lab table. "Shadow goblins, then, probably have an actual, rather than potential, form. To put it simply, you were all supposed to be mortal. It was only a fluke in the process of your creation that caused your immortality."

"The edge of existence and nonexistence," Sebastian said, quoting what Alistair and Inez had said dozens of times.

"Indeed. You were brought into existence using a combination of two acts of the will, one that humans call magic, and another called love. But your creation, brought about by imperfect beings, was imperfect."

Her tone was absolutely serene, but it captured his attention more than anything Inez had explained to him. It was as if she understood what had happened implicitly. She was, he reminded himself, the person who had given Inez and Alistair the idea to create him in the first place.

"I say imperfect," she continued, "because the students' so-called 'love' hardly fits the definition. Alistair wanted to heal people, just not *you* people. Jurek wanted to give something life… never mind what happened afterward. And the other students wanted to create some amazing new creatures… but only so they could make a name for themselves. I'm surprised it worked at all, though I shouldn't have been. Mankind has always had a knack for creation."

Sebastian noted a hint of bitterness in her voice, but she quickly returned to her calm explanation.

"The only reason the others started showing mortal tendencies was, according to Alistair's reports, because they 'became more and more insular and tried to disrupt the experiments by taking each other's places.' Apparently they began to truly love each other, and their genuine, selfless love finished what the students' pseudo-love could not."

"Then what about me?" Sebastian asked. "You said I'm becoming mortal, but…" But what? He'd always felt separate from the others, and until today had shown no mortal tendencies. If the others' love for each other had turned them mortal, what did that mean for him?

"You want to know for sure?" With a twist of her wrist, she conjured a small sewing needle. "Hold out your hand."

He hesitated a moment, knowing from his observations of the experiments that pain was something to avoid, but his curiosity got the better of him. He did as Hollyhock said, and she stabbed the needle into his palm. He whipped his hand away, shocked by the sharp sting, and watched as gray smoke flowed like a spider web from the pinprick in his palm to the needle, then returned and disappeared.

"You're not mortal yet," Hollyhock said, "but your hunger indicates that you're headed that way. It makes sense, given that you're a copy of Sebastian Galimatias."

"What do you mean?"

"Inez has fancied him for a while now, from the one time he gave a guest lecture last year to when we studied his advice on magic that he gave to Melieh. The reason she and Alistair chose your statue was because they thought her love for his image would give their spell the greatest chance of success. Though I can't say your personality matches Sebastian Galimatias at all, your physique and intellect certainly do. Inez was thrilled that you turned out to be so intelligent. It seems the more you fit her image of the original Sebastian, the more she loves you, and the closer to mortality you come."

Hollyhock was smiling slightly, but Sebastian didn't share her enthusiasm, understated though it was. What she had just disclosed explained many of Inez's actions that had confused him before: why he was the only member of the control group, when a proper experiment would divide the subjects evenly; why she had given him a coat designed to look like what Styxian royalty might wear; even why she had seemed so eager to educate and spend time with him.

And yet, despite all this, he only recently showed signs of mortality. The whole thing seemed off somehow, and he couldn't help but ask himself which was worse: being created as an experiment, or a copy.

He didn't have long to muse over this, because Inez came through the door carrying a plate of pastries.

"Jurek's pretending to help look for the other shadow goblins," she explained. "Also, I saw Olivia when I was getting these. She said Alistair's talking about making more experiments. I don't know how he intends to do it, but—"

"I'll take care of it," Hollyhock said, and strode through the doorway.

"Here," Inez said, handing a pastry to Sebastian. He smelled it curiously, took a bite. "Well?"

"It's good," he said quietly.

"What's wrong? Is it too sweet?"

"No, it's all right… What's it called?" he asked, trying to focus on something other than what Hollyhock had just disclosed to him.

"A chocolate éclair. It's pretty good, though lemon cream would be better."

"I thought lemons were sour."

"You don't even know what 'sour' tastes like. I had lemon flavored things all the time at home, and they're really good. It's just too expensive to buy lemons that have been shipped here."

He nodded, and continued eating in silence as Inez told him all about her family's orchard where citrus was in plentiful supply. He vaguely recalled telling her, long ago, that he wanted to visit where she lived, and how she had seemed embarrassed by the suggestion. It made sense now.

"Inez, um…"

"Hmm?"

"I think I'm… I think I'm getting tired."

"Really?" she asked, clearly eager to figure out what was bringing on this sudden bout of fatigue and hunger.

"I think so. So could you go back to your dormitory? I just want to stay here and…"

"Oh, of course! I'll bring you some more food tomorrow. And we'll keep Alistair away until we figure everything out."

She left with a wave, but Sebastian didn't move. He wasn't tired at all.

In the next two days, no students came near the laboratory except for Jurek and Inez, who brought various types of food and drink. Sebastian assumed that Hollyhock had managed to keep Alistair away from the laboratory somehow, though he wondered why she was being so helpful, given her apparent fascination with immortal beasts. She couldn't keep him away forever, though, and one evening Sebastian heard voices growing louder outside the door.

"I think we should just stop for a while," Inez was saying, "a-and the lab, I don't think, is secure enough to hold new experiments."

"We can make it secure," Alistair said, opening the door to the laboratory, "so when we make more immortal beasts they can't—"

He stopped in his tracks when he saw Sebastian, who had made no effort to hide. Inez looked nervously between the two of them as she shut the door behind her.

"So you are planning to make more of us," Sebastian said coolly.

"What… what are you doing back?" Alistair asked. "Where are the others? What happened?"

"I helped them escape."

Alistair looked at Inez for support, but she couldn't hide her guilty expression.

"You knew he was here?" he asked, sounding hurt.

"His being here doesn't change anything."

"It will when we start the experiments again. What if he interferes?"

"I'm not sure we *should* start them again."

"What!"

"It was wrong, Alistair. You have to see that. We had no right to treat them that way."

"You're one to talk, Inez. You claimed Sebastian like a pet."

"He's not a pet!"

"Oh, I'm sorry, you're right. What would you call him, exactly? Well, you dressed him up like a doll, so there's that. I wanted to use these experiments to be able to heal people who were dying, but you just used them to make a handsome goblin to talk to. So don't preach to me about how I should treat anyone!"

Inez had balled her hands into fists by this point, and looked like she would strike him if he said another word. Still, they had finally arrived at what had been plaguing Sebastian's mind for the past few days.

"Then," Sebastian said softly, "then you did make me to be a copy of Sebastian Galimatias?"

"See, Inez?" Alistair said. "Even he figured it out."

Inez glanced guiltily at Sebastian, then stared at the floor. "I did use my love for him to cast that spell, but that's not why…"

"Then what was it?" Alistair prodded.

"It was just an experiment! You asked me if we could create an immortal beast and I wanted to see if we could. That was all."

That was all, Sebastian thought. Of course, he'd always known he was an experiment, like the rest, but to hear her come out and say it, to use it as a defense…

"Sebastian," she said, "that's how it started out, but I…"

"You fell for him," Alistair said with disdain. "That's the real reason you wanted him to be the control, right?"

"That's not…"

"Oh come on, Inez. You didn't care what we did to the rest of them. You were just as interested in the experiments as I was; you just didn't want to try them out on his pretty face."

"It wasn't like that."

"Then why let the others suffer?" Sebastian asked. He

had formulated his own theories on that, but wanted to hear the answer from Inez's own mouth. He didn't get one.

"I… I helped them escape," she muttered, not meeting his eye; she knew that was no excuse.

"What!" Alistair said. "You helped him? But after everything we worked on, everything we were learning… You just threw it away?"

"You were going to kill one of them," she responded, "just to see if you could."

Alistair paled, losing all the self-righteousness he'd had a moment ago. With a tremor in his voice, he said "No, we… that wasn't what the experiments were about. We wouldn't have done that."

"No?" Sebastian asked, picking up a scalpel with his shadow. He examined its blade with an air of revulsion. "How else would you test if they were mortal or not? You'd already been slicing away at them for weeks. Killing them was just the next step."

"That wasn't the point of the experiments," Alistair said, looking uneasily at the scalpel.

"It doesn't matter either way. Nothing could justify the way you treated them, even if none of them actually died."

"Nothing?" He took a step forward, finally pulling his eyes away from the blade Sebastian held aloft. "I think saving lives justifies it. Increasing the stores of human and goblin knowledge justifies it. The Styx goblins would have done this years ago if they could. They understand that in research, you can't stop just because some people might object."

"If that's so, why not show your 'research' to the Styx goblins and say how it came about? Tell the president of the

Academy all about it, if you're so proud of what you've done... unless there's something holding you back."

"Th-there aren't any rules against it, if that's what you mean."

"Why would there be?" Sebastian scoffed. "It's so obvious that it needn't be spoken. Aside from the simple matter of toying with the laws of nature and harming innocent people, there are other negative effects of your actions."

"Meaning what?"

"You didn't seem like a violent person on the first night we met. And yet, the more of us you created, the less we seemed to matter to you. After all, if you can make a life artificially, why not do what you want with it?"

"Exactly my point."

"I disagree. We don't exist as objects for you to manipulate and use as you wish," he said to Alistair, but glanced at Inez as well. "But that's all you see us as. This being the case, I cannot allow you to continue."

"You don't get to decide that. As Sebastian Galimatias said, 'Knowledge can't be confined to one race or people, or even one man. Knowledge does not have limits.' I'm not going to stop experimenting just because you tell me to. The Styx goblins never feared knowledge, so I won't either."

"I don't fear *knowledge*," Sebastian said, and snapped his shadow forward, throwing the scalpel past Alistair's face, leaving a single, small cut on his right cheek. Inez and Alistair both froze in place "*That's* the sort of thing I fear. So I suggest you rethink the idea of doing these experiments before something unfortunate happens."

"But…" Alistair said, shaking.

"Because if you do start them again," Sebastian continued, "I'll see to it that they stop."

"I… I have to go," Alistair said, backing out of the room.

Sebastian let his shadow sink back beneath him while Inez retrieved the scalpel and leaned against the table beside him.

"That was unnecessary," she said after a while.

"You said it yourself; he was going to kill someone. What would you do if he wanted to kill a human in an experiment?"

"Well, that's… different."

Sebastian bristled at this, but decided to change tack. "Then what if it were me? What if he wanted to use me in an experiment?"

"I wouldn't let that happen! And I wouldn't do it by threatening him," she said, folding her arms. "Actually, I've been thinking of a way to get you out of here. If we could somehow get you to Nopali, you could live on my family's orchard. It's out of the way, and I could just tell my family that you're a Styx goblin, since they've never seen one."

"But I'm not a Styx goblin."

"No, but—"

He moved a few inches away, then turned to face her. "And I'm not just a copy of one, either."

For a moment she looked as if she were going to defend herself, but then she bit her lip instead.

"Look, about what Alistair said… I really *do* care about you."

She laid a hand on Sebastian's arm.

"I care about you, too," he said, pulling away from her.

"But not the way you want me to."

Her eyes widened in shock, then brimmed with tears.

"I-I know I messed up," she said, pleading with him. "I should have stopped the experiments sooner, but please don't let that change how you feel about me."

"It's not that, Inez. I'm glad you ended up helping the others. They wouldn't have gotten anywhere without you. But that's not what I'm talking about. The way I feel about you… is different from the way you feel about me."

"You mean you don't…"

"I love you, but… not like that."

She studied his face, as if she could somehow find an alternative meaning to his words there, but after a moment, the truth sank in. Her lips trembled, and a tear rolled down her cheek.

Sebastian was at a total loss for what to do. The only time he'd ever seen anyone cry was when they had been injured during the experiments, which had little to do with him. He hated to think that this time, he was the cause of whatever pain Inez was feeling.

"Ine—"

But she ran out of the room, slamming the door behind her before he could even finish saying her name.

For several days, Sebastian did nothing but stay in the laboratory and watch snow fall in the courtyard through the street-level window. His only visitor was Jurek, who brought him food and kept him updated on what was happening in the Academy. Alistair had not told the other students that

Sebastian had returned, but other than that, Jurek didn't know much. When asked about Inez, he merely said that she was quiet. Sebastian missed her, but he also had other things on his mind, namely Alistair and his plans for further experimentation.

He had caught a glimpse of him the day after their confrontation, studying the ground beneath the statue of Sebastian Galimatias. When a professor walked past, Alistair quickly jumped up and sped away; whatever he was doing, it was something he didn't want anyone else to know about.

On the third night, Sebastian again spotted the boy skulking around the edges of the courtyard, long after most other students had retired for the evening. He bent low to the ground with his arms in front of him, as if he were spreading something on the pavement, but Sebastian couldn't see anything else from his angle. Before he could figure out what these strange actions might mean, Jurek came through the laboratory door.

"…because I'm sick of being your go-between," he was saying, pulling a reluctant Inez behind him by the arm, "and because if we're talking about what to do next, he should be part of it."

Inez glanced at Sebastian as he turned away from the window, then dropped her eyes to the ground. He wanted to speak with to her, but she didn't look as if she wanted to hear anything he had to say, so he addressed Jurek instead.

"What do you mean, what to do next?"

"With you," Jurek said. "It's not like you can stay here forever."

"What about Alistair?"

"We haven't talked much."

"But you're aware of what he's been up to?"

Jurek shrugged. "I know he tried to come down here yesterday, but I headed him off. Why? Do you think he's going to try something?"

"See for yourself."

The two students climbed onto the table beside him to look out to the courtyard. Sure enough, Alistair was still wandering around, every so often stopping to touch the ground.

"What's he doing?" Jurek asked.

"What do you think?"

"It's got nothing to do with the experiments," Inez mumbled, staring at her left shoulder. "He told me he was going to stop."

Sebastian doubted that. Whatever Alistair was up to, it certainly fit the same motions that were used in the spell to create shadow goblins. But there were no other statues in the courtyard for him to use except his own, which no longer had a shadow… or did it? Alistair crouched down beside it, brushing snow away from the pavement, and holding his hands to the ground. Sebastian had watched the students create all the other shadow goblins in the same way, and he wasn't about to let another person become a tool to be used for Alistair's designs.

He pierced his shadow through the window, turned to smoke, and issued through the hole, ignoring Inez and Jurek's cries to wait.

He rematerialized in front of Alistair, who jumped to his feet and backed away.

"I should have known you'd be watching," the boy said, brushing snow from his gloves. "Really, you saved me the trouble of getting back to the laboratory; Jurek wouldn't let me near there, you know?"

"You told Inez you wouldn't create any more of us."

"Creating more? No, I know you wouldn't sit still while I did that. I have been experimenting, though."

He cast his hand around the courtyard, and Sebastian couldn't figure out what he meant. There weren't even any other shadows that one might experiment on. There weren't any shadows at all, save the one beneath his own feet.

With a chill, Sebastian realized that the courtyard was unnaturally bright, with no shade to be seen, despite the fact that the full moon shone down through patches of cloud.

"Hold out your hand, Sebastian." He spoke in a calm voice, the way he had when he told the other shadow goblins to sit still while being cut up, yet his face was full of malice. Sebastian took a step back, knowing that something painful always followed those words.

"Are you afraid?" Alistair said, walking toward him. "You can't die. What could you possibly be afraid of?"

Sebastian didn't know, but refused to offer his hand.

"Don't be difficult, Sebastian. This is the sort of thing you were created for."

"I'm not an experiment. I'm a person."

"Are you? Is something that's just smoke and shadow *really* a person?"

"I'm not…"

"Of course you are. Right on the edge of existence and oblivion, just like all shadows."

Sebastian wanted to argue, but he couldn't. He knew he was a shadow brought to life, and not even full life like the others; he was still immortal, because no one had wanted him to become anything more than an experiment, or an idea, or a copy—just a shadow of Sebastian Galimatias.

"Now hold out your hand."

"What's going on?" Inez cried as she and Jurek burst into the courtyard.

"I was hoping to do this without an audience," Alistair mumbled, "but it's too late now. Sorry, Inez."

He held his hands together in front of him so that his thumbs and index fingers touched, forming a spade-like shape. Sebastian stepped back further, out of his reach, but Alistair knelt down to the ground, laying his gloved hands on Sebastian's shadow.

If he was part shadow, then his shadow was part of him, and if Alistair vanished it…

Terrified, Sebastian ripped his shadow up from the ground and slashed it into the statue of Sebastian Galimatias. The stone figure slid in half at the waist and came crashing to the ground where Alistair knelt. The boy screamed in pain as the stone pinned his right arm that he had been about to cast the spell with. He shrieked something unintelligible through sobs, as he desperately tried to push the stone off his arm. Inez ran to help him, but Jurek bolted into the academy.

As Inez pulled pieces of statue off of Alistair's arm, Sebastian glared down the boy who had created him. He hadn't meant to hurt him, but he also didn't feel a shred of regret for it happening. Alistair had been trying to erase not only Sebastian, but with him, all evidence of the experiments, but there was no way he could keep an injury like this a secret.

"Don't worry," Inez said to Alistair, "I'm sure Jurek's bringing someone down. They'll… They'll be able to heal this."

She sounded unsure, but Alistair nodded, looking for an instant like nothing more than a frightened child, until his eyes fell on Sebastian. His face became the embodiment of hatred, contempt, and accusation.

"Don't blame me for this," Sebastian whispered.

"Be quiet, Sebastian," Inez said.

"But he…"

"Just get out of here!"

Seeing the fearful look on her face, he nodded to her and turned away from the broken statue and toward the gate of the academy. As he walked away, he heard Alistair mutter the same rhymed healing spell he had used on Midori a month ago. The experiments had been quite a success, Sebastian thought bitterly.

As he reached the gate, he felt a sharp pain in his side like nothing he had experienced before. He looked down and saw a dagger, as magicians often conjured in their tricks, clatter to the ground. When the gray mist rose off it and returned to heal his side, he turned to Alistair. The magician held his left arm out before him; the right was shredded and broken, but glistened with blood that was magically prevented from running.

"You think I would just let you leave?" Alistair managed to say between shallow breaths. "I should have unmade you months ago. You—you ruined everything!"

Sebastian knocked him face down on the ground with one wave of his shadow and advanced on him.

"Sebastian, stop!" Inez said, conjuring her own dagger.

"I'll stop when I'm sure that there will be no more experiments," Sebastian said. "And I'm certain there's only one way to do that now."

"I never killed anyone," Alistair said, looking helpless yet defiant on the ground.

"Neither did we, no matter how much you hurt us," Sebastian said, fuming.

"My research would've saved lives. Hundreds of lives. The experiments would've just been a price we had to pay."

Unable to control his rage any longer, Sebastian swept his shadow up, then down in one fluid motion. Alistair screamed, and Sebastian looked down to see Inez kneeling in front of him, holding the hilt of her conjured dagger above her in defense. The steel blade, which had been no match against shadow magic, lay on the ground at her feet. A deep, flowing gash went from her left shoulder to her stomach.

Sebastian stepped back in horror. Why? Why had she gotten in the way?

Alistair froze for a moment, then sat up to catch Inez as she fell back. He laid her limply on the ground before him and said his healing spell once again, causing the blood that was soaking into her clothes to return to her body, but he could not keep the wound shut, nor stop all the bleeding. He repeated the spell over and over, but Inez's face grew paler and her eyes lost focus.

Sebastian could do nothing. He stood watching Alistair, unable to fathom what had just occurred. He didn't know how much time had passed when he heard footsteps. Jurek had brought two middle-aged men, presumably faculty, into the courtyard. Upon seeing Inez, Jurek turned away and vomited, while one of the faculty, a cadaverous looking man, ran to Inez and Alistair.

"Get me a box," he shouted at the other man, who ran inside at once. "Keep doing that spell," he told Alistair, "whatever it is."

He stood and faced Sebastian, looking him over repeatedly.

"Are you a Styx goblin?" he asked.

Sebastian shook his head, unable to speak.

"What are you then, and why are you in the Academy?"

Sebastian looked past him to where Alistair continued his spell, tears streaming down his face.

"Did you attack that girl?" the professor asked.

"Yes," he said at last.

"What?" Jurek asked. "But why? She was just…"

Professor Leech gestured for them to stop and pointed to the door behind them, out of which came the other professor, carrying a large, foldable wooden box. They gently folded it around Inez and cast a healing spell, but the girl did not wake up. Though Alistair's spell had kept Inez alive, the blood-soaked snow and pavement around him was a testament to how much blood she had lost

"Take her to the infirmary," Professor Leach commanded. The other man took Inez's limp body in his arms and went into the academy once again, accompanied by Jurek. Professor Leech stayed and began to examine Alistair's arm with a doubtful expression.

"Alistair… with this much damage I… I'm not sure we'll be able to save it."

Alistair did not seem to have heard him, and instead turned to Sebastian with a look of absolute hatred.

"Why?" he said. "She never did a thing against you, and you…" he sobbed, but continued. "You ruined everything! I just wanted to end this!"

He broke down once more, and Professor Leech draped an arm protectively over his shoulder, then stared at Sebastian, at a loss for words.

Sebastian stayed in the laboratory under the supervision of three magicians in red accoutrements. He knew they could not stop him from escaping, but he intended to do nothing of the kind. He sat in his usual corner, staring at the wall without seeing it and wishing, for the first time, that he could sleep like the humans. As it was, there was nothing to keep him from thinking of the night before, of shadows and daggers and so much blood. He imagined the scene over and over again, seeing their faces, until he lost track of time altogether.

Finally, the door to the laboratory opened and Professor Leech stuck his head in. He surveyed Sebastian with a guilty expression and told the magicians to bring him. They led him through the academy, up to the highest floor, and into a large room. There was a desk at one end, and Sebastian realized this must be the office of the president. It was nothing like he had imagined. The room seemed cold, lit by oil lamps along the walls and a single fireplace. There were a few wooden shelves occupied by books and sinister looking metal devices, which reminded Sebastian of the experiments that had started months ago. In front of the desk, a row of six people sat, though there was a seventh chair on one end left empty. Facing them, on the side of the room nearest the door, stood the students who had participated in the experiments. Only Jurek and Inez were absent. In the center, there were two chairs. One was taken by Alistair, whose right arm was nothing but a bandage-wrapped stump below the shoulder.

The professor led Sebastian to the other chair, where he remained flanked by the three magicians, then took his own place at the end of the row of seven. The center-most seat was occupied by a dark-skinned woman in magnificent green robes who looked the room over. She seemed calm, though slightly perturbed, and nodded to the man on her left, who was clad in fine magician's regalia.

"Let us begin," he said. "You were all told the situation before you arrived here. Now we must decide what's to be done."

"Question, President."

The man on the woman's right, an unctuous looking nobleman in embroidered silk clothing, was raising his hand next to his face like a school boy.

"Yes, Karolek?" the president said.

"Before we decide what to do with the shadow fellow, I was wondering about the explanation of events you gave us. See, it doesn't add up."

"Oh?"

"How is it that a group of twelve children, none over the age of seventeen, managed to hide… how many did you say there were?"

"Twenty," a voice from behind Sebastian said. He recognized it as Kibwe's.

"Thank you. How did they create and experiment on twenty of these people, and then let them escape, without you noticing?"

"The students went to lengths to hide their experiments, for obvious reasons," the president replied.

"You mean you didn't even have an inkling?"

The cadaverous professor stood up, bowed, and said, "If I may… I suspected that there was something going on months ago and informed President Folio of my suspicions. As I could gather no concrete evidence of anything illegal happening, he thought it better to let the matter slide."

"Thank you, Professor Leech," President Folio said, sounding tense.

"See," the nobleman continued, "that seems like, forgive the term, incompetence. Imagine if all the creatures had the violent tendencies of this one. You could have had twelve dead students on your hands."

"On the contrary," the president said. "Though I did not know of the specific activities of the students, Professor Hollyhock kept me informed, in the most general of terms, of their experiments. I thought it best to let the students have some amount of freedom, as Professor Hollyhock did not inform me of anything illegal."

"Hollyhock?" the nobleman said, looking worried. "And where is this woman now?"

"I'm afraid she hasn't been seen since the attack. I certainly would have brought her to this conference, as she clearly knows far more about this matter than I do."

The nobleman was about to say something else, but the woman in green glanced at him, so he merely straightened his cravat, said, "Just getting that cleared up, thanks," and jotted down a note in a small book he held.

"Now," the president continued, "you have all had an account of these creatures' powers. I believe that retrieving the escaped creatures is of utmost importance. We assume that they went to Ataxia, likely through the Wastes. I have since sent a message to Styx to be on the lookout for them. There are some patrols on the northern side of Styx, so if they haven't left that country yet, they will be apprehended, and brought back here.

"Now, we must discuss the future of what to do with these creatures. I believe the solution is quite obvious," he said, pausing briefly to glance at the unctuous man two chairs to his right, who was poised to write more notes. "We must see what exactly this creature is made of, and how he exercised the power he did."

"I don't think experimentation of that sort is very wise," Karolek said without looking up.

"Nor, my friend, is fear of knowledge. I would have thought you would know that. Correct me if I am mistaken, but didn't your grandfather write the famous book, *Flora, Fauna, and Fungi of the Goblin World*?"

"He did, but he also abhorred vivisection. But I suppose you have to have your hobbies."

"One of the students attested," the president said, as if there had been no interruption, "that with the knowledge gained from your experiments, Alistair, you learned a new form of healing. Is that correct?"

Alistair said nothing, so Olivia spoke up; her choked voice made it clear that she had been crying.

"He saw how the smoky stuff from the creatures went back into their bodies, and he learned to do it to blood."

"Those results cannot excuse what was done," Karolek said.

"What was done," Folio replied, "was a great advance for magical healing methods. I have long thought that box-healing is too unreliable in real-world emergencies. I was proven correct, rather tragically, last night. But with Alistair's new spell—"

Karolek cut him off, saying, "If you could cure the plague by drinking an infant's blood, would you go for that as well?"

"I feel you are being a bit rash."

"You would."

The woman in green softly cleared her throat and the room went silent. All eyes fell on her.

"I agree with Karolek."

"But, Empress!" the president began, but was stopped by her gaze.

"What was done here was inexcusable, and has shamed not only the Academy, but the entire Empire. There will be no more experiments of this nature at this school, nor anywhere else."

Folio continued to smile, but his jaw seemed to clench as he spoke. "That being said, Empress, what ought we to do with this creature?"

"We have to destroy him."

It was not the empress, but Alistair, who had spoken.

"If I… if he'd never existed, Inez wouldn't have…" His

whole body shook, but he continued speaking. "I was wrong to ever have created him! I understand that now. He can't be killed, so we have to undo his existence through magic."

The group fell silent and seemed to consent, but the nobleman would have none of it.

"That's charming," he said, "but do you know how to do that?"

"I tried to do it last night. I have a theory—"

"No? Well then, let's think of a better option."

"What do you suggest?" the president asked.

"Explain exactly what you did to Miss Bustan," the nobleman said.

Alistair looked taken aback, confused as to what the man meant, but then saw that he was not the one being addressed.

"Inez Bustan. Did you mean to do it?" Karolek continued, speaking to the goblin with an almost conversational air.

"I meant…" Sebastian began, and the row of men gathered there began to mumble, as if it were unnatural for him to be speaking at all. "I meant to kill Alistair… with my shadow. I-Inez was protecting him."

It was all he could bring himself to say.

After a moment, the nobleman nodded, saying, "I understand."

"You see?" Alistair said. "His powers are too dangerous to be left alone."

"In that case, we'll seal them. If he was once a shadow, it may be that he and his shadow are now one and the same, so his magic is tied to his form directly. So his form will have to be contained somehow."

"The Styx goblins," Professor Leech offered. "I have heard of a curse goblins use. It turns the victim into an animal of some sort. I'm sure they would do this for us, if we explained the situation.

"Very well," the president said, sounding slightly annoyed that he would have to give up such an intriguing test subject. "Alistair, because you made the creature, you will accompany it to Styx."

"That sounds like a great idea!" Karolek said, unable to contain his sarcasm any longer. The empress gave him a warning look and he returned an obsequious smirk. "By the by, what's going to happen to the students who caused all this?"

"I think what has happened to Miss Bustan is quite enough punishment for them all," the president said.

"I disagree."

"Then what would you suggest?"

"Expel them, especially that one," he said, pointing to Alistair.

"Boys will be boys, Karolek."

"Perhaps, but when their school hijinks result in casualties, perhaps it is time for boys to start acting like men. I understand that he is only sixteen, but that only brings up more questions. You let him and his classmates have free run of the Academy's laboratory at night? That doesn't seem like a bad idea to anyone else? I don't want to tell anyone how to do their job… Well, actually, as I'm the Overseer of Imperial Assets, I guess I *do* want to do that. Silly me."

"I am doing what is best for the Empire," the president began, but Karolek silenced him.

"Empress, may I speak openly about the subject?"

She nodded.

"Ignoring the matter of gross negligence, I believe that there should be measures put in place to stop such an incident from happening in the future. Keep the curfew and expel the students who flouted not only the doctrines of this institution, but also the very laws of nature. I further recommend instituting a test, evaluating which students hold these," he said, gesturing at Alistair, "sorts of ideas. This Academy and its students are the pride of the Empire, so we cannot allow such criminal activities and philosophies to be part of it."

"Is that everything you have to say on the matter?" the president asked, seething.

The nobleman nodded and once again flashed his sycophantic smile.

"Then allow me to respond. You may not agree with my methods, Karolek, and you may have a certain amount of sway, but I am still the president of this school—"

"Speaking of which," the empress said softly, "tomorrow, in fact, I would like to find out exactly how much you knew about these students' activities, and how much you ignored."

The president paled as the woman stood up.

"But I believe tonight's proceedings are concluded. The president of the Academy," she said ominously, turning from Folio to Karolek, "will decide what's to be done with the students at a later date. But tomorrow, Alistair, you and a retinue of magicians will accompany this creature to Styx, as President Folio has suggested. For now, he shall be taken back to the laboratory and kept under guard."

Alistair stared straight ahead as the magicians led Sebastian out of the room, never giving his creation a second glance.

Twelve

Last Request

Sebastian took his shaking hand away from Millicent's forehead and changed back to his true form. Millicent could feel herself crying and wiped her tears away with her glove. Other than this, she didn't know how to react. What Sebastian had tried to do to Alistair was awful, but the fact that he had instead inflicted it on Inez had to be unbearable. All she could think to do was try to talk him past it.

"So Alistair brought you to Styx?"

"Yes," he said quietly. "I could have escaped before then, I suppose, but I didn't think I had the right to. The Styx goblins were shocked to hear what I was, and never felt the need to question whether they should seal my powers or not. The last thing I saw with my true eyes was Alistair turning his back on me, leaving me in the hands of the Styx goblins, who locked me away in the dungeon."

"Did they just leave you down there?"

"Not entirely. I had been imprisoned for what must have been several days, contemplating what Alistair had said about me and what I'd done, when a Styx goblin came down and talked to me. It was my namesake, Sebastian Galimatias."

"What did he want?"

"He said he didn't know how long I would have to be kept down there, and he didn't want me to go mad, so he put me in a trance. It wasn't exactly like sleep, I suppose, but something similar. The next thing I knew, I was waking up to a sneering, pink-haired monster."

"Oh…"

He turned and walked to the balcony. She followed him. Seeing the beautiful city that the shadow goblins had created only made Sebastian's story more miserable, Millicent thought, because he might never have tried to attack Alistair if he had gone with the other Ancient Shadows.

"So, Millicent, now do you understand?"

She tried to think what he could want, but she had no idea how she could help him. After everything that had happened, she wished she could somehow make up for what Alistair had done or allow Sebastian to forgive himself, but she was just one magician, and a novice magician at that.

"I don't. I'm sorry."

"Millicent, I need to finally put an end to what happened. I want to redeem myself for what I did, but I need your help. I believe that after he was expelled, Alistair wrote those magic books you read when you were younger. Even then, what happened at the Academy must have weighed heavily on his mind. He wrote down the healing spell he learned from the experiments, but there were others you read about as well."

"Which one do you need?"

"You mentioned it in passing once: the spell that made shadows disappear."

"I remember it. But wouldn't that be bad for the city?"

"Not for the city," he said quietly.

"You mean…? But you're not a shadow anymore!" Millicent said, fearing what he would say next.

"In a way, I am. You heard what Alistair said about me. I'm sure that the spell you know was the one he intended to use on me that night."

"So you want to make it so you don't exist anymore?"

"After what I did, I don't deserve to exist."

"But it's over. That all happened hundreds of years ago!"

"It's not that easy."

"Yes, it is!" she said, reaching out for him, but he drew back.

"You don't understand. Alistair was right about me," he said in a choked voice. "I tried to murder the very man who created me, though he was no more than a boy, and I ended up… killing Inez." He doubled over, blinking back tears. After a few deep breaths, he straightened back up. "And even hundreds of years later, I'm no better. I lied to you and Bostwick just so I could fulfill my own plans."

"But you chose to do that! You didn't have to. If you'd just—"

"Just what? Forgotten? I can't forget, Millicent. Every day, I remember what I've done and wonder how things would have been different if I were never created. Certainly Inez would have…" he trailed off, looking up into the blackness above the city. "This is what I want, an end to all of my regrets. Alistair's spell can give me that."

"But when I read Alistair's books, I guess in the first two volumes, he seemed sort of like he did in your memories, but the writing seemed to get more normal over time. Isn't it possible that he… he forgave you—and himself—and moved on?"

"I suppose that he may have considered his expulsion to be a sufficient punishment and gone on to lead a normal life. He never killed anyone, after all. The only way to atone for what I did is for me to be destroyed."

"So you want me to kill you!"

"I can't be killed."

"Well, I certainly can't… can't… unmake you."

"Why not? Hollyhock theorized something about the link between existence and love," he said, as calmly as if they were discussing the weather. "It's an ancient philosophical idea. The way she explained it, because of the students' pseudo-love, I still remain on the edge between existence and non-existence. It's why I've lived for hundreds of years, and why I can't be harmed."

"But what about Inez?" Millicent asked, trying to sound respectful of the deceased, though she knew everyone she had seen during the memories had technically died long ago anyway.

"She loved the idea of me," he said. "I was nothing more to her than a fantasy. In the end, she sided with Alistair, and died to save him."

"I don't think that's true."

"No? Then why didn't her love make me mortal?" He sounded hurt as he said it and clutched his arms like he was cold. "Regardless of a reason, I'm still alive, and immortal. But that doesn't mean I can't be unmade. If I was willed into existence, can I not, then, be willed out of it?"

Millicent could barely comprehend what he was asking.

"Even if that's possible," she said, "are you really all right with just ending it? I can't imagine not wanting to exist. I just can't. Don't you like, well, everything?"

Sebastian stood in silence, gazing at the city below. When at last he spoke, he did not look up.

"Life is painful. Mine is doubly so. And yet, when I look at this city, I think it's quite beautiful. And I did enjoy my time with you and Bostwick. I think, despite everything that's happened, I enjoy existence… but that makes no difference. Technically, I shouldn't have existed in the first place, and after everything I've done, I have no right to do so now."

He then threw his arm out over the white edifices of the city and said, "But all of them are innocent! If I can do anything to at least partially make up for my crimes, it will be to give my people a chance at a normal life, at a future outside this shadow."

"But your dying won't change any of that," Millicent said. "Or does Alcea want you to die, too?"

"On the contrary. If you must know, in exchange for bringing Chiaroscuro out of this shadow, I'll become bound to serve her for as long as I live. Knowing Alcea, I shudder to think what my service might entail."

"So if I… vanished you from existence…"

"You would save me from whatever Alcea has in store."

"Wouldn't that be breaking the deal?"

"She said 'as long as you live.' I made sure she specified."

"But… if we found a way to save Chiaroscuro without Alcea's help, then you wouldn't have to die."

"I deserve to, after everything I've done. It may be difficult for you to understand, but I want it this way."

Millicent wished that she could have called him mad, or senseless, but his face had become perfectly serene. It was obvious now that this was what he had wanted all along. She felt like crying, but held back her tears. He'd told her before to try to remember all those spells, back in Styx, when all she was supposed to do was learn simple magic tricks. Even then, he'd expected her to be his savior… or his killer.

"Please, Millicent."

"I won't do it."

He looked slightly confused, but pressed on.

"You saw what happened. You saw what I did."

"I won't unmake you." she said again, and followed the intricate designs of Chiaroscuro's buildings with her eyes while she thought. "Maybe the students did do something wrong when they created you. I don't know if you'd call it black magic, or twisting nature, but I agree, it wasn't right. And you did intend to kill Alistair." She paused, took a breath to steady herself, then somehow managed to smile. "But I don't agree that your life itself is wrong. Despite what happened a long time ago, and what you did in Styx… well, after spending all those days practicing magic with you, and seeing your memories… I'm glad I met you."

He stared at her in complete disbelief.

"I really am," she continued. "I'm glad you exist."

"How can you—"

He swayed in place and fell to his to his knees.

"What's wrong," Millicent asked, rushing to him.

"I… I'm not sure."

"You should rest."

"I don't rest."

Millicent paused to consider this, but Sebastian had already stood up and returned to his inner chambers. He walked unsteadily, and eventually sat on one of the many couches that occupied the room and held his head in his hands, pressing his palms to his eyes.

He seemed to be staying in one spot, so Millicent ran to his bed, balled up the blankets, and brought them to him. She handed him the bundle, half spreading them over him, while he continued to hold his head.

"Does it hurt?" she asked. "Maybe you showed me too much for one day. Or maybe you're sick. I mean, maybe you can't die, but you could still be sick, right? You should try to get some sleep, or well, you know what I mean."

She paced back and forth, pulling nervously on the fingers of her gloves.

"I could ask Misha to bring you some soup or something, or a doctor."

"I'll be fine," he said. "For now, you should probably return to your room."

She was about to protest, but Sebastian fell to one side against the arm of the couch. She shook his shoulder gently. He appeared to be asleep, but didn't look ill. Nevertheless, Millicent straightened the blankets around him.

How could he possibly expect her to unmake him, she wondered. Even now, she debated whether she should stay by his side till he woke up or fetch a doctor immediately. Of course, she thought, there probably wasn't a doctor in Chiaroscuro equipped to tend to an Ancient Shadow, but simply standing around wouldn't do him any good either. She checked outside the chambers and sure enough, Misha was there, leaning against the wall with a vacant expression.

"Misha, I need your help."

Millicent informed him in the simplest terms what had happened.

"Well, maybe he's just tired."

"I don't think he gets tired."

"Well, maybe he started to. He never used to eat either, or so Heidi tells me."

"That's true," Millicent said, considering. "He started eating when we were in Styx, but he only ate a little at the Academy. But why would he just start sleeping all of a sudden?"

She remembered Hollyhock's theory, but she didn't understand it very well. Inez, and now the whole city of Chiaroscuro, seemed to love Sebastian, and that had never made him mortal, which, considering his suicidal intentions, was a relief.

"Misha, do you know why Sebastian brought me here?"

He shook his head, and Millicent explained the situation as best she could. Misha was as surprised as she was, but seemed to understand Sebastian's motivation better.

"It's a little heroic, really," he said, "to sacrifice himself to that Alcea person for the sake of the city. And since he's suicidal anyway, he might as well escape from her by ceasing to exist. Still, vanishment isn't a fate I'd wish on any Chiaroscuran. And he wants you to do it?"

"He said it wouldn't be the same as killing, but I don't see much of a difference." When Millicent pictured Sebastian, asleep and helpless in the next room, the request seemed even more deplorable.

"Well," Misha began timidly, "if you don't kill him, then there will be no way for him to die, right? So why don't you just *not* kill him?"

"Then he'll be obligated to do whatever Alcea wants, and I'm pretty sure that wouldn't be anything good. But more importantly, I don't just want to not kill him. I want him to live, and be happy that he's alive. I just wish… I wish things could go back to the way they were before, when we would all practice in the library and be happy together. I can't believe that Sebastian wants to give up that sort of life."

"Maybe he *doesn't* want to," Misha said, sounding serious. "From what you told me, it sounds like he thinks this is for the best. For atonement and all that. Of course it's the wrong way to go about it, but I don't know if you can change his mind. Maybe if you just talk to him?"

Millicent sighed. Misha expected everything to work out so easily, but she knew it would not be so simple. Sebastian had been planning this for years, perhaps even dreaming of it while imprisoned in the dungeons of Styx. Her wanting him to live would never be enough. She needed someone who could do something constructive, who could change his mind, and perhaps even save Chiaroscuro before Alcea did.

"I have to escape."

"What? But you're not—"

"I need Delilah's help. I want to stay and make sure Sebastian is all right, but that won't help him in the long run. I need to get out of Chiaroscuro."

"But you can't," Misha said, following her down the stairs. "You're a human. The only reason you got in was because Sebastian brought you with magic."

"Then can't you help me?"

"What? No! I know I'm not the most reliable steward in the world, but that would just be crossing the line."

"But you want to save him, don't you? And Chiaroscuro?"

"Of course I do! But… Well, I suppose his hating himself isn't exactly what you'd call healthy."

"Please, Misha? I can't do this by myself."

He glanced around suspiciously, though they were alone, then whispered, "I'll help you, but you have to stay with me, so I can bring you back here once you talk to Delilah. That way, you only sort of escaped."

Millicent smiled despite the dire situation. They continued down the stairs, stopping at the floor her room was on.

"I'm still worried about his falling asleep like that," she said.

"He'll be all right. Plus, if he's asleep, he can't stop us from escaping."

"So how do we get out of the city?"

"We need to use a top hat. See, we can travel to other places through hats, but when the Ancient Shadows came here, they discovered that they could even go into shadows using the hats."

"Sebastian destroyed the hat in his room, though."

"There are others in the city, at the hat station. Hat travel is strictly regulated here, so the authorities can keep track of who leaves and make sure they're allowed to."

"Will they let us out?" she asked, turning Misha away from the door to her room as they passed it. "Where is the hat station, anyway?"

"At the base of the palace. The northern stairs should take us right there."

Millicent had never gone below her room before, and found that the staircase had more traffic the further down they went. After a while they came to a wide room that served as an entrance hallway, which Misha walked down purposefully. Many Chiaroscurans surged past them in both directions, most clad in black, white, and light blue, though a few were wearing red.

"You're sure this is the way?" Millicent asked, hurrying to keep up with Misha.

"Oh, yes. I don't know why, but I seem to remember my way around fairly well, despite everything I've forgotten."

They went through a large archway and Millicent looked up to see a maze of walkways and platforms above them, and beyond that, blackness. She was finally out of the palace and turned to see the building she had been imprisoned in for so many days. It was enormous, kept up by numerous flying buttresses, under and around which were a plethora of clustered-together, multi-story buildings. The entire palace was white and had intricate, yet glassless, windows that made it seem like lace.

There were even more Chiaroscurans on the streets, clad in clothes that Millicent could tell were based on the uniforms worn at the Academy, though the years had caused a great amount of variation. As Misha turned and walked towards one side of the palace, Millicent tried to drink in as much of the city as she could. On a low wall, three girls with bright blue and yellow hair sat giggling, while a stocky man sold glass sculptures to a couple holding hands; the woman had a sling holding a large, leathery black egg against her stomach.

"I wish Sebastian would let himself be part of all this," Millicent said, noticing a small boy gazing at her with large yellow eyes before he was dragged back into the fray by his father. "I understand that he's trying to save it, but… I hope Delilah will know what to do.

"Hopefully." Misha pulled her towards a smaller domed building that was nestled against the base of one of the buttresses. Inside were three top hats on pedestals, and three shadow goblins clad in green at a desk in front of these.

"Hi!" Misha said, waving to the woman on the left.

"Hello," she said good-naturedly. "I'm sorry, but right now, we can't allow anyone to leave. There have been people spotted outside."

"Oh," Misha said, then turned to Millicent. "See, whenever there are non-Chiaroscurans around, we have to stay inside. A shadow flowing out of a top hat and turning into a person would make people too suspicious."

"Do you know what they looked like?" Millicent asked the woman at the counter.

"There are two of them, a man and a woman, both blonde. That's all the information we have."

"Oh. I guess it wouldn't have been them," Millicent said. "But, um, do you know when we can get out?"

"We have to wait till they leave," the woman said, sounding slightly exasperated, as if she'd had to explain this several times already that day. "We'll make an announcement as soon as it's safe. I'm sorry for the inconvenience."

"I guess we'll wait," Misha said as they went back to the street.

"There aren't any other hats?"

"Hats are a rarity in Chiaroscuro, and it's illegal to make them, for the sake of public safety, you understand."

"Then why did Sebastian have a hat in his room?"

"The king and the Council are allowed special hats. Sebastian had the king's hat, and the Council's is in another part of the palace."

"Misha!"

"Sorry, I forgot. But it wouldn't be of any help. That hat's in the Document Chamber; only the king and members of the Council are allowed in because it's where we keep official stuff. It always has a guard."

"Just one?"

Misha nodded.

"Let's go," Millicent said, leading the way back to the palace entrance.

"What are you going to do? Use magic?"

"I don't know any spells that would make a guard leave, but we'll think of something. Could you slide under the door with your shadow?"

"Nope. The door is made of this special metal; I don't remember what it's called. It's supposed to stop us from using our magic."

"Do you think it would stop mine, too?"

"We use it to stop shadow magic, but it might work on a human's also."

Once they crossed the threshold of the palace, Misha led her up the staircase yet again, but did not go as high as the floor Millicent's room was on. From where they stood, it seemed they were exactly halfway up the palace. He continued on, but stopped when a young Chiaroscuran approached. She was carrying a broom over one shoulder and a bucket in the other hand. Her pace was hurried, and she seemed altogether disgruntled.

"H-Heidi?" he said.

"You remembered my name. Great. But I don't wanna talk right now, Misha. I just finished cleaning the Council Chamber. Apparently Councilmen Noh and Sfumato were arguing, so Sfumato threw red wine on Noh's dress, so she smeared his shirt with curry, and it somehow devolved into an all-out food fight. I'm all for debate, but when it involves more condiments than conversation, I think you've crossed a line.

"Um…"

"Sorry, Misha. I'd stay and talk, but I'm going to go have a bath and sleep and never wake up. Besides, you seem like you're in capable hands."

She breezed past them but Millicent called after her. "Are you done with that broom?"

Heidi stopped, turned, and raised an eyebrow.

"A-and the bucket?" Millicent continued.

Heidi shoved them into her hands, spun on her heel, and continued away, saying simply, "Good luck cleaning. Poor sap."

"What are those for?" Misha asked, continuing to the Document Chamber.

"Even if they say only officials are allowed in," Millicent said, "someone has to clean the room, every so often, at least."

"What if it's already been cleaned today?"

"Then we'll play it by ear."

Before long, they arrived at a large double door made of a luminous green metal with etchings of a forest scene. There was only one guard, in a red uniform, standing before it. He stood extremely straight, adding a few inches to his short stature, and followed Misha and Millicent with his eyes. As they approached, his fingers went to the hilt of his sword.

"Good day," he said, though it sounded like a threat. Millicent noticed that although he seemed to have a serious demeanor, he could have been no older than she was.

"Hello," she began, holding up the bucket and broom for him to see. "We're supposed to clean this room."

"This room? The Document Chamber?"

"Yes."

"Oh, really? Are you a member of the Council?"

"No."

"Then why would I let you in, hmm?"

"Because we need to clean it. We're maids, or well, I'm a maid. He's—"

"Ah-ha!" the guard said, but did not elaborate.

Misha and Millicent exchanged glances.

"If," the guard continued, "you really were sent here to clean, then of course I'll let you in. But that's just the thing, isn't it? Supposing you're only saying you're going to clean as a clever attempt to make off with official documents."

"What would we do with them?" Misha asked.

"I don't pretend to understand the criminal mind," he said with a sniff.

"But I really am a maid!" Millicent said.

"And therein lies the problem. You say you are; I say you

aren't. There's only one way to prove it, and that is… a maid test."

"A…"

"Maid test, yes. If you really are a maid, you'll be able to answer my… three challenges."

"Oh, dear."

"I can see you're worried, 'maid'." Here he removed his hand from the sword hilt to make quotation marks in the air, but returned it quickly after. "The first question is this: do you have calloused hands?"

Millicent held hers up for him to see. After three years of cleaning Styx Castle from top to bottom, they were quite calloused. The guard looked impressed, then turned to Misha. He held out his hands, which were comparatively soft and smooth.

"We'll have to see about you," the guard said. "Next question: if we had a phantasmal jellyfish loose in the palace, and it got its gunk everywhere, how would you dispose of the mess?"

"Honey, egg yolks, and oil," Millicent said without hesitation.

"Very impressive. But how would you then clean up the very materials that once helped you? You, the one with the vacant expression."

"I don't know," Misha responded.

"Neither do I," the guard said. "All right, now your last question is… if you really intend to clean this room, then why are you using a bucket with a broom instead of a mop, or alternatively, a broom with a dust pan?"

"Heidi gave it to us," Misha explained. "Although, it is

kind of weird that she would have that particular combination. Maybe her dust pan broke, or perhaps the mops were being used."

"Thinking out loud, are you? Can't even get your story straight with yourself. Pitiful."

He tapped the hilt of his sword in warning. Millicent realized she had to make up some sort of excuse before someone got hurt.

"Cobwebs!" she cried.

"Eh?"

"That room hasn't been cleaned for so long that there are cobwebs all over, and thick dust, and it's just easier to dump it into a bucket instead trying to keep it in a dust bin. See, there're already bits of, uh, lobster in here."

"From the councilmen's fight?" he asked. "I heard it went everywhere. Well, if you cleaned that up, I suppose you know your stuff. Congratulations, miss, you are clearly a seasoned maid. But it's obvious that this fellow hasn't cleaned a day in his life."

"Oh, but it's… it's only his first day on the job."

The guard looked at Misha suspiciously, then smiled and relaxed.

"Hey, it's my first day, too! Sorry to give you such a hard time, but you know, I have to do my duty."

"Of course," Millicent said. "So, could you let us in?"

"Sure, sure," he said, taking a key from around his neck. He unlocked the door and held it open for them. "Here you go. How do you think I'm doing, by the way?"

"Oh, you're doing really well," Millicent said, feeling a little guilty.

"Well, I'll leave you to your cleaning. Just knock when you want out, as I have to keep this door locked." He shut them in with a cheery wave.

Millicent looked around at the walls, which were covered in narrow file shelves. A silk top hat occupied a table in the middle of the room, along with something that looked like a bulky, vaguely crescent-shaped sculpture that seemed to act as a sundial, with five shadows drawn on a chart around one side of it.

"What's that thing," Millicent asked, turning the top hat upside-down.

"Oh, that shows the city limits. See, we can only build it as far as the shortest shadow on the summer solstice, otherwise, parts of it disappear when the shadow moves. There were quite a few disasters before construction was regulated, which is why all of our buildings are built so close to the palace, which the Ancient Shadows constructed first. It's turned into a real crisis since parts of the mound have started to rot away, so the limits keep getting smaller."

"The mound?"

"Yeah. When the Ancient Shadows first saw it, it was just a big old pile of junk—which is where they found the first pair of top hats—but then they added more and more to it, as the population got bigger. Why do I remember so much history?"

"Junk?"

"Yeah, junk. Stuff no one needs anymore."

"Who threw it out?" Millicent asked, already hoping for the answer.

"The Styx goblins. Oh, I guess I shouldn't have said—"

But Millicent threw her arms around him before he could say anything else.

"We're in the Wastes! We've been in Styx the whole time!"

"Yeah," he said, coughing. "I guess you would have found out anyway, so…"

"If we're in Styx, maybe Delilah can find us, or we can find her, and then we'll think of some way to save Chiaroscuro together."

"Right. Uh… could you let me go?"

"Oh, sorry," she said, releasing him and stepping back. Something crunched under her foot. Millicent was used to scattered papers from her days of cleaning Styx Castle's libraries, but she still didn't like the idea of official documents being left all over the floor. The scrap of paper she picked up, however, was no council transcript or government record. Instead of text, she saw sketchy images of mountains, trees, and what looked like a coast line, as well as a compass rose that was so blotchy it could only have been drawn by one person.

"It's the map!" she cried, hugging Misha again, though not as tightly. "Sebastian must have hidden it in here for safe keeping."

"I feel bad stealing it."

"It belongs to Heather," Millicent said, folding it and putting it in her pocket. "Besides, if we bring this to Delilah, it might make her less angry about Sebastian."

"What do you mean?"

"Considering everything he did, and considering Delilah's… well, considering Delilah, she might not be willing to help him. But I'll be able to talk her into it. Everything will work out. Let's go!"

"All right," Misha said, taking her hand. He turned into smoke, and Millicent saw darkness surround her.

Thirteen

Unexpected Reunions

The first thing Millicent did after she and Misha materialized out of the hat, which stuck out of a mass of discarded clothes, was collapse.

"I don't feel so good."

"What happened?" Misha asked. "Did I forget how to do it?"

"No," Millicent said, lying flat on the ground. "I fainted when Sebastian brought me through a hat the first time. I just don't think humans are supposed to do that." She took a deep breath, blinked, and looked up. "That's a big pile of garbage."

The mound which she referred to dwarfed the hills of black stone around it, more like a mountain than a rubbish pile. It was composed of everything from moldy books to broken doors, a great mass of gray and brown against the blue sky that Millicent was glad to see after so long. One side had been molded into something like a curved wall held up by a cage of pipes, ropes, and boards, so that the entire mound resembled a great crescent-shaped dome, the interior of which would be in shadow at all times of day and year.

"We've been adding to it for two hundred years," Misha said, sitting beside her. "Although the area inside the shadow has no maximum height, we still needed a fairly large base for our buildings.

"What's that sound?" she asked, noticing a faint creaking noise that seemed to be ever present, interrupted every so often by a snap.

"Parts of the mound are rotting away on the inside, so trash on the outside sometimes falls off. A lot of the furniture on top used to rest securely against older garbage, but since that's decomposed, the only thing keeping the wooden pieces up is that they've wedged against each other. So sometimes, part of the pile can't hold the weight and breaks down."

"That does seem pretty dangerous for the shadow."

"Very much so. So, what do we do now?"

Millicent sat up slowly, though she still felt woozy, and looked around. Apart from the huge mound beside them, the Wastes looked the same in every direction.

"Well, we could try going to Catawampus."

"That'll take months by foot."

"We could go to the Empire."

"Too dangerous."

Millicent stood up with a wobble and brushed herself off.

"We have to do something, and we have to hurry. That guard might get suspicious after a while, and if Sebastian wakes up he'll—"

"Wait!" Misha whispered, freezing. "Someone's talking. Someone's here."

He ran and hid behind a table that stuck out sideways from the mound. Millicent followed, falling over as soon as she reached him.

"This is just awful," a female voice said. "Are you sure this is Styx? I mean, at night it's not so bad, but now it seems so desolate."

"I don't know," a male voice responded. "I think it's very picturesque. Of course the rest of the country is nicer. Not that we had much of a choice, eh?"

"Wait a minute," Millicent whispered. "I know that voice."

"I've decided I'm cursed," the woman said, "You really ought to know that that bar fight was only one in a long line of disasters I've helped cause. Still, you didn't have to follow me."

"Nonsense. A young lady can't wander around alone, especially if she's just been banished."

Before Misha could stop her, Millicent stepped out of hiding and went toward the voices.

"Clarence?" she asked. Sure enough, the magician stood there, his hat and coat as shabby as ever, with his jackalope, Jill, in one arm. Beside him was a blonde goblin with floppy ears and a staff.

"Hello? Who are you, then?" he asked without losing his smile.

"It's me, Millicent."

He squinted at her, then snapped his fingers.

"So you are! But what the deuce happened to you? You look like you've seen a ghost. About a hundred ghosts by the look of it."

"Oh, my skin," she said, and quickly turned it the right color and changed her hair back to its usual green.

"Ah! It's you!" the woman cried. "I found you! My quest is over."

"Told you it would all work out," Clarence said. "Millicent, meet Dolly. Dolly, Millicent."

"A human named Bostwick sent me to find you. Speaking of which," Dolly said, removing a pair of opera glasses from a bag that hung from her staff, "do you have any paper?"

"No, sorry," Millicent said. "So you met Bostwick? Is he all right? Did he have a white rabbit with him, and—"

"Hold on a moment. I need paper. Clarence?"

"Fresh out," he said. "Why don't you point it at a landmark or something?"

"What landmark? We're in the Wastes."

"Oh! I know someone who can help," Millicent said, running back to where Misha hid. "Misha, it's all right. I know these people."

"But I don't have my cloak on. What if they see me?"

"They're going to see you. They're friends of mine, or at least Clarence is. But the other one knows Bostwick. Please come out."

"Well… all right."

She led him forward, though he tried to hide behind her, and introduced him.

"So you're that white-haired goblin, eh," Dolly said, sounding unimpressed, then muttered something that sounded like "Hmph. 'Dangerous', my hoof". She coughed into her hand, then went on. "So, as a native, do you know any landmarks? Places that say, 'This is the Wastes'."

"The only thing that an outsider would recognize is a signpost. It's not far from here."

"Let's go!" Clarence said, and urged Misha to lead the way. As they went, Millicent again asked about her friends.

"So yes, I met all three of them," Dolly said. "Though as to the circumstances of our meeting and parting, I have been sworn to secrecy."

"But are they all right? They weren't hurt, or… inordinately depressed?"

"Well, Bostwick seemed upset. Though that was my fault," she added in an undertone.

"And he sent Dolly to find you," Clarence said. "And that's when she met me. I was performing in a town on the Gammon Coast, you see. At first goblins would throw things at me as soon as I even mentioned magic, but they warmed up to me. I'm not what you might call skilled, see, and they thought my act was quite hilarious. Some even gave me a few pointers."

"On magic?" Millicent asked.

"On comedy. So anyway, I met Dolly at one of my performances, as a dove I conjured flew for her face, and she mentioned magicians and Bostwick and whatnot and I've been traveling with her ever since to help her find you."

"But why are you here?"

"We flew by carpet to Bombast, the country just to the north of Styx. While there, I accidentally started a bar fight and Dolly knocked over a bunch of casks, which broke through the wall into the capitol building. We were summarily banished and found ourselves here."

"So what are those glasses supposed to do?" Misha asked, staring at them suspiciously. He still hadn't let go of Millicent's arm.

"They're mine," Millicent supplied. "Delilah must have found them in my room. I assume she has the other pair."

Dolly nodded and said, "As soon as we prop these up so they can see where we are, your friends will come right here."

"They'll be here in no time!" Clarence cried happily.

"Not necessarily. They're probably miles and miles away, even as we speak."

"So, where am I supposed to land?" Emmaline asked. She had navigated through the buildings of the Capital and was now circling the Academy. The square below them was full of awed citizens who gazed up at the flying device.

"For full details on how to purchase your very own flying airship," Delilah called down to the street, "contact Bedlam Lesse of Lesse's Moor. Lesse's Airships, for all your air travel needs."

Bostwick glowered at her in mild disbelief.

"What?" she said. "What kind of daughter would I be if I didn't take advantage of a free advertising opportunity?"

"But even at a time like this?"

"I'll just hover over the roof," Emmaline said to no one in particular.

"Good thinking," Delilah said, "but how will we get down?"

"There should be a stairway from the roof leading down to the dormitories over there," Bostwick said, indicating the spot.

"And why do you know about that, hmm?"

"Let's just say one of Clarence's many adventures

involved climbing over the roof and dropping into the restaurant next door while carrying an unconscious waiter, and leave it at that."

"I really need to meet this Clarence of yours," Emmaline said, steadying the ship over the sloped roof. She threw one rope around a chimney, secured the ship, and began to climb down to the metal staircase below.

The door to the dormitories was unlocked. They slipped through one of the bedrooms, which was empty except for unmade beds and messy dressers. Bostwick explained that classes would be getting out in about an hour's time so they should hurry and see the president before the rush of students came. He led the way out into a bright hallway paneled in cherry wood and lit by square, green lanterns. They passed a few closed doors and one class that seemed to be in session, but went by, unnoticed. Eventually, they came to a large, spiraling staircase that led to the top story and, continuing up this, came to a large double door. Bostwick stopped outside this, hesitating.

"What's wrong?" Emmaline asked. "Isn't this the president's office?"

"It is, but… well, should we knock? What if he's in a meeting or something?"

"Oh, Bostwick," Delilah said, "still thinking like a student, I see. Styx goblins need no invitation."

She burst through the door and marched into the office as if it was her own throne room. Bostwick and Emmaline followed. The president rose from his desk, where he had been conversing over tea with a well-dressed man who looked at Delilah as if she was a mildly interesting insect. His expression changed when he saw the two humans behind her.

"Emmaline?"

"Mr. Charles!" she said, and ran past Delilah, who pouted at being ignored. "Look, I'm human again!"

"So I see. But what in the world are you doing here?"

"It's a long story. Actually, we came to speak with the president about someone Melieh may have known."

"That's an odd request," the president said, "but I'll try to be of help, especially if it's to aid one of our alumni." He nodded to Bostwick. "That is, if you don't mind the interruption, Mr. Charles?"

"Not at all." He gave a deferential wave of his hand and picked up his tea cup once more.

"Sebastian Galimatias taught Melieh magic, correct?" Emmaline asked, and the president nodded. "What happened to him after that?"

"He remained friends with Melieh until his death; he died in his sleep… Please don't tell me you plan on exhuming any bodies, Your Majesty," he said, turning to Delilah.

"Of course not," Delilah answered. "Everyone knows we cremate our dead, anyway. We were just wondering if Sebastian left any weird white doppelgangers running around or anything, because we've seen one."

"You've… seen one?"

"Specifically, he used to look like a cat, then he stole my Domino and transformed into a Sebastian lookalike, then he kidnapped Millie. You remember Millie?"

"Miss Minikin has been kidnapped?"

"You certainly do repeat a lot of other people's statements," Delilah said with a smirk.

"It's called back channeling, Your Majesty, and falls under the category of being polite," the president said wryly. "As far as Sebastian goes, I have no idea who this imposter might be. But if Miss Minikin is in trouble, I feel some responsibility for that, having sent her to Ataxia in the first place. Where has she been taken?"

"Sebastian turned into some sort of black mist shadow-type thing and disappeared into Bostwick's hat with Millie"

The president seemed mildly surprised at this story, while Mr. Charles choked on his tea and coughed several times, waving away Emmaline's offer of assistance.

"They went into a hat?" he said between coughs.

"Have you ever heard of a goblin like that, Mr. Charles?" Emmaline asked.

"Well, there's certainly no such entry in *Flora, Fauna, and Fungi of the Goblin World*, that's for sure. Where did this fellow come from?"

"My dungeon," Delilah said matter-of-factly. "And we were thinking, or I was at least, that maybe there is some sort of alternate dimension or something inside of magicians' hats that he took Millie to."

"But magicians' hats have no magical properties," the president said. "They're no different from any other hats."

"Well, then, the dimension can be accessed through all hats," Delilah declared.

"I'm afraid there is no such place."

"Then where are the rabbits from?"

"It's magic."

"Easy for you to say."

"Yes," he said, "because it's true. You take rabbits out of

hats and put them back in, and you can carry a certain number of items in a hat, but there is no extra space inside them. That's magic."

"Then where is Millie?"

"If I might make a suggestion," Mr. Charles said. "Mightn't a certain kind of goblin be able to use hats to create a portal, not to another dimension, but to another location? Goblins have been known to summon objects from a set place, so perhaps this person you've described did something similar, only in reverse."

"That may be the case," Bostwick said, "but it still doesn't help us find out where he went. A portal like that could lead anywhere."

"Not necessarily. Gremlins can only summon items from within their own houses. Magicians can only conjure man-made objects that they, themselves, have vanished first. Goblin magic, human magic: it all has limitations. You just need to figure out the limits of this man's magic."

"But we don't even know what type of magic that really is," Emmaline said. "I thought he was a Styx goblin, but that's obviously not the case, and if he's an immortal beast…"

"But beasts can only use the magic of whatever form they've taken, so there must be some sort of creature that already uses this sort of hat-shadow magic," the tea inspector mused.

"Well, he did say that his people live somewhere to the west of Styx, but we don't know if he took Millicent to them, or somewhere else. The only limit that his magic seemed to have was that he can probably only travel to other hats, but there are hats all over the world."

Mr. Charles mulled this over, sipping his tea thoughtfully, then held up his finger as if he'd come to a conclusion.

"I need another cup, Wilfrock!"

"One moment," the president said in polite exasperation, then addressed Delilah. "As much as I would like to help you, Your Majesty, I'm afraid I can't think of a single solution at present. If you would let me finish my business with Mr. Charles first, I could then focus on helping Miss Minikin."

"Oh, yes," Emmaline said, turning to the tea inspector. "Why are you here, anyway?"

"To tell the truth," Mr. Charles said, sounding embarrassed, "I was sent to find a replacement for Dogsbody. We didn't know when you were coming home, see. But now that you're here, and human, we can all go back to Camellia together."

Emmaline looked at her feet as she spoke.

"I do miss home, and I'm sure everyone wants to see me, but I can't abandon Millicent. I don't know how much help I'll be, but if I can do anything for her, I want to be there."

"I understand. But Dogsbody, surely you can return. I think Emmaline and the queen can handle things on their own, don't you? And you can go back to your job as our court magician."

"Hey!" Delilah said. "He's my butler. I saw him first."

"You did not!" Bostwick said. "The fact is, Mr. Charles, Delilah will curse me if I leave before… what was it now? Eighty years?"

The president covered his eyes. "Your Majesty, you can't go around cursing magicians. It just isn't done."

"I'll curse whomever I wish," she said.

Mr. Charles raised his eyebrows. "Oh, really? And how were you going to do that?"

"Why, whatever do you mean? With my amazing magical prowess, of course."

"That's interesting," Mr. Charles continued, "because all my research shows that the Styx goblins' magic is limited to floating and creating balls of energy. I suppose they're rather good in the area of magical research, but that doesn't mean they can go around cursing people left and right."

All eyes fell on Delilah, who, though smiling widely, looked like she wanted to murder the tea inspector.

"You can't curse people?" Bostwick asked.

"Well, not as such, but—"

"You can't curse anyone, and you mocked *me* for not pulling a rabbit out of my hat?"

"Now, now, like he said, I can float and use that glowing shield spell. But that's not to say I couldn't curse you."

"I could have just walked out of Styx, scot-free, the whole time!"

"On the contrary, Bostwick, I could have used the Domino to curse you. See, if one transforms into a different sort of goblin, like the imp who cursed Emmaline, for instance, one could curse anyone one wished. So I most certainly could have cursed you before. So there."

"But as soon as I gave it to Sebastian, I just could have left."

"Technically speaking…"

"So why couldn't you have removed the curse on me?" Emmaline asked.

"As I have said before, goblin curses are a familial sort of magic. I wasn't part of Drollery's family, so I couldn't do a thing about it. If my mother had cursed you, I could have removed it faster than you could say 'piffle', even without the Domino."

"So you see, Dogsbody," Mr. Charles said, sounding amused, "you could leave right now and be our court magician. It would make my job a lot easier, unless you have some other objection?"

"I'm going to stay until we find Millicent, of course," Bostwick said, then turned to Delilah. "After that, we'll see."

"Yes, indeed," Delilah said, wrapping her arm around Bostwick's shoulders. "Good old Bostwick. As much as I would wish to delay your departure from my employment, I really must insist on finding Millie."

"We still have no idea where—"

"Well, check the glasses again!"

"I didn't bring them," he said, but she shoved them into his hands. "Thanks. But you know it probably won't…"

He trailed off as he looked into the glasses, for they had finally shown something other than darkness. Dolly's glasses were apparently lying sideways on the ground, pointing up at a wooden signpost. Bostwick thought that she had dropped them, but then considered that the name of the place might be on the signs themselves. The top two, pointing left and right, said *That Way* and *This Way*, while the one below that, with arrows on all sides of it, read *Which Way?*. The bottom one simply pointed at the ground and read, vertically, *Here!*

"What is that supposed to be?"

"Let me see!" Delilah said, grabbing the glasses. A smile

spread across her face and she handed the glasses to Emmaline to look as well.

"That's in the Wastes!" Delilah said. "We must have just missed her before!"

"If you've never been in the Wastes, then why do you know an obscure sign like this?" Bostwick asked.

"Oh, Inattentive Bostwick! My parents mentioned this in their long and rambling tale of their marriage. It was at this signpost that the third duel to the death happened."

"Does this mean she found Millicent?" Emmaline asked.

"Of course it does!" Delilah said. "To the airship!"

She dashed out of the room before anyone could stop her. Bostwick turned to face the tea inspector.

"You should probably look for a new court magician. Sorry that I bothered you, President Wilfrock."

With that, he bowed quickly and followed Delilah.

"Mr. Charles, tell my family I said hello," Emmaline said, "and that, when everything is sorted out, I'll come home. But even after we find Millicent, I don't know if that will be the end of this. We still have to figure out who Sebastian is, and what he's up to."

"I shouldn't wonder. But I'm sure they'll understand. After all, a princess's first duty is to the people, and in this particular instance, yours is to the people in Styx."

"Thanks for understanding," she said, hugging him goodbye.

"Ah, but I think you have time for a small suggestion."

Emmaline nodded eagerly. It had been some time since she had taken advice from Mr. Charles, but she'd always found it helpful.

"Always remember, there is no such thing as false tea."

"What?"

"The other day I found myself on the train, and they were out of tea, that is, dried leaves of the *Camellia sinensis* plant. But not entirely, see. They had some herbal varieties—rooibos, matte, and something involving chamomile flowers—so I accepted them, because I get a little depressed without my tea, but that's beside the point. Now, my traveling companion, a self-professed tea connoisseur, was disgusted by my choice, and warned me against this vile drink, saying it was nothing but an imposter that could never substitute for 'true tea' of the Camellian variety, and would only bring heartbreak. I'm paraphrasing, mind you.

"But the tea came, and you know what? It was every bit as delicious and tasty as any true tea I've ever drank… drunk? What a horrible word. Regardless, the lesson I learned that day was this: tea is more than the plant it comes from. Are these 'false' teas any different from the teas of the camellia bush? If you soak them in water, will they not steep? I think tea is what you make of it, and thus, there is no such thing as a false tea. Just don't tell any tea connoisseurs I said that."

She stared at him.

"Tea connoisseurs are very finicky people. Often they judge a poor little cup of herbal tea too harshly. I, for one, think they're simply snobby," he explained, "if that's what confused you."

"That has nothing to do with it. I thought you were going to tell me something important."

"That is important. There is no such thing as—"

"I mean something important to the situation at hand!

Something deep and meaningful to help me before I go off to who-knows-what."

"It is meaningful. It's a *secret metaphor*," he said, waving his hands in what must have been meant to be a mystical way.

"For what?"

"If I told you, it wouldn't be a secret metaphor. You should figure it out for yourself, and all that jazz that they tell young people nowadays."

"You're not that old," she said with a laugh.

"Oh, I could you tell you stories, but I think your friends are getting impatient."

He looked over her shoulder, and Emmaline turned to see Delilah, who marched up and grabbed her by the arm.

"Let's go. Chop-chop. No more chitchat," she said, leading Emmaline out of the office.

"Goodbye, Mr. Charles," she called over her shoulder.

"Bye, Emmaline. Remember, secret metaphor-phor-phor-phor."

"Did he add his own echo?" Delilah asked as they went back to the dormitory. "What a lovely fellow."

"So," Emmaline asked, "what are you going to do when we find Sebastian, since you can't curse him?"

"I'll have Bostwick conjure some sort of weapon for me. And who knows, maybe Sebastian's out of commission already."

"You think so?"

"Well, the Academy test said Millie was the evil overlord type. Who knows what she's capable of."

Fourteen

This Way. That Way. Which Way? Here!

"Those glasses have been up for hours. They must have seen them by now," Clarence said.

"Yes, but the question is, how close to the Wastes are they?" Dolly said. "It took us days to get here, even by magic carpet. Although they do have an airship."

"Really?" Millicent asked excitedly and began to scan the skies. "Do you think they'll see us? Maybe we should make a flag or a fire or something."

"We're the only moving things in the Wastes. I'm sure we're plenty noticeable."

"Is that them?" Misha asked, pointing to a small black speck against the blue. It got larger as it approached, until they saw that the speck was in fact a tub-like basket suspended from a large balloon.

"That's them all right."

"Um, I'll just wait over here," Misha said, standing behind the signpost in an attempt not to be seen.

"Millie!" they heard a voice scream as the ship began to

descend. When it was still thirty feet up, something pink jumped out and floated to the ground, then ran and leapt onto the bewildered Millicent, knocking her to the ground.

"Millie!"

"Good to see you, too, Delilah," she said, standing up.

"Are you all right? What did that horrid cat do to you?" Delilah asked, linking arms with her. "Good job Dolly… and Clarence?"

"It was nothing," Clarence said.

"But what are you doing here? And who's the fellow behind the signpost?" She walked arm in arm with Millicent up to Misha. "Wait a minute. I recognize that coloration. You're one of *them*."

"Wha-what do you mean?" he said, and ran around to grab Millicent's other arm, keeping her as a shield between himself and Delilah.

"One of the magical white cat-type hat living people!" she said accusingly. "You do live in a hat, don't you?"

"D-do I?"

"You live in Chiaroscuro," Millicent assured him. "There's a whole city here, Delilah. It's pretty amazing."

The queen looked around, as if a city would spring forth out of nowhere. By this time, the ship had landed and Emmaline and Bostwick climbed out.

"Millicent!" Emmaline said, running up to her.

"Emmaline, you're human! When did that happen?"

Bostwick approached more slowly, looking both nervous and relieved at the same time. Millicent was seized by the desire to run to him, and was grateful that both Delilah and Misha's hold on her prevented her from embarrassing herself.

"Bostwick," Delilah said, "have you seen a city lying around here?"

"It's inside a shadow," Millicent said. "There's a lot to explain, but first, how are all of you? Is Styx all right?"

"It's all over the place, but don't worry, we've got most of it. Emmaline?"

Emmaline brought out the three map pieces and showed them to Millicent.

"We just don't have the last piece, but I don't know where exactly it would be in a place like this."

"Maybe the last place you look?" Millicent said, taking the folded map piece from her pocket.

"Brilliant!" Delilah cried. "Now let's bring Styx back."

"What if that lets Sebastian know that we're here?" Emmaline said. "He could come and make trouble for us."

"Who cares what he thinks. Besides, we know his silly tricks now, so we're ready for him. My snakes, pineapples, and populace are in danger, so my country is getting repaired now. And dash the consequences!"

Delilah placed the map of the Wastes on the ground then arranged the rest of the pieces together like a puzzle. There was a slight rumbling where they stood, and suddenly the eastern horizon was filled up with forest, and just above the tree line, the towers of Castle Styx were visible.

"Yes! Victory! Now how do we get it all to stay together?"

Bostwick wordlessly swept his hands over it several times, and handed it to Delilah, back in one piece.

"Why, thank you, Bostwick! Now that that's taken care of, I believe you had something to say, Millie?"

"I'd prefer to go back to the castle to talk. I've been sort of homesick, and we should probably get as far away from Chiaroscuro as possible, just in case Sebastian comes looking for us."

"Of course! We'll take the airship. My dad made it, you know? You three shall also come," she told Dolly, Clarence, and Misha.

The trip to Castle Styx was spent recounting the search for the map pieces. Delilah embellished wildly, and left several key events out, but Emmaline filled in some of the gaps. Millicent was content, for the moment, to relax and enjoy the company of her friends and look around at the different parts of the airship, but was also anxious to get back home. There were too many things to be discussed, she thought. And Bostwick still looked unnerved about something, and even demanded that Delilah skip to the next part of the story a soon as she mentioned kobolds.

Delilah insisted they fly over the town to see how the people were getting on. A few of the newly erected shops had fallen to the ground, but most seemed no worse for wear. Many of the citizens waved happily at them, and Delilah and Clarence waved back.

When they finally did reach the castle, Heather met them at the door. While Delilah hugged the doorframe with a contented smile on her face, Heather ordered them to show her the map.

"What on earth is this hideous smudge?" She indicated a spot on the Wastes where someone had written *Chiaroscuro.*

"I wonder if Sebastian did that," Misha asked, then shrank before Heather's angry stare.

"There's no respect for cartographers these days. I didn't have a spare moment to draw any maps in Catawampus. People came by every few minutes, some trying to loot the place no doubt, while others were convinced it was the Eastern Hall of Bureaucracy. Somebody even came around asking about the map piece. Librarians! Thank goodness she left when I told her you'd already taken it out of the city. I eventually had the capybaras patrol the perimeter, so that seemed to keep people away, although we might well have some very confused Catawampians who got stuck in the castle or the hedge maze by mistake."

"Why didn't you have Spleenbeck order people to stay away from the castle?" Emmaline asked.

"In the beginning I did, but one week into the job, Spleenbeck decreed that the kingship points be set back at zero and quit. Apparently, he couldn't handle it."

"Big surprise," Bostwick said. "Anyway, shouldn't we sit down somewhere so we can sort everything out?"

Delilah chose the ballroom, as it was large enough to fit everyone comfortably inside, and insisted they pull the chairs away from the long table and sit in something like a circle. She herself sat on top of a large harpsichord that had been there since the last ball.

"So," Delilah said, "my first question is: who's this guy, really?"

"His name's Misha," Millicent explained. "He helped me escape from Chiaroscuro, which is that place inside of the shadow."

"We've technically met before," Misha said. "I sold you some memories."

Delilah looked at him suspiciously, until he held a hand over the top half of his face.

"Ah yes! The memory merchant. You remember him, Emmaline. So you're telling me that you live in a shadow?"

"I live in a city that was built in a shadow."

"And how'd you manage to build it?"

"I don't remember."

"He got rid of his memories," Millicent said, "so there's a lot he couldn't tell me."

"And you told Delilah how to do it, too," Bostwick said, finally realizing who was ultimately responsible for the loss of Millicent's memory and the troubles that followed. "What made you think that was a good idea?"

"Well, I had to, you see," Misha said, "to get her to buy some memories. I'm pretty sure it was important. There was this note that I wrote… It didn't cause any problems, did it?"

Bostwick was about to articulate just how many problems it had caused in the strongest of terms, but stopped when Millicent jumped up.

"Misha! That's it! You must have sold Delilah your own memories. I don't know why I didn't realize it before!"

"You really think so?"

"You must have. Your note said to sell them to her at all cost. A fake memory wouldn't be that important, but your own would. Maybe there was something you wanted her to see, something you couldn't tell her because the shadow goblins are supposed to stay secret."

"That could be the case, and since she knows about us

anyway, then I can get my memories back and tell her in person. Can I please use them?" he said, turning to Delilah hopefully. "It would mean a lot to me. I'll even refund your money."

"Well, of course. They should be on my dresser."

Misha stood and walked toward the door, but stopped mid-stride.

"Show him where it is, Heather," Delilah said with a wave of her hand. When they'd left, she leapt off the harpsichord and took the newly vacated seat next to Millicent. "Now, Millie, I want to hear everything. Time is no object. Also, feel free to do impersonations if you must."

Millicent's story went well into the evening. Delilah stopped her once so they could get something for dinner, but other than that, and the occasional clarifying question, Millicent continued uninterrupted until the clock struck eleven.

"And then you found us," Millicent concluded, looking at the expressions of her friends. Emmaline, Clarence, and Dolly looked concerned, while Bostwick brooded thoughtfully. Delilah seethed.

"How dare he!" she said at last, drawing herself up to her full height and pacing in the small space between their chairs. "Asking a young lady to do him in. The... the... Clarence, what do you call a man like that?"

"Well, I've never met him, but he sounds like a bit of a cad."

"The cad!"

"But Delilah," Millicent said, "think about what he told me about Alcea."

"You made it sound like he wants to die, Alcea or no Alcea. What a coward! What a… I don't even know what!"

"But consider his… his upbringing."

"Upbringing is no excuse. Besides, I had a hand in his upbringing. And then he dares to accuse Styx of brainwashing his precious little Aloysius!"

"Alistair."

"Ali-whoever obviously had his mind made up about the world before he ever learned about the Styx goblins, causing him to misinterpret our words. That little wretch! But Sebastian is worse! He plays the woe-is-me mistreated card, then turns right around and tears my country to pieces, then tries to save his own people by making empty promises, all the while whining about being evil and pretending like suicide is the answer to everything. Faulty logic! Or at the very least, faulty premises. What a beast! What a mongrel!"

"That's why I need your help."

"I understand. You think we should use some kind of blunt instrument, or maybe do it quick with one of the swords from the treasure chamber?"

"You don't mean that, Delilah."

"Don't I?"

"No. I know you're upset about what he's done, and you have every right to be, but I also know that when you really think about it, you'll realize that…"

"That?"

"I don't know. That he doesn't deserve to die. That he's wrong and confused, and that if we could just convince him of that, then, maybe… I know things can't go back to the way they were with him, but maybe he might want to live."

Delilah still looked furious, but gradually grew calmer and sank down in a chair until she was lying sideways across the seat.

"Well, Millie, I suppose that as a welcome home present, I could spare Sebastian's life. But I still get to punish him somehow. A pity. I was looking forward to stabbing him with some sort of pointy object."

"I'm sure you'll think of a suitable punishment, but what about saving Chiaroscuro?"

"We could always try evacuating everyone," Emmaline said, "although the buildings would still be in jeopardy."

"Alcea said she knew a way to remove the entire city from the shadow. There must be some kind of spell or something, but I can't think of any that powerful."

"I don't know of any spells that could do it," Dolly said. "At least not from my tribe."

"Human magic is a bit of a wash in this case, too," said Clarence.

Everyone was silent for a moment, contemplating how to extricate a city from a shadow, until Emmaline said, "Maybe we should sleep on it. I, for one, am far too exhausted to think clearly right now."

"I guess so," Millicent said, sounding disappointed, then addressed Dolly and Clarence, who both looked tired and disoriented. "I'll go ahead and show you two to your rooms."

The queen, Emmaline, and Bostwick waited quietly until the three of them had left.

"Speaking of sleeping arrangements," Emmaline said,

breaking the silence, "I've just realized that I'll need a larger, non-rabbit-sized room now."

She glanced at her companions, both of whom seemed dazed.

"So…"

"So?" Bostwick said.

"What should we do?"

"Can you believe her?" Delilah said, leaning over the arm of her chair. "Maybe he put some kind of spell on her. Or that syndrome, you know, where you become chummy with your kidnapper. Isn't that a syndrome?"

"Considering everything she told us," Emmaline said, "I'm not so sure I can just write Sebastian off as evil myself."

"Still, that's no reason to get all buddy-buddy with him. So what if he has to work for that Alcea woman?"

"It would be easier just to let *her* raise Chiaroscuro, since she knows how."

"Absolutely not! Although it would amuse me greatly to see Sebastian become someone's slave, I can't hand over the fate of my people to some mysterious woman who obviously has ulterior motives."

"*Your* people?" Bostwick asked.

"Of course," she said benignly. "They've lived in Styx for centuries, and even the stones that cast their original shadows were from the Wastes. They're as Styxian as they come, and are thus my responsibility. I suppose the same goes for Sebastian, making him a rebel, which means I must think of how to make him pay for all this." Her face suddenly became serious. "To ask Millie to do something like that. Unacceptable!" she cried, marching out of the room.

Emmaline turned to Bostwick, who was slowly making his way to the door while staring into space.

"Are you going to bed?" she asked him.

"I will in a bit. I want to talk to Millicent first, but I don't know what to say."

"Tell her you love her!" Delilah yelled, peering in from the doorway.

"Would you just leave!" he said angrily.

"Don't deny it! We all know it's true."

"I'm not telling her something like that at a time like this."

"Very well then. Make yourself of use and convince her that Sebastian is not worthy of her concern and should be summarily whacked."

"Don't make me do your dirty work!"

"But you can get through to her," she said seriously. "You're a maid, she's a butler. Oh, what am I saying? You're both magicians! You can see things eye to eye. Make it so!"

With that, she bounded away.

"Bostwick," Emmaline said, "she actually called you a magician."

"I know. I think the stress is finally getting to her."

Bostwick knocked on Millicent's door and received no answer. He assumed she was asleep, but peeked in just in case, to find that the room was empty. At first he panicked, thinking that Sebastian had taken her once more, but quickly realized that made no sense whatsoever. She was probably just getting a snack or something, he thought, and paced the hallway several times. When she did not show up, he went to the Hall of Portraits two floors below to see if she might be on her way back from the kitchen, but noticed a light in the greenhouse at the end of the hall.

Millicent was there, sitting on a wicker bench with a flame spell in one hand and a deck of cards in the other. She seemed tired and pensive, and though the cards were rearranging themselves in small circles in the air, it looked as if she were performing the spell without much heart.

"Millicent?" Bostwick said.

She jumped in surprise, letting her cards fall to the floor. She knelt down to pick them up, but Bostwick had already cast a spell to make them fly into his hand one by one.

"Thanks," she said, sitting back on the bench. "I was just wandering around the castle. I've really missed this place. But what are you doing up so late, Bostwick?"

"I wanted to make sure you were all right." He handed her the deck, then took the seat next to her.

"I am. A lot has happened, but now that we're all together again, I think everything will be okay." She paused, then asked, "Do you think Delilah will be able to save Chiaroscuro before Alcea does?"

"She'll think of something. Considering that she managed to get Styx back from all over Ataxia, I don't think there's much she can't do, which is sort of a scary thought."

Millicent chuckled, but then uttered a worried "mmm".

"I hope everything works out," she said. "I know it sounds stupid, but I… I wish things could go back to the way they were. I just want to learn magic and cook and clean and not worry about k-killing anyone," she finished in a teary sob.

Bostwick conjured a handkerchief and handed it to her. As she took it, her flame spell flickered out, so that the room was illuminated only by the moon outside, which was half obscured by clouds.

"That's not stupid," he said. "I think we all want things back to normal. I want to start teaching you magic again. And I'm sure Delilah is feeling the same way. I don't think she really hates Sebastian; it's more likely that she expected finding you would somehow make everything that's happened in the past few weeks not matter anymore. Unfortunately, things don't work that way."

"It's not all bad, though. I can't say I was happy being kidnapped, but at least now the shadow goblins will finally be able to live in Styx without fear."

"That doesn't justify what Sebastian did."

"Of course not, but—Bostwick, what's wrong?"

"It's my fault," he said, unable to meet Millicent's eye. "All of this. It's my fault you had to go through it. I don't know how much he told you, but… I gave him the Domino."

"He said you gave it to him so I could escape."

"That's what I wanted…"

"Sebastian used you, Bostwick. I'm sure he would have stolen the Domino anyway. He had this plan for years, even before he met me. And he would have found someone else to… you know," she said, dabbing her eyes with the handkerchief.

"I wish you wouldn't cry so much."

"I know. I'm being silly."

"No, I meant… I wish you didn't have reason to cry so much. I hate seeing you sad."

Millicent looked at him questioningly, and he could feel his face coloring.

"I mean, well, it doesn't seem right, now that you're finally safe, you still can't relax. I've been really worried about you this whole time."

"I was worried about you too, Bostwick."

"You were? About me?" he asked, forgetting his guilt for a moment.

"A-about all of you." She got up and walked to one of the hanging plants. "I didn't know where Catawampus was, or if it was a dangerous place or not, or if I'd ever see you again. And… and I worried that you'd blame yourself for what happened."

"How could I not?"

As she turned to face him, the clouds outside moved away, flooding the conservatory with light.

"Well, *I* don't blame you," she said with a reassuring smile.

It took a moment for her words to sink in, but as they did, it seemed that whatever had been plaguing his thoughts for the past week vanished. Bostwick had hoped she might be able to forgive him for his role in her abduction, but thinking about it now, with her gazing back at him, he realized that there was nothing to forgive.

Bostwick felt a lump in his throat, and muttered, "R-right."

"And it seems like Delilah doesn't mind not having the Domino, so…"

"Well, it's not like she could make me her butler for a hundred *more* years."

"I wouldn't put it past her to try."

She was finally starting to sound like her old self, but her contented expression quickly faded into a far off, agitated look. "Um, speaking of Delilah, do you know if, uh, she ever took a memory… from me?"

"How did you know about that?" Bostwick asked, dreading what she might say.

"Sebastian told me."

"Oh. How much did he say exactly?"

"Only that."

Bostwick breathed a sigh of relief. He had planned to tell her what happened, but he wanted to do so tactfully, for once.

"You remember back when you wore that pink dress?"

"You saw that!" she said, panicking. Bostwick nodded.

"So, anyway, you asked what I thought of it, and I said I didn't like it."

"Me neither!" She laughed self-consciously. "It was awful, wasn't it? I tried explaining that to Delilah, but she… she gets these schemes into her head. Oh, but please go on."

"So I said some pretty uncomplimentary things—but about the dress, not you!" he added hastily, although Millicent didn't look as if she'd taken it that way at all. "But I think I embarrassed you, and then you ran off crying."

He had skipped the part where Emmaline had exposed Millicent's crush; revealing that he'd seen her in a strange outfit was one thing, but admitting that her secret affections had been brutally exposed was a different matter altogether.

"Then what happened?" Millicent asked, looking concerned.

"Well, Emmaline made me follow you, and then I apologized. And later, Delilah took your memory, using something Misha sold her. I was furious, but now I realize she was just trying to spare your feelings. Not that that makes it all right, but still…"

"That's all?"

Bostwick nodded, and to his surprise, Millicent smiled.

"Sebastian made it seem like she did something awful!"

"It was pretty awful at the time. I mean, it may not seem like a serious situation, but you were really crying, and then to just act like it didn't happen… Never mind the fact that she literally stole your memory."

"I guess Delilah has always tried to ignore unpleasant things. Still, if you apologized, I don't see why it was so important for me not to remember."

"Who can say?" Bostwick said with a nervous shrug. "It's like you said, she gets these schemes."

"Yeah." Millicent said, pulling on the fingers of her glove absentmindedly. "Um, thanks for talking with me, Bostwick. I feel a lot better."

"I'm glad," he said, standing. "We have a lot to talk about tomorrow, too, but for now, we should go to bed. I don't know how much sleep you got in Chiaroscuro, but you look exhausted."

"A little." She paused and brushed her hair behind her ears. "Um, Bostwick…" She fiddled with one of her gloves, looked at him, then at her shoes, and finally spoke. "I'm really glad you're back, I mean, that we're back—"

They heard a soft footstep and saw Emmaline in the doorway. She mumbled an excuse and was about to turn around, but Millicent said, "Is there something you needed, Emmaline?".

"Oh, I was just… Actually I was wondering if I could borrow some pajamas, but if you're busy…" she added hastily, but Millicent had already breezed to the door.

"I have some in my room," she said.

"I can find them by myself."

"It's all right, Emmaline," Bostwick said. "We were basically done talking anyway."

"Well, goodnight Bostwick," Millicent said, shrugging bashfully, and walked up the hallway. Emmaline attempted to sign an awkward apology, then spun and followed Millicent up to her room.

"I forgot that you never had to bring any clothes with you as a rabbit," Millicent said, opening a drawer in her wardrobe. "Let's see… These yellow ones are cute. Ah, but these blue ones are really soft."

"I'm sorry I interrupted your conversation."

"Oh, no, it's fine. We really were about finished anyway. And you've been sleeping in your clothes for days. It's about time you got some pajamas. Here, these are nice and warm."

She handed Emmaline the blue pair, then took out the yellow ones for herself.

Without warning, Emmaline threw her arms around her.

"I missed you."

"Oh, Emmaline. I missed you, too," Millicent said, hugging her back.

"Sorry," Emmaline said, releasing her and sitting on the

bed. "I just… The whole time, I told Bostwick and Delilah that we'd find you, but… I'm just relieved it's true."

"I bet you kept their heads on straight."

Emmaline nodded. Millicent noticed that she, like Delilah and Bostwick, seemed shaken by their search across Ataxia.

"Do you want to sleep in here tonight?" Millicent asked. "There are plenty of spare rooms, but…"

"I'll stay here."

"Great!" she said, folding back the covers of her bed. "I feel better having someone else around, after being away for so long. But still, we should try to get some sleep. We have a lot to discuss tomorrow."

Delilah sleepily walked up to her bedroom, but was met on the stairs by Heather.

"Ah! I was just coming to see you, Delilah."

"Oh yeah, you came here with that memory guy. Can you make him leave? I wanna go to sleep."

"That's just it. He's in there babbling about something. He's not making any sort of sense."

"I'll talk to him. You can go back to your map shop, since I'm sure you've been… Wait. Wait a moment! Do you still have the map of Styx on you?"

"Of course. I don't think I'll ever let it go again." She pulled it from her pocket and held it out for the queen to see.

"That pathetic cat! How could he not have thought of something so obvious?" Delilah said, pointing to the scribbled *Chiaroscuro*. "Heather!"

"Yes?" she asked, sounding annoyed.

"You absolutely must draw up a new map of Styx at once, only in the Wastes, right at that spot, draw a city, maybe label it something like 'Chiaroscuro, no longer in shadow' or something. Yes, and maybe extend the river a little more, and add some grassy hills, and maybe a lake."

"Anything else you want?"

"Make it nice for them, Heather. Millie said most Chiaroscurans have never been out of that shadow. How awful would it be if the first thing they saw was the Wastes? They'd surely think Styx was as bad as every other goblin nation says it is."

"Well, we can't have that! And I have been itching to get ink on my hands again. I'll do it!"

"Excellent. Have the first draft ready before the sun comes up. That mound of trash could already have collapsed for all we know, and one more dawn could be disastrous. Ta-ta."

Delilah continued up the stairs, feeling extremely pleased with herself, and pushed her door open to find Misha pacing around the room. He ran forward when he saw her, looking half excited and half terrified.

"Oh, Delilah! It's you! So yes, those were my memories. Wow, just—and you know—well, that can wait for a bit."

"You mind making sense?"

"All right! So, those were my memories, and the reason I gave them to you was to ask you for help, indirectly, because I couldn't talk to you about the shadow goblins, by law."

"As Millie theorized," she said, floating to one of the chairs in front of the empty fireplace. "Well, before you go on with requesting what I'm sure will be an easy task for a

Styx goblin, might I ask why you came to me?"

"You're the only one who can help!"

"Well, obviously."

"Because you have the Domino."

"But I don't have the Domino."

Misha's face fell for a moment.

"Well, you did at the time, so I made my mind up to give you my memories, except, being an inexact science, I leeched out far more memories than I intended. Does that make sense?"

"No. And what else doesn't make sense is how you knew about the Domino in the first place. Don't you live in a shadow in the middle of nowhere?"

"Chiaroscurans are allowed to interact and do business with other goblins, so long as we don't reveal what we are. That's how we acquired most of the materials we use in our city, and how I learned about your mask."

Delilah raised an eyebrow and Misha took the chair across from her and endeavored to explain.

"Do you remember the night, about ten years ago, that Sebastian left you?"

"Nope."

"Oh," Misha said. "Well, long story short, your mother was throwing you a coronation party—"

"Domination."

"…What?"

"Styxians wear dominos, not crowns. Hence, it was a domination party."

"Uh, right… so your mother invited royalty from across Ataxia, and she hired my sister and me to make a fake memory of a really good party for her guests to remember, in case things didn't work out."

"Sounds like Mom."

"Anyway, I met you and Sebastian in this castle. He recognized me as a shadow goblin and followed me back to Chiaroscuro."

"Hmm…"

"But during the party, you gave a speech, and said that if anyone tried to harm Styx, you'd use the power of the Domino to make them pay. Apparently, Bombast was threatening war."

"Mm-hmm."

"So you told the guests about all sorts of things the Domino would let you turn into, and how you'd let no harm come to anyone within your borders, no matter who they were, and… You really don't remember this at all, do you?" Misha asked, sounding a little disappointed.

"Nope. But then, I have a notoriously awful memory."

"I remember you saying so."

"I don't. There, you see? Now, not to interrupt your rather interesting story, but why can't you ask Sebastian for help with whatever this is about? Don't you all just love him to pieces?" she said moodily.

"He'd already gone back to Styx before I could warn him… but I'm getting ahead of myself. It all started with Alcea. Millicent told you about Alcea, right?"

"She did."

"I always felt there was something off about her. I've heard her talking with Sebastian a few times, and she always says that he's too attached to us, or that Chiaroscuro won't matter in the long run. I told Sebastian to be careful of her, but he said that he needs her to save the city, no matter how suspicious she is.

"Anyway, it was just after he left for Styx to try and find a way of getting his true form back that Danika—that's my sister—told me something I couldn't ignore. My sister works as an experimental chemist at the edge of the city, and it's widely known that she's studied magichemical literature from across Ataxia. Well, it seems that Alcea came to her and asked for a very specific mixture of chemicals, the kind used in massive Gremlin bombs."

"And your sister gave them to her?" Delilah said, starting to wake up a little.

"Yes… a-and put them into an old Gremlin-made bomb that Alcea had somewhere."

"What?" Delilah said in a deadpan.

"Danika assured me that the bomb is somewhere far outside the city and too big to move anywhere, but I think her excitement over seeing that big of an explosion is blinding her to the obvious danger of it all."

Delilah's jaw clenched for a moment, then she relaxed, leaning her head on her hand.

"Well, I suppose I'd want to see that sort of explosion, too. And anyway, if Alcea used such a device on Chiaroscuro, wouldn't it void her deal with Sebastian?"

"I don't think so. Danika said that due to some magical component of the chemicals, the explosion would only affect living matter, not stones or steel. So the city would technically be safe, but we'd all be dead. It all seems too convenient to be a coincidence"

"Hmm… and I don't suppose you tried to warn the authorities before coming to me?"

Misha shook his head, then hopped up and started pacing again.

"Sebastian was gone by the time Danika told me about it, and I couldn't go to the police or the Council because, well, selling those kinds of chemicals isn't exactly… legal. There would be trouble for Danika if anyone found out. I didn't know what to do, but with all of Chiaroscuro at stake, I had to try something, even something desperate. Telling you about Chiaroscuro would have only gotten Danika and myself into more trouble with the law, but I thought, if you had my memories, you would remember how dangerous Alcea was and go to investigate the bomb plot on your own…"

"Seems like a bit of a gamble."

"Yeah… to be honest, I thought you would have used my memories months ago."

"I suppose they completely slipped my mind. But that's neither here nor there. I have heard your belated plea for help, and can see that I'm clearly the only one for the job," Delilah said, cracking her knuckles. "After Heather saves the city—did I mention she's going to pull the city out of its shadow with her map-drawing powers? Well, she is—we shall work on thwarting this bomb plot. I already have some experience in that area, you know? Oh, but, um, don't tell Millie, all right? She's already fretting over Sebastian. I'm sure she'd just gloom all day if I told her about this."

"I won't have the opportunity," he said, going to the door. "I need to get back to Chiaroscuro. Now that Sebastian has the Domino, he might be able to deal with the bomb himself, especially if he won't be indebted to Alcea since you're saving Chiaroscuro in her place."

"I suppose… Ah! Why don't you take one pair of the opera glasses—they're in the airship—that way you can leave us a note if there are any further developments. Do you need a top hat?"

"It's too far to go by hat."

"Sebastian went all the way to Pandemonium, I'll have you know."

"I think that's because he's immortal. He doesn't quite exist, or rather, he exists potentially—"

"Enough! Enough! Enough!" Delilah said, pushing him out of her room. "It's too late for an existential discussion. Just wake the capybaras up and take the jaunty car. Tell them time is of the essence."

"Oh, um…"

"They'll be sleeping in the garden, most likely."

"Right! Well, uh, thanks again," he said, and proceeded down the stairs.

"First my country was going to be blown up, then it was torn apart, and now it's going to be blown up again!" Delilah said to the empty room. "For chaos' sake, can't I have a single moment of peace?"

Sebastian paced the Document Chamber, seething. When he'd woken up to find Millicent gone, he had assumed she had simply returned to her room, but if Misha was also missing, then she could very well have made it out of the city.

He'd already been told that no one had used the citizens' hats all day. The current guard of the Document Chamber had seen nothing, but when Sebastian found that the map of the Wastes was missing, he knew what had happened and sent people to search for the guard who had let Millicent and Misha inside.

No doubt Millicent had wanted to run as soon as she learned what he intended her to do. How she could refuse, after seeing everything he had shown her, was beyond him. An irrational part of him wondered why, if she cared so much about him, had she left him alone, to fester in an unending, miserable existence. *Why not, though?* he asked himself. *Why should she stay when Alistair had turned away?*

He checked for the map once more, then stormed out of the chamber, only to see Alcea leaning against the wall staring at him.

"How did you get here?" he asked, not even pausing on his way down the hall.

"I've been here for hours," she said, following him. "I got in through the Document Chamber hat, then chased that pitiful little guard away. So much for security…"

"So you've been wandering around the palace all this time?"

"Indeed. It seems there's been some commotion about Misha. Did he take your human away? Or maybe your map?"

"What have you heard?"

"Oh, just a few snatches here and there. I've also seen Styx's eastern horizon."

Sebastian stopped walking.

"What did you see?"

"The Forest of Infinite Horrors is back, as is Styx Castle. I can only assume the queen came with it. Now let's go to your chambers to talk in private," she said, glancing at one of the servants in the hallway.

Sebastian led her up the staircase, eager to hear any news about Styx's reunification.

"You know," she said as they went, "I didn't expect everything to fall into place so fast."

"What do you mean?" he asked sharply. "You didn't intend this to happen?"

"Intend? Well, the part about Styx getting back together, yes. The part about the human betraying you was a happy accident."

"Alcea," he said through clenched teeth.

"Shh," she said as they passed a goblin on the staircase. "Let's wait until we get behind closed doors, shall we?"

When they finally arrived at the king's chambers, Sebastian shut the doors and locked them. He turned around to find himself face-to-face with a giant white spider.

"Charming," Sebastian said, walking past her to a chair.

"This is much better," Alcea said through her fangs and scuttled over to him. "I hate staying in one form that long. I can still feel the shadow goblin clinging to me!"

"I'm glad to hear that you think so highly of the people you'll be saving. Now what is this about Styx returning?"

"Oh, yes. I realized some days ago that for the mapmaker of Styx, bringing Chiaroscuro into the light would be a simple matter, so I went to seek out that Heather woman." She changed again into a gray fox and coiled her tail around herself. "I suppose I could have just snatched the mapmaker, brought her here, and forced her to draw Chiaroscuro outside of the shadow, but I thought, wouldn't it be more interesting if I let Delilah get her map back together and raise Chiaroscuro for me? I paid her a visit in Catawampus, in disguise, of course, to perhaps clue the queen in on how to go about doing that, but Heather informed me that she was already well on her way to bringing Styx back together."

"And I suppose you gave them your part of the map?" he said, fuming.

"For a price, Sebastian, everything for a price. And I had even come here to fetch your piece of the map from the Document Chamber, when who should burst into the room but your human?" Again she changed, into a tiny, white moth, and rested on the post of Sebastian's bed, flexing her wings. "It seems she was thinking the same thing as I, namely getting the map into Delilah's hands somehow. Since the queen was already on her way here, I allowed your human to make off with the map. I had originally hoped the Styx mapmaker's curiosity would cause her to draw Chiaroscuro into the light by accident, but now it seems your human will tell her to do it for me."

"You could have just brought Heather here! You didn't have to let Delilah get all of Styx back together!"

"And you didn't have to bring a human here," she said nastily, and transformed into small purple serpent. "I hope this teaches you not to go behind my back, Sebastian. Not that it matters. Soon, you won't be able to."

"You mean the terms of the contract?"

She nodded. The rage Sebastian had felt a moment ago disappeared in a wave of anxiety. With the shock of

Millicent's escape and Styx's return, he hadn't thought about Alcea's real purpose in coming here.

With shaking hands, he retrieved a paper from a shelf beside his bed and glanced over the swirled black letters that specified the length of his servitude, the fact that he had to obey Alcea, and that the terms must be met so long as she orchestrated the city's removal from the shadow and its continued protection. He had placed his paw print on it years ago, shortly after seeing Alcea for the first time in her shadow goblin form. He had been in the Wastes, waiting for Misha to gather ingredients for memories and had noticed her watching him from the sea shore. His paw print was something like an incentive for the immortal beast to wait, to give Sebastian time to get his true body back and, unbeknownst to Alcea, find a way to make lifelong slavery as short as possible.

Without Millicent's help, the contract seemed worse than a death sentence.

"Heather will be the one who saves Chiaroscuro," he said, grasping for his last chance to get out of signing.

"I showed her exactly where to put it."

"Millicent's the one who gave her the map. She'll explain about what's happening to Chiaroscuro."

"And will she protect it from Delilah? Can she stop some creature…" Alcea turned into a wyrm and breathed a thin stream of flame. "…from burning down that pile of trash that casts the city's shadow? From knocking over a palace support beam?" She flicked her tail against a stool, upending it. "From anything that might happen to this delicate little city?"

Sebastian had never known Alcea to use threats before, but he didn't doubt for a minute that she would carry them out. He imagined everything that the Ancient Shadows had worked to create being annihilated, then resolutely signed his name to the paper. His only consolation was that his people would be able, after nearly three hundred years, to live in safety.

He placed the contract on a table for Alcea to sign, wondering what she would change into to seal his fate. She laughed softly as she turned into her human form—a tall woman with glasses and long black hair—and signed *Hollyhock* next to his signature.

"So you still go by that name?" Sebastian asked as she rolled the contract up.

"I have many names, but I've always had a fondness for the dear professor. In fact, I think that's how you should address me from now on."

"Once the city is safe."

"Of course," she said. "It could happen as early as tomorrow. And then, after years of waiting, I'll finally have what I want."

"You know I'm not really an immortal beast."

"I knew that before you were ever created. There are only a set number of us," she said bitterly. "We have existed for millennia, always a part of the world, yet never to take part in it. Able to observe, but never create. Trapped in a thousand true forms that have never been our own. But you? You are *my* creation. A new immortal being."

"Inez and Alistair made me," he said, as she changed back into a shadow goblin.

"I gave them the idea." She flitted to the door in her shadow form and unlocked it. "I gave them everything. Alistair learned how to heal, Inez got to make the man of her dreams, and you got existence. And after two hundred and sixty years, I finally get you."

She smiled briefly, then turned to face the door.

"Don't worry, Sebastian. The end of your freedom marks the beginning of Chiaroscuro's," she said, glancing at him over her shoulder. "Enjoy it while it lasts."

The story continues in
The Styx Trilogy Book Three
Recast Light

available for purchase in 2018

In the meantime,
find more information about
the Styx Trilogy (including bonus
stories about the characters)
at rosecorcoranwrites.com

Acknowledgements

Thank you to all the people I thanked before in the Acknowledgment section of *Miscast Spells*, but also to Sabra, whom I forgot to thank in that book but should have! I knew I'd miss at least one person, and I was right.

Thank you, also, to Shannon, who changed both the files for *Miscast Spells* and *Outcast Shadows* into their ebook formats. I'd also like to thank the customer service people at Ingram Spark and Createspace for helping me with all the odds and ends of self-publishing. You were all very kind and understanding.

Thank you to everyone who bought *Miscast Spells*, wrote reviews, and gave me feedback. Thank you for coming back for round two!

Last time I acknowledged Lewis Carroll, which I will do again. Much of the experiment arc in this book was inspired by his essay "Some Popular Fallacies about Vivisection", which among many other interesting points, notes that vivisection causes a moral degradation—a deadening of empathy to the suffering of others—in those who participate in it. Lewis Carroll may have often been silly, but his serious pieces are also worth a read.

In chapter 9, page 158, Bostwick's poem about Emmaline is paraphrased from Christina Rossetti's "Goblin Market", from which Lizzie and Laura also get their names. He goes on to claim that there simply aren't a lot of nice things to compare brown to. It should be noted that his repeated references to people's eyes while under the influence of love potion are my own little commentary on the YA genre's obsession with describing characters' eye colors when trying to make them seem attractive. Strikingly blue, sapphire, grass green, emerald, slate grey, and so on are all used ad nauseum, with only the occasional underwhelming "warm brown" or "golden brown" thrown in. I've always found it insulting to brown-eyed people, thus Emmaline's reaction to Bostwick (and really, the YA genre as a whole). A sensible person, such as Clarence, could tell at a glance that Emmaline's eyes are, in fact, the exact brown of well-steeped tea.

About the Author

Rose Corcoran substitute teaches by day, studies library science by night, and writes whenever the mood strikes her. *Outcast Shadows* is her second book. She lives in Flagstaff, Arizona and continues to drink an outrageous amount of tea.

To contact her, write to
rosecorcoranwrites@gmail.com